"Luke...they say Mike killed himself."

"Oh, God," he whispered.

Luke stepped closer and put his arms around her. For a moment, Caitlin tried to ignore the way being in the warm shelter of Luke's arms made her feel. It had been such a long, long time since a man had held her. And it felt so good to have someone care enough to comfort her.

Finally, reluctantly, she eased away. "I'm all right now. I'm over it—I really am. I'll never forget Mike, and part of me will never stop loving him, but I've accepted the fact that he's gone. Still, it's hard to talk about the way he died."

"Because he killed himself?" Luke asked.

"That's the conclusion the sheriff came up with, but I just don't know." Taking a deep breath, Caitlin continued. "Luke, I think Mike may have been murdered."

Dear Reader,

The idea of a hero who is a Navy pilot came to me in midair. About thirty-five thousand feet midair, to be precise, while I was flying home from Mexico.

Luke Dakota had popped into my head the first day of my vacation. But for two weeks he'd stubbornly refused to tell me a single thing about himself. Once we were airborne, though, he let slip that he'd just learned a baby had been named after him. As soon as I knew that, all the whys and wherefores of his story began falling into place.

By the time my plane landed in Toronto, the idea was well enough developed that I called my editor about it the next day. And when I did, I discovered that Superromance had decided to do a promotion featuring men in uniform. (Life is just full of coincidence, isn't it?)

At any rate, I hope you enjoy reading what happened when Luke met Caitlin Alexander—and his little namesake, her baby son.

Sincerely,

Dawn Stewardson

Dawn Stewardson

Big Luke, Little Luke

Harlequin Books

TORONTO • NEW YORK • LONDON
AMSTERDAM • PARIS • SYDNEY • HAMBURG
STOCKHOLM • ATHENS • TOKYO • MILAN
MADRID • WARSAW • BUDAPEST • AUCKLAND

ISBN 0-373-70653-7

BIG LUKE, LITTLE LUKE

Copyright © 1995 by Dawn Stewardson.

To John, always.

With special thanks to:

Peggy Algeo, who gave me a Desert Storm T-shirt to wear for inspiration. It is now a very well-worn shirt.

Pilot Terry Algeo, who edited the flying scenes and helped out with the technical "stuff."

And, last but not least, friend and fellow writer Vicki Lewis Thompson, my Arizona adviser. Any errors in the setting are entirely her fault. Hey, Vicki, just joking.

PROLOGUE

OVER THE YEARS, Luke Dakota's life—like the lives of all men—had been irrevocably altered by certain events and decisions.

Had he chosen to, Luke could have looked back and easily identified those specific turning points in his life. Most people don't do that, though, and Luke Dakota was no exception. But if he *had* drawn up such a chronology, he would have included the following:

On August 2, 1990, in the Persian Gulf, the armed forces of Iraq invaded neighboring Kuwait.

On August 7, 1990, George Bush, president of the United States, sent the first troops and planes to the Persian Gulf under Operation Desert Shield—which subsequently escalated into the conflict known as Desert Storm.

On December 27, 1990, while in the Persian Gulf, Luke Dakota saved the life of fellow navy pilot, Mike Alexander.

On January 4, 1994, in Culpepper, Arizona, Mike Alexander died.

On June 7, 1994, Caitlin Alexander, widow of Mike, gave birth to a baby boy.

On June 26, 1995, in Pensacola, Florida, Lieutenant Luke Dakota received a letter that changed his life forever.

CHAPTER ONE

LUKE AWOKE IN a cold sweat. He could still hear the roar of explosions all around him, still see flashes of fire streaking through the darkness.

For an instant he was back in the Persian Gulf. Then the frayed curtains of sleep fully parted, the relentless heat of the Middle East dissipated, and the only audible sound was the faint hum of the air conditioner.

With his heartbeat gradually slowing, he propped himself up and switched on the light.

Back in '91, when he'd first shipped home, he'd had frequent nightmares. But that had been four years ago, and he'd thought they were gone for good. Then Caitlin's letter had arrived, and the memories of those months he'd spent with Mike had brought back the horrors of Desert Storm to haunt his sleep again.

Reaching into the bedside table, he fumbled for the envelope. It was pale blue, scented ever so faintly with an enticing fragrance that made him think of meadows in moonlight, and addressed in a feminine hand:

Lieutenant Luke Dakota, Flight Instructor
c/o Pensacola Naval Air Station
Pensacola, Florida

He pulled out the contents, set the snapshot aside and looked at the letter one more time.

Dear Luke,

We've never met, but perhaps you'll recall my name. Mike often mentioned that he talked about me when the two of you were flying together in the Gulf.

I should have contacted you long ago, but the last little while has been very difficult, and I hope you'll understand why it's taken time to write. I guess you may have already heard from someone else. But in case you haven't, I'm afraid I have some bad news. Mike died eighteen months ago....

Luke stopped reading, wondering again what had happened. What had Mike died of?

He could write back, *should* write back, telling Caitlin he was sorry. After all, he and Mike had been best buddies in the Gulf. But pressing her for details she hadn't volunteered just wouldn't seem right to him.

His gaze returned to the page, and he picked up where he'd left off.

...died eighteen months ago. His death was unexpected, and hard for me to cope with for many reasons. But there's one thing I know Mike would have wanted me to tell you about.

When he died, I was three months' pregnant. And as soon as we learned about the baby, Mike said he wanted to name him after the man who'd saved his life—assuming it was a boy, of course.

So when our son was born, I named him Luke Michael Alexander.

Luke stopped reading again. His thoughts drifted back to the time when he and Mike had been flying reconnaissance missions off the *USS Saratoga*. They'd gotten a rare three-day pass and had wanted to see some of Saudi Arabia. But they'd driven a little too close to the Iraqi border, up to Al Khafji. And even though the ground war hadn't officially started, nobody'd thought to mention that to the sniper they ran into.

Mike almost bought it that day, caught right out in the open the way he was. But Luke had gotten off a couple of lucky shots and they'd hightailed it back to their jeep—damn scared, but both still in one piece.

He turned his attention back to Caitlin's letter, wondering about the "many reasons" Mike's death had been so difficult. Were she and the baby okay now? She didn't really say, just closed the letter.

So you have a namesake out here in Arizona. I only wish he could grow up with his father still here.

Well, Luke, I apologize again for not letting you know about Mike's death before this. But I'm sure, from everything he told me about you, you'll forgive me for the delay.

Warmest regards,
Caitlin Alexander

Luke exhaled slowly. The last time he and Mike had talked on the phone, Mike had just been discharged from the navy. He'd said he and Caitlin were thinking about moving but they hadn't found a place yet. So, when Luke had next tried to reach him and found the number was disconnected, it hadn't been a major surprise.

He'd just assumed Mike would get in touch again, once he got his civilian life organized. But now he wished to hell he hadn't simply left it at that.

Reaching for the snapshot, he glanced at the back, where Caitlin had written *Luke's first birthday, June 7, 1995.* Then he turned the picture over and studied the baby once more. He was a typically cute one-year-old—brown hair, round, rosy cheeks and chubby little arms waving at the birthday cake sitting on the coffee table in front of him. Just a cute one-year-old Luke hadn't been able to stop thinking about.

Not that the reason was any mystery. His sister Sarah still lived in Denver, where they'd grown up, but he called her regularly. And the odd time he'd mention something, then immediately regret it. This was one of those times.

But how could he have known that talking about the baby would get her started on that myth? Or old wives' tale, or whatever people called it. Whatever the appropriate term, he was sure only a philosophy major like Sarah could have made such a crazy concept sound almost plausible.

"Luke, it's a really common belief," she'd insisted. "If you save somebody's life you become responsible for them. And for the results of everything they do from then on."

"That's nuts," he'd told her.

"No, it's not. It makes perfect sense. If you hadn't saved Mike's life, nothing he did after that would have happened. His baby would never have been conceived, so—"

"So you're trying to tell me I'm responsible for a baby I've never seen?"

"No, I'm only telling you about a common belief. But, thinking in cosmic terms, it does seem kind of meaningful that he's named after you...doesn't it?"

Maybe it did, Luke silently admitted. But he wasn't a man who thought in cosmic terms.

He looked at the snapshot again, this time studying the woman who held the baby. She was in her late twenties, he'd guess, and pretty in an untamed sort of way—her face framed by such a wild tangle of long brown hair that, at first, he hadn't noticed how big and dark her eyes were.

She was smiling in the picture. A warm smile that made her look... He knew *nice* wasn't much of a word, but he wasn't the greatest guy in the world with words.

Still gazing at the snapshot, he grinned ruefully. His positive impression of Caitlin's photograph didn't count for much—not given his track record at judging women. The only saving grace was that he'd never married any of the ones he'd ever been involved with.

Oh, he almost had, once. But both of them had been far too young, and luckily the girl had realized that before they actually made it to the altar.

In hindsight, of course, he knew it was a good thing she'd dumped him. But at the time he'd been heartbroken. And since then, with every woman he'd dated, he'd always held back. And he'd always ended up glad there'd been no promises, no strings.

So even though Sarah still claimed that someday the right woman would come along, he was starting to wonder if Ms. Right existed.

He folded the letter around the snapshot once more, put them back in the envelope, then glanced at the return address. Route 2, Box 16, Culpepper, Arizona. It had to be a rural address. Did that mean...?

One of the things Mike had mentioned the last time they'd talked was that he and Caitlin were thinking about starting up a dude ranch. So did the country address mean they'd gone ahead with that?

Staring at the envelope for another minute, Luke told himself that what he was contemplating was insane. Hell, he'd checked his atlas, and this Culpepper was in the Sonoran Desert—about fifty miles south of Tucson and practically on the Mexican border. It had to be even hotter there than it was in Florida.

So not having any specific plans for the month of July, other than just spending his leave wherever the road took him sure didn't mean he should let it take him to Arizona. Not during the hottest month of the year.

"Nah," he muttered, turning off the light. "The idea's insane."

"SURE ... SURE, I understand. But you'll still have time to bring it back out here once it's fixed? Fine, see you later, then."

Caitlin switched the phone off and put it back on the kitchen counter, wondering how such a small animal could cause such a big problem.

Most of the time, she loved having wildlife living virtually on her doorstep. But when the neighbor-

hood pack rats chewed the wiring in your engine—
especially to the tune of four hundred dollars—things
were getting out of hand.

"Haven't rodents heard of live and let live?" she
asked, looking over at her son. "What if we'd really
needed the van today?"

Little Luke grinned happily at her from his high
chair, then turned his attention back to mashing a
chunk of banana into his hair.

As usual by the end of lunchtime, bits of food were
smeared liberally across his bib. And when she saw
Sam sniffing around the chair legs, Caitlin guessed
that the baby had sent a goodly part of his food to the
floor, as well. If Luke didn't get his eating act together soon, they'd have the fattest dog south of
Tucson.

"So what do you think, Chief?" she asked, grabbing a washcloth and starting across the sun-drenched
room to clean him up. "Think if you just cut down on
wasting food we'll be able to pay that garage bill?"

He shook his head vigorously—an attempt to avoid
getting his face washed, not in answer to her question—and she couldn't help laughing. He was becoming more of an independent little person all the
time.

Just as she removed the final bit of banana from his
hair, Sam started to growl and Luke cried, "Oh-oh!"

By the time Caitlin could make out the faint sound
that told her a car was coming up the driveway, the
dog was already on his way to the front door.

"Ghaaa," Luke said, giving his best imitation of
Sam's growling.

Caitlin unsnapped his bib and lifted him from the
chair. When she set him down, he took a few steps

then dropped to the floor and started scooting along in Sam's wake. As steady as he was getting to be on his feet, he could still move faster on his hands and knees.

Heading for the sink to rinse her hands, she watched a black Mustang come up the driveway. It continued past the kitchen, then stopped by the front door.

She waited, wiping her hands dry, as the car door opened and the driver emerged.

In his early thirties, he was a couple of inches over six feet, with a square, chiseled face—a face her grandmother would call manly. His eyes were hidden behind his sunglasses, but his nose was straight, his mouth was wide, and he had a pronounced cleft in his chin.

She'd have to agree with her grandmother. Manly was the word—and not just for his face, she decided, noting his broad shoulders and muscular arms.

Something about him struck a familiar chord, but she didn't think she'd seen him before. And she doubted he was from around Culpepper.

He was as tanned as most locals, but his dark hair was shorter than the norm. And instead of wearing cowboy boots with his jeans, he had on taupe deck shoes.

Then he turned toward the front door, squaring his broad shoulders as he moved, and she realized what it was that seemed familiar. His posture said "military" loud and clear. T-shirt and faded jeans or not, she'd bet money he was one of *them*. The realization made her wince.

Since Mike's death, she'd had her fill of the military. She might not know what this out-of-uniform representative wanted, but odds were against its being anything she'd like.

When he shoved the car door closed, Sam took the sound as his cue to begin barking.

"Quiet," she called, starting out of the kitchen. "He doesn't look at all like an ax murderer." And even on *her* scale of undesirables, being in the military didn't rank with serial killers.

She scooped up the baby just before he got through the dining room, tugged down the cuffs of her shorts, then continued on toward the door.

Outside, Luke headed slowly for the house, suspecting there was nobody home except the dog he'd heard barking. There was no car in the carport, and this didn't seem like a place anyone would live without transportation. And it didn't look like the mental image he'd formed of it—back in Florida.

Of course, the entire state of Arizona hadn't turned out to be much like he'd expected. Oh, there were a lot of cactuses, especially the tall straight ones with chubby arms that made them look almost human. Saguaros they were called. At least that's what the waitress who'd given him directions back in the Culpepper Café had said. But aside from the cactuses, most of what he'd encountered in Arizona had surprised him.

After driving through the parched flatness of Texas, and even flatter New Mexico, Arizona seemed mountainous in comparison, with far more vegetation than he'd imagined.

And this property of Caitlin's wasn't on the stretch of barren desert he'd expected. Instead, it sat in a river valley, bordered by the rolling foothills of what the waitress had told him were the Santa Rita Mountains.

He glanced beyond the house to where a couple of weathered outbuildings stood. They showed no signs of being in use, and the corral was unoccupied. All in all, this sure as hell didn't look like a dude ranch.

In addition to the lack of animals, there wasn't a single *dude* in sight—and the house wasn't big enough to accommodate many of them, anyway. It was just a long, low, rambling house. White with a red tile roof, typical of what he'd seen while driving through the state.

Reaching the front door, Luke took off his sunglasses and stuck them into the pocket of his T-shirt. Climbing out of his air-conditioned car had been like climbing out of a fridge and into an oven. The Arizona heat was one thing his imagination had been bang on about.

Just as he was about to knock, the door opened and he was face-to-face with Caitlin Alexander. She had the baby braced against her hip and one tanned leg was angled to block the path of an extremely large dog. The beast seemed intent on displaying all its teeth, but Luke risked taking his eyes off it to focus on Caitlin.

He barely had time to think that the picture she'd sent hadn't done her justice before the baby shouted, "Da-da," and Luke glanced at the little guy. His eyes were large and dark, like his mother's.

"Don't worry," Caitlin said. "He calls everyone Da-da. Even me, half the time."

Luke looked at her again, realizing he hadn't introduced himself. When he did, it was obvious his name didn't register for a second.

Then she murmured, "Oh, my," and quickly brushed her tangle of hair back with her free hand. "I'm sorry, I should have recognized you. Mike had snapshots of the two of you... but you were always in uniform. And when I saw you arrive, I thought you were somebody from... You got my letter, then."

He nodded.

"And you're here all the way from Florida?"

"All two thousand-plus miles—including a couple of little detours."

"Oh, my," she said again, but at least she was smiling this time.

It was the same inordinately warm smile from the snapshot. In real life, though, it drew his attention to the fullness of her lips.

"I was kind of in the neighborhood," he offered. "On my way to San Diego to spend my leave with a couple of navy buddies stationed there." He stopped himself before he let it slip that Culpepper was actually his primary destination, that San Diego was only an add-on. "So," he continued, "since I was driving through Arizona..."

"Well... please, come in."

When he stepped past her into the relative coolness of the house, he smelled a trace of the same enticing fragrance that had scented her letter. Even in the middle of the day it made him think of a spring meadow by moonlight. And because he recognized it, he felt as if they weren't total strangers.

But the feeling lasted only for a second. Only until Sam began to growl at him.

Caitlin told the dog to be quiet, then closed the door against the heat. "Don't mind Sam," she said, glancing at Luke once more. "The part that isn't hound is rottweiler, so he has strong protective instincts. But the vicious routine is mostly an act.''

The beast shot him an evil look that suggested *mostly* was a far cry from *entirely*. Then it trotted about three feet away and flopped on its stomach—without taking its eyes off him for an instant.

"And this is Luke, of course," Caitlin said, smiling at the baby. "Little Luke, I guess in this context. I usually call him Chief, though."

Luke looked uncertainly from the baby to her. "That was my call sign in Desert Storm.... I was squadron leader."

"I know. Mike started referring to the baby as the Chief from the moment he knew I was pregnant. He said you'd get a kick out of that. It would be like we'd be naming him after you twice. And even though Mike was...gone, before the baby was born, the Chief thing stuck."

Even though Mike was gone. They'd reached the part Luke was dreading. He hadn't had much experience with grieving widows. And even though it had been a year and a half since Mike's death, he really didn't know what to say to Caitlin about her loss.

Was *Sorry about Mike* the right phrase? It sounded pretty damn lame, yet what other words were there?

Caitlin brushed her hair back again, obviously ill at ease, and he wished he'd let her know he was coming. But he hadn't been sure how long he'd take to make the trip, and...

Hell, why was he trying to kid himself? The truth was, right up until the last minute, he might have decided to pass on this entirely.

Only half an hour ago he'd been sitting in the Culpepper Café, thinking about heading straight through to California. And he still hadn't figured out why he'd driven across the entire continent to see a baby he knew nothing about—simply because the little guy was named after him.

Luke looked at his namesake again. Little Luke was drooling, but before he could mention that to Caitlin, she said, "Why don't you go on into the living room and I'll get you something cold to drink. Beer? Lemonade?"

"A beer would be great."

Caitlin put the baby on the floor. "And you, Sam," she said to the dog, "can come with me and go outside. Go scare up some coyotes or something, huh?"

Sam seemed decidedly put off by that suggestion, but followed along after her when she started away.

"Ta-ta!" the baby yelled.

Caitlin stopped, retraced her steps, and gave him the plush bear that had been sitting on the hall table. "Ta-ta's as close as he gets to Teddy," she explained before heading off again.

LEFT ALONE WITH THE BABY, Luke watched him for a minute or two, but he simply sat gurgling at the stuffed toy.

Finally, Luke turned his attention to the house. The open-concept interior was filled with sunlight and bright colors. Indian rugs lay scattered here and there, partially covering a terra-cotta floor the color of burnt sand.

On one side, the front hall flowed directly into an L-shaped living-dining-room combination, while the hall on his left had to lead to the bedrooms.

Straight ahead was the family room, where a gun case containing a couple of rifles stood against one wall. Absently, he wondered if Caitlin could shoot or if they'd belonged to Mike.

On the far side of the family room were sliding glass doors. Beyond them, a deck ran across the back of the house. It stepped down to an inground pool surrounded by a garden.

As he wandered into the living room, Caitlin materialized with a Lone Star beer in one hand and a glass of lemonade in the other.

"I'm glad you got the letter," she said, gesturing him toward the couch. "I wasn't sure you'd still be risking your life training pilots."

"Well, I do everything I can to keep the risk factor minimal. The navy's happier that way."

She laughed, then handed him the bottle and sat down on one of the chairs facing him. "I hope you don't prefer cans. Mike always used to say beer tasted better from a bottle, so that's what I still buy."

"He was right." Luke took a swig of the beer, knowing the moment had come. "I... Caitlin, I hadn't heard about Mike until your letter came. I'm sorry. He was a terrific guy."

Caitlin forced a smile, remembering that Mike had used the same phrase to describe Luke. "It's hard to know what to say, isn't it. I just... for the first few months I wished people wouldn't say anything at all. I'd break into tears anytime his name was mentioned. But it's been long enough now that... hey, look who's coming to check you out." The baby had crawled in from the hall, and it was a good excuse to change the subject.

For a moment, she watched Luke Dakota studying her son. Luke's eyes were a grayish steel blue. Not a cold steel blue, but a soft, muted color, almost the same shade as his T-shirt. And he was looking at the baby with a friendly gaze, as if he liked children.

The baby still had his teddy clutched in one hand, but he let go of it to grab the end of the coffee table. Then he hauled himself onto his feet and used the table as a handrail while he edged along to his mother. Once he reached her, he wrapped his arms around her bare legs and stood staring at Luke.

"He takes a while to warm up to strangers," she said. "Do you know much about babies?"

"My sister has three little boys, so I know some. But . . . I've never had one named after me before."

"Well, you do now, and—" Caitlin stopped mid-sentence as the front door flew open.

CHAPTER TWO

CAITLIN'S HEART SANK when Billy-Bob burst into the front hall.

"Da-da!" the baby cried.

Luke leapt to his feet, obviously assuming Billy-Bob was an intruder.

"It's all right," she quickly murmured, but she knew that it wasn't. Sooner or later, Billy-Bob would come home in one of his snits and she wouldn't be able to talk him out of it. Then what would happen?

"Billy-Bob? What's wrong?" she asked, even though she didn't need to.

"Look, I've really had it this time," he muttered. "I'm just going to get my things together and take off." He turned away and began stomping toward his bedroom.

"Ghaaa," the baby said.

"Oh, Lord," Caitlin whispered. She unwrapped the baby's arms from around her legs and scrambled to her feet. "Keep an eye on the Chief, will you, Luke? I worry about him hitting his head on the table."

Putting down his beer, Luke watched Caitlin hurry after Billy-Bob. The baby followed her with his eyes for a couple of seconds, then started making his way back along the coffee table. Once he reached the end, he took a few tottering steps after his mother, then dropped onto his hands and knees and began scuttling across the floor.

Luke followed along. After all, Caitlin had told him to keep an eye on the little guy. Besides, he was damn curious about what was going on.

So much for his concern about not upsetting the grieving widow. This Billy-Bob character was obviously living with her. Or *had* been living with her. Now he was apparently packing his bags. So what the hell was the deal?

Caitlin had stopped at one of the bedroom doorways. Not wanting to seem too nosy, Luke paused halfway down the hall.

She stood silently staring into the room, her hands on her hips. Finally she said, "Billy-Bob, can't we at least discuss this?"

"Look, I'm sorry to bail out on you," he muttered from the bedroom, "but we both knew it was only a matter of time."

The baby reached Caitlin and started to pull himself up, using her legs for support.

When she glanced down at him, she caught sight of Luke. The color rose in her cheeks and she gave him a look that seemed half embarrassed, half defiant, as if warning him against offering sympathy.

It made him feel guilty about witnessing the scene. It also made him wonder what the hell Billy-Bob's problem was. What could possibly have him so steamed at Caitlin? There sure didn't seem to be anything wrong with her that Luke had seen. And he could see a whole lot that was right.

He wasn't sure what it was about her... her long dark hair, those eyes, her full lips, or the way her high cheekbones hinted at something exotic in her heritage... But hell, if *he* had a woman like her begging him to discuss things, he'd have a tough time saying no.

"Billy-Bob?" she pleaded.

"No!" the guy snapped. "Let it go, okay? I've made up my mind this time. I hate to leave you in the lurch, but I'm not putting up with all the garbage any longer."

"But—"

"Uh-uh! That guy's a maniac in the air. He's going to kill somebody one of these days, and it's damn well not going to be me."

Caitlin hesitated, then reached down, picked the baby up in her arms and started back along the hall with him.

"I'm sorry, Luke," she said, not even breaking stride as she passed him, "but I've got to go out."

She stopped at the hall closet to grab a diaper bag, then opened the front door. "I really am sorry to be so rude," she added, pausing to glance over her shoulder at him. "It would be nice to talk a little more, so if you have time to wait, help yourself to another beer and I'll be back in just a... Oh, damn!"

She turned around to face him. "Luke? I forgot that my van's in the garage. Would you mind giving me a ride?"

IN THE SHORT TIME Luke had been in the house, the temperature inside his Mustang had become unbearable. Another degree and the leather would probably melt.

He started the engine, switched the air conditioner to full blast, then glanced at Caitlin. She was coping

with the lack of a baby seat by adjusting her seat belt
to protect both herself and the Chief.

Waiting until she finished, Luke mentally replayed
that scene in the house. She hadn't offered a word of
explanation, and he was damned curious as to what
it had been all about.

When the seat belt was finally in place, she glanced
over at him, her dark eyes luminous. He wanted to
say something to make her feel better, but he couldn't
come up with the right words.

"I'm really sorry to put you to all this bother," she
murmured after a moment. "But my van won't be
ready until later this afternoon, and the only thing
that's going to take Billy-Bob much time is packing
up his stereo equipment."

"Hey, no problem. Just tell me where we're heading."

"The Culpepper City Airport. If you go back to
the main highway, you'll see the Airport Road turnoff about halfway into town."

"Yeah, I noticed it on my way out." He started
down the drive, relieved that she hadn't dissolved into
tears. But was she going to fill him in on what was
happening, or leave him in the dark?

Trying not to let his curiosity get the better of him,
he concentrated on the surrounding landscape. The
farther they drove away from Caitlin's place, though,
the less interesting it grew.

The terrain was arid, flat and brown, not much
more than a level stretch of sun-baked sandy clay,
with little vegetation except for scattered clumps of
dried grass and the odd cactus and scrub bush.

By the time they reached the highway, his curiosity was back to full force. Surely it wouldn't hurt to ask an innocent question or two?

"So," he ventured, as he made the turn toward Culpepper, "we're heading for the airport because...?"

"Because Sky Knights operates out of it."

"Ahh...and we're going to Sky Knights so...?"

"So I can kill Lonnie McDougall—unless I can convince him to phone Billy-Bob and apologize."

"And this Lonnie? He's the one your friend back there said was a maniac in the air?"

When Caitlin merely nodded, Luke realized this approach was getting him nowhere fast. Since she didn't seem to mind his questions, he decided he might as well go for broke.

"Caitlin, do you think you could bring me up to speed here? Until a few minutes ago, I'd never heard of Billy-Bob or Lonnie McDougall or Sky Knights or—"

"Mike didn't tell you about starting the business?"

"You mean the dude ranch?"

"No, I mean Sky Knights."

Luke shook his head. With every word Caitlin said, he was feeling farther out in left field. "The last time I heard from Mike, he was talking about buying a dude ranch."

"Oh, then I'd better tell you what..."

The baby began to whimper, and she stopped talking to settle him down. A minute later, she said, "I think he'll be all right. He's just wondering what happened to his afternoon nap."

"It's okay. Fussing babies don't bother me."

From what she'd noticed about Luke, Caitlin suspected there wasn't much that did bother him. If only that were true of Lonnie and Billy-Bob, her life would have been a lot easier lately.

"So... you're going to fill me in on things?"

She nodded, even though she was far too upset to feel like telling him the story—hardly surprising, considering that her world was collapsing around her.

"Well, to start way back," she began, "Mike and I did buy the ranch. I mean, we bought the place you just saw, with the intention of turning it into a guest ranch. They aren't usually called dude ranches anymore, because...oh, that's not important. The point is that Mike decided having a guest ranch was a great idea. So I quit my job—I was a teacher—and we bought our place. But before we could even start working on it, Lonnie heard about—"

"I don't know who Lonnie is, remember? Or why you want him to apologize to that guy you're living with."

Living with? She stared across the car, certain Luke couldn't have meant that the way it had sounded. Then she realized he had.

"What?" Luke asked, noticing her looking at him.

"You assumed I was *living with* Billy-Bob Wiggins?"

"Well . . . yeah."

"Oh, Lord," she murmured. That was either totally mortifying or hilariously funny, but she wasn't sure which.

"What?" he said again. "I didn't hallucinate his hollering about leaving you, did I? Or heading into the bedroom to pack his bags?"

"Luke...I haven't even looked at another man since Mike died. Billy-Bob is a pilot, and he flies for Sky Knights. Or maybe I should say he did, until this afternoon. Either way, he's not from around here so he's been boarding with me."

"Oh," Luke said. He kept his gaze straight ahead on the road, but his neck got slightly red.

Despite the way she was feeling, it almost made her laugh. She'd never have suspected a man as unmistakably masculine as Luke Dakota ever blushed— even if it was barely perceptible.

"So, about that deal back at the house?" he finally asked, glancing at her. "You're saying it was his job he's had it with? That's what he was ranting about?"

"Yes. Lonnie's not the easiest guy to get along with, and he and Billy-Bob have been at each other's throats from day one."

"Which gets us back to the question, Who the hell is Lonnie? And what have they been at each other's throats about?"

CAITLIN TOOK A MINUTE to organize her thoughts before trying to explain things to Luke again. So far, she hadn't managed to sound very coherent.

"All right," she began. "Let's start with Lonnie McDougall. He and Mike were cousins. And then they ended up as partners in Sky Knights. You see, Lonnie used to be a pilot in the air force. After that, he flew air cargo for a while, but then he heard about a fellow in Texas who'd set up a mini Top Gun school...you know the sort of thing I mean?"

"Jet flight instruction? For civilians? That's what Sky Knights is about?"

"Partly. Flying lessons are the more mundane side of it—the bread and butter. The real money-maker is taking people up for mock air combat."

"Yeah?" Luke grinned. "You mean those deals where a couple of pilot wannabes go up and have dogfights with each other? While the *real* pilots are right behind in the rear seats?"

"Exactly. But I'm surprised you've heard about it. There can't be more than half a dozen companies doing it in the whole country."

"Well, there's one in Montana, and I know a guy who's flying for it. He says he loves it. Instead of life and death, it's fun and games. And he says it's a hell of a lot easier on the nerves than the real thing."

Caitlin nodded. "The customers love it, too. We fly trainers, so there are dual controls, and they can do some of the actual flying if they like. Most of them just want to play shoot-'em-up, though. At any rate, getting back to the story, when Lonnie heard about the operation in Texas, he figured it would be a great business for him and Mike to set up. And Mike figured that making his living by playing games in the air was a great idea."

"They've got to be *expensive* games, though," Luke said, as much to himself as to Caitlin. Mock combat meant a minimum of two aircraft and pilots, a mechanic constantly checking the planes, hangar space, plus all the costs involved in getting any new business venture off the ground—so to speak.

"Yes, very expensive," Caitlin agreed. "They started off as small as possible, planning to expand later. But even so, the costs were really high. I...well, to be perfectly frank, I was never in favor of Mike's getting into it."

"Oh?" Luke prompted when she paused.

"No. When Lonnie suggested it, Mike and I had barely taken possession of the ranch. And coming up with half the money for Sky Knights meant we had to turn around and mortgage it to the hilt. Plus it took serious bank financing."

"That must have been tricky—finding a banker to go for the idea of playing games in the air."

"Normally, I guess it would have been. But Lonnie's father, Mike's Uncle Quentin, is the president of Culpepper's local bank. And since he was willing to approve a loan, on top of the mortgage he'd given Mike and me, they were off to the races."

"Da-da!" the baby interrupted, grabbing a handful of her hair.

"No, I'm Ma-ma," she corrected him. "So the guest ranch went by the boards," she continued, freeing her hair as she spoke. "Mike and Lonnie were suddenly flying every day, and I ended up getting involved too. I was in charge of everything they figured I could handle—scheduling, looking after the books, promotion, whatever. But then ... Mike was gone. And since I was his beneficiary, I ended up as Lonnie's partner."

Luke waited. "And without Mike?" he finally asked when Caitlin didn't go on. "Has the business been doing all right?"

"Well, there've been problems, but so far we've coped. The work divides up pretty well. Lonnie spends all his time at the airport and handles everything to do with the actual flying. Most of the administrative things, I can take care of from the house—with the odd trip to the hangar. So between us we've been keeping our heads above water. But we don't have much in reserve, and if Billy-Bob really does leave..."

"He's the only pilot? Aside from Lonnie?"

"Yes, and without him we'd be operating at a loss. Lonnie could probably cover most of the flying lessons, but we'd have to cancel all the bookings for combat missions. And there'd be a plane sitting idle, and... and I just don't think we could survive long enough to find a replacement for Billy-Bob."

"He's not the only pilot in the world," Luke said quietly.

"No, but we need someone with combat experience. And you don't find too many fighter pilots growing on trees in the middle of Arizona."

Luke looked back at the road, wondering how the situation had become so bad. If she and Mike had mortgaged the ranch to the hilt, as well as hitting the bank for a loan, that had to mean she'd lose everything if Sky Knights failed.

They'd almost reached the airport turnoff, so he eased up on the gas and flicked on his turn signal. After they'd left the highway he looked at Caitlin again—and caught her wiping away tears.

It gave him a strangely hollow feeling in his chest. And for some reason it made him think back to that conversation with his sister.

"If you save somebody's life you become responsible for them," Sarah had said. "And for the results of everything they do from then on."

Luke considered the logic of that one more time, but it still struck him as an awfully warped way of looking at things. *He* wasn't responsible for Mike's business venture. Or for whatever became of Caitlin and the baby, because of it.

Hell, he'd like things to work out for them, but they were barely more than strangers to him. And he was a stranger to them. Just a stranger passing through.

But if it turned out that Billy-Bob really was packing things in for good, there had to be some way of sorting out the problems his leaving would cause. And if Lonnie's father was president of a bank...

When he raised that, though, Caitlin merely shook her head. "Not even his father is going to loan us more money at this stage. Either we make it or we don't."

Luke nodded, then forced his attention back to his driving. Just as he did, a low-flying Piper Cub veered in their direction.

"Bhhrrrrr," the baby sputtered.

"That's his engine noise," Caitlin murmured.

Luke glanced at the two of them once more, unable to keep from worrying about what would become of them if Sky Knights went belly-up.

"IT'S HANGAR A-6," Caitlin said, pointing ahead as Luke drove past the airport's small terminal building. "And that's Lonnie's pickup. You can park beside it."

Her stomach in knots, Caitlin had the seat belt undone before Luke had even stopped the car. She didn't know how long it would take Billy-Bob to get everything packed up, but the faster she convinced Lonnie to phone the better. Assuming, of course, that she'd be *able* to convince him.

With the baby squirming in her arms, she climbed out of the Mustang into the sweltering afternoon sun. It was so hot that the heat from the tarmac began seeping through the soles of her sandals the second her feet touched the ground.

She looked around for Lonnie, but the only person outside the hangar was Trout. He was busy tinkering with one of the engines and hadn't noticed their arrival.

"Bhhrrrrr," the baby said, jabbing his fist toward a Cessna that was taxiing to a runway for takeoff.

"You going to be a pilot when you grow up?" Luke asked him, coming around the car.

The Chief gave another emphatic "Bhhrrrrr," then made a grab for Luke's sunglasses.

"He's decided he likes you," Caitlin said, intercepting his little hand. "I wonder..."

"Uh-huh?"

"Would you mind holding him while I talk to Lonnie? He has a loud voice. And a tendency to yell. The Chief's not too fond of either."

"How about it, ace?" Luke said, holding out his arms.

"It's okay, Chief," Caitlin assured the baby when he looked at her uncertainly.

Luke took him, jiggled him up and down a few times, and he began gurgling in delight.

"Hey," Luke said to him, "you and I are going to be just fine. We can talk spiral dives and half rolls while your mom's gone."

"Ga!" the baby agreed.

Spiral dives and half rolls. For a moment, Caitlin couldn't help wishing that Mike was still alive, talking about planes to his son. Then she forced the thought away and did her best to ignore the lump in her throat.

Mike was gone. It had been more than a year and a half now, and she'd come a long way in working through her grief, and had pretty well gotten over the feelings of abandonment and rejection she'd had for so many months. Still, when she let herself think about the baby growing up without his father... But loss was forever, and thinking about what might have been couldn't change what was.

"That's Lonnie?" Luke asked, nodding toward Trout as they started away from the car.

"No, that's Trout Hoskett, our mechanic."

"And how does he get along with your partner?"

"Oh, they're just fine. He's been with us from the very start. Lonnie and Mike hired him when things were barely beyond the planning stages."

"So, what's with this problem between Lonnie and Billy-Bob? Most of the blame lies with Billy-Bob?"

"No, it wouldn't really be fair to say that. You see, both Lonnie and Trout are good ol' boys from right around here. They went to school together, played on the same football team in high school, you know, those kinds of things. And Trout really feels he's part of Sky Knights. If you talk to him you'll see what I mean. You'd almost think it was his company. But Billy-Bob's from Texas, and Lonnie's just never treated him... well, he never really considered Billy-Bob one of them, and Billy-Bob always resented that."

"Bit of a closed shop around Culpepper, is it?"

"More than a bit. Even Mike was never quite one of the boys, because he was originally from Michigan. Even though he used to spend part of every summer with the McDougalls when he was growing up. That's how he and I first met."

Luke nodded. During their months in the Gulf he'd heard bits and pieces of Mike's life story, and he remembered something about that.

As they neared the open door of the hangar, Caitlin glanced out toward the planes and called, "Trout?"

The mechanic looked over and gave her a laconic wave.

"Do you know where Lonnie is?"

"In the office, I think."

She looked at Luke again, saying, "I won't be long," then blew the baby a goodbye kiss and started away.

"Ma-ma!" he yelled after her.

"Hey, attaboy," Luke told him. "You got it right this time. That's Ma-ma."

He watched Caitlin disappear into the hangar, thinking he'd like to trail along and see how she made out with Lonnie. Then he decided he'd better mind his own business, and took a slow look around to see what he could of the setup.

The two planes in front of the hangar were T-34 trainers—high-performance little prop jobs that actually felt just about the same as jet fighters. They were a little slower, but you could easily hit six Gs in them, which would knock the socks off most amateur pilots.

The hangar, with Sky Knights emblazoned above the door, was easily big enough to house half a dozen T-34s. They'd probably leased it with a view to that expansion they'd planned on. But there were no planes inside, only the two sitting out on the apron.

They had custom paint jobs, white with dark blue trim, and Sky Knights lettered in red along their sides.

On one of them, Lonnie "Terminator" McDougall was written in script beneath the cockpit. On the other plane, the pilot ID read Mike "Phantom" Alexander.

Phantom. Mike's call sign from Desert Storm. That sure brought back memories. "Phantom," he said to the baby. "That's what we called your daddy when we were flying off our aircraft carrier in the Gulf."

"Ghaaa," the little guy said.

"Well, actually our carrier was the *Saratoga,* but I guess that name's a little tough for you yet." He glanced back at the planes, wondering how Caitlin felt when she saw Mike's name, then noticed that Trout had stopped what he'd been doing and was sauntering over, eyeing him curiously.

Luke eyed him back.

Caitlin had mentioned he'd played football with Lonnie, but now he looked like a jock beginning to sag into middle age. About thirty-five, he was a large man with close-cut reddish-brown hair and a beer belly that he must have been devoting a fair amount of time to developing.

"Da-da!" the baby called at him, punctuating the greeting by smacking Luke's shoulder with his fist.

"How ya doing, Luke?" Trout said.

For an instant Luke wondered how the guy knew his name, then he realized Trout was talking to the baby.

"You a friend of Caitlin's?" Trout asked, reaching them.

He didn't bother to introduce himself, so Luke merely nodded.

"Where y'all from?"

"Florida."

"Yeah?"

Luke nodded again.

Trout wiped his palms on his coveralls and glanced over at the Mustang. "You drive all the way cross country?"

"Uh-huh."

"You plannin' on stayin' long?"

Resisting the urge to point out that this was sounding like a round of twenty questions, Luke said, "Uh-uh. Just passing through."

Trout seemed to like that answer and began to look almost friendly. "So," he said after a minute, "you want a tour? While you're waitin' on Caitlin?"

"Sure."

"Come on, then. We'll have a look at the hangar first," he said as they began walking. "It's pretty ordinary, 'cept we put in a classroom. We start people off with a little ground school. The combat mission customers, I mean. Caitlin tell you about that side of things?"

"Yeah, she did," Luke said. "And I've heard a little about this sort of thing before. I've got a buddy up in Montana who's—"

"Well, you oughtta give it a try while you're here. Beats the hell out of bungie jumpin'."

They stepped out of the burning sun and into the hangar. More than half of it was just a big empty space that made Luke think of a mountain cavern— except that he always thought of caverns as cool, while the temperature in the hangar wasn't much lower than outside. The baby was starting to wiggle around, so he tried jiggling him again while Trout continued talking.

"Usually, when you first mention the combat missions, people figure you mean a simulator or video games or that virtual reality stuff—not the real thing."

"Yeah ... I guess that's what most people would figure."

"But it's real, all right. You can't pull six Gs in a video game. You know what I'm talkin' about? *Six Gs*—six times the force of gravity? I mean, you can really hit that up there in our planes."

"Uh-huh, I know exactly what you're talking about. I'm—"

"And," Trout interrupted once more, "the planes are really jazzed up—equipped with laser units that sound just like machine guns. And when you score a hit there's a blast of smoke from the other plane. It's a real rush for folks. But it's in here that we start them off. See, there's the classroom over there." He pointed across the hangar. "Next to Lonnie's office."

Luke looked over. The upper halves of the walls on both the classroom and office were glass—allowing whoever was inside to look out into the main hangar area. Or, as the case might be, allowing anyone outside to look in.

"That's Lonnie?" he asked, nodding toward the man standing in the office with Caitlin.

"Yeah, that's him."

Trout started to say something about the classroom, but Luke stopped listening. He was far more interested in what was going on with the two people in the office.

Like Trout, Lonnie was in his early-to-mid thirties. He didn't have a beer belly, though. And his blond hair, rather than being short like Trout's, was about three times as long as the air force would ever have allowed.

But aside from that, Lonnie was one of those clean-cut, good-looking Nordic types—even though Caitlin had said his name was McDougall, which was about as Scottish as it got.

Caitlin was talking to him with her hands on her hips and a glare on her face. Clearly, she didn't like the way the conversation was going.

Lonnie apparently didn't like it, either. He was crowding her, his body language menacing, and even through the glass Luke could hear him yelling.

It was hard to make out the words, but the expression on his face was plain enough. He looked as if he wanted to wring her neck.

Glancing around, Luke scoped out a safe place to put the baby down, just in case Lonnie got carried away. That done, he forced himself to stay where he was—reminding himself Lonnie was Caitlin's partner. This was between the two of them, and it was none of his business.

But if Lonnie moved one inch closer to Caitlin, he'd damn well make it his business.

CHAPTER THREE

"HEY," TROUT SAID, glancing at Luke. "Don't sweat it. Lonnie just likes to yell."

Luke nodded. Caitlin had told him that, too. Maybe he *was* reading more into the scene than he should.

"So, like I was sayin'," Trout said, starting in on his tour spiel once more, "after folks have had an hour or so of ground school, they get into the planes for a little cockpit trainin'. After that, they take off with our pilots in back and go one-on-one in dogfights. If we head outside again, I can show you the planes. They're real nice two-seaters with an intercom between front and back, so—"

"Yeah, I noticed them before we came in. Beechcraft T-34s. One of the hottest little trainers ever built."

Trout's expression went from friendly to suspicious in the blink of an eye. "You know planes?"

Luke nodded. "I'm a pilot. A naval flight instructor now, but I flew with Mike in the Gulf. That's how I know Caitlin."

Trout just stared at Luke for a minute. "Well, shoot, why didn't you say so right off?" he muttered at last.

Before Luke was forced to come up with an answer, Caitlin stormed out of the office with Lonnie on her heels.

"Oh-oh!" the baby cried.

"Dammit, Caitlin," Lonnie was shouting at her, "we'll get somebody in no time flat. I'll phone Tucson right now. We can have an ad in the *Daily Star* tomorrow."

Caitlin stopped and whirled around to face him. "It would be one hell of a lot easier," she snapped, her volume only a decibel or two lower than his, "to just phone Billy-Bob. So why don't you get back in the office and do it?"

"No way! I told you, I've had it with that hot dog."

The baby started making noises that sounded like he was thinking about crying.

"Hey, it's okay, ace," Luke whispered to him. "Your mom's doing just fine."

She was, too. From the looks of things, she had ten times more spunk than most women he knew. The way she was sticking to her guns made him feel damn proud of her.

Where the hell had that come from? He had no call to feel proud of her. He'd barely met her. He tried to ignore the feeling and listen to the argument like a detached observer.

"I wouldn't take him back if *he* phoned *me* and apologized!" Lonnie was yelling. "I'll call the *Star* and—"

"And what if there's nobody in Tucson who can fit the bill?" Caitlin demanded. "What if there's nobody in Tucson who even wants to fly for a tiny operation like ours? Last time, we had to advertise in Houston before we got someone, remember?''

''And we'll do that again if we have to. In the meantime, everything's going to be just fine.''

''In the meantime, everything is going to go to hell in a hand basket! Maybe we don't have a mission booked for tomorrow, but what about the one the day after that? Are you going to have somebody to fly it with you?''

''If I don't, we'll cancel.''

''Oh, terrific. That's a great way to run a business. And what about the next day? That's the booking that could get us all kinds of referrals from Phoenix. Do I just call those guys and tell them sorry, no can do?''

''Well—''

''Well nothing! Lonnie, listen carefully here. If we have to cancel things, it not only costs us a lot of money but it's hardly a gold star on our reputation. And I'm the one who looks after the books. I'm telling you we just can't stay afloat with only one pilot. Not even for a little while. So you'd better just get on the phone and call Billy-Bob.''

Beside Luke, Trout muttered, ''No way ol' Billy-Bob's ever comin' back. Not if Lonnie went crawlin' after him on his belly like a snake.''

Having seen the mood Billy-Bob was in, Luke didn't doubt Trout was right.

''Well?'' Caitlin demanded, still glaring at Lonnie.

Luke cleared his throat. ''I...ahh...'' He stopped himself, knowing the impulse that had seized him was totally insane.

Then damned if he didn't hear himself saying, "Caitlin, I was just thinking... I'm kind of at loose ends for the next couple of weeks."

LUKE TURNED OFF the main highway, and the Mustang's tires began kicking up clouds of dust that drifted along behind the car.

Caitlin sat watching him surreptitiously. The idea of his wasting his leave on her account made her feel guilty as sin. So, if she was going to be able to live with her conscience, she had to give him a chance to back out. Even though the thought he might take it terrified her.

If he didn't stay... well, she was sure Sky Knights would go under.

Finally, as they were nearing her place, she forced herself to speak up. "Luke, you can still change your mind, you know. I'd understand if you did. You've got those friends you were on your way to see, and you probably weren't thinking about them when you said you'd stay." She held her breath, waiting for his reply.

"I don't want to change my mind," he said, allowing her to start breathing again. "Playing those combat games sounds like too much fun to pass up. I told you, my buddy in Montana says he loves it. And like I said, it's not as if anyone's actually expecting me in San Diego. I was just going to surprise them. It's no big deal."

"It *is*, Luke. I know Lonnie acted pretty cavalier about taking you up on your offer, but that's just his way. He never likes to admit needing anything. But your helping us out *is* a big deal."

Luke shrugged. He wasn't helping *them* out. He hadn't much liked either Lonnie or Trout. What Caitlin called Lonnie's way, he'd call an attitude. And he wouldn't bother crossing the road to do either of those guys a favor. He was helping out Caitlin... although he wasn't even entirely sure why he was doing that.

Maybe because he and Mike had been friends. Or maybe just because he liked Caitlin and he was the only one around at the moment who could fly their damn planes.

"Well," he said, glancing over at the baby, "I've got this little namesake, here, who might grow up to be a pilot. So it would be nice for him if Sky Knights was still in business. Besides, if it turns out Lonnie's right, if that ad of his gets you somebody right away, you'll need me only for a few days. Then I'll hit the road again."

They lapsed into silence until they reached Caitlin's drive and turned in. As she'd expected, Billy-Bob's car was gone. Her van was in the carport, though. The garage had delivered it as promised.

Luke parked and they climbed out into the heat.

"Cah!" the baby said, pointing at the minivan.

"That's right," she said. "They fixed it and brought it home. Next time we go out," she added, reaching into the back for the diaper bag, "you'll be in your car seat again."

"How much of that does he understand?" Luke asked.

"I'm not really sure. But the pediatrician says the more you talk to them, the more you're teaching them to communicate."

"Ahh...well, I'll try to have some lengthy conversations with him while I'm here."

"Good. He'll like that. Billy-Bob didn't pay him much attention."

Luke smiled. He had an easy smile she'd been aware of right from the start. But this time it made her feel a little anxious. She'd only met the man a couple of hours ago, and all of a sudden he was her houseguest.

She reminded herself that giving him a place to stay was the least she could do. It was nothing more than she'd done for Billy-Bob. And he'd only been an employee, not someone doing her a favor.

Luke Dakota, though, was not Billy-Bob Wiggins. And for some reason, the prospect of spending the next few weeks with Luke under her roof was a bit unnerving.

For *some* reason? an imaginary voice asked.

She glanced at Luke again. He was hoisting a large duffel bag from the trunk, and she let her gaze linger on his muscles—silently admitting she knew exactly what the reason was.

Luke Dakota stirred her. The very first time he'd smiled at her, she'd felt a fluttering inside, and that hadn't happened in an awfully long time. She hadn't felt a twinge of interest in any man since Mike had died. Not until Luke had walked into her house and smiled.

It made her feel guilty. She'd loved Mike, and the fact that another man could cause that fluttering seemed somehow wrong.

Luke slammed the trunk shut, bringing her back to the moment. A second later Sam appeared around the side of the house and greeted them with his whining-wiggling performance.

"Zam!" the baby cried in greeting.

"What happened to the vicious routine?" Luke asked.

"I told you, it's mostly an act. He tries it on everybody once, then usually forgets about it."

Starting for the house, she was very aware of Luke walking beside her. He was too big and solid and blatantly masculine for her not to be. And even if she hadn't felt anything at all, she was sure she'd still have noticed that the cleft in his chin was sinfully sexy.

She snuck a sidelong look at him, liking the way he moved. That military bearing made his stride purposeful. And those hard muscles and chiseled features...

The problem was, she decided, the mere fact she was aware of a man wasn't something she'd anticipated. It was like the first time she'd laughed after Mike had died. She'd thought she'd never laugh again, and it had taken her completely by surprise.

But this... this didn't really mean anything. People had told her she'd eventually start becoming aware of attractive men again. So she'd simply reached that stage. It certainly didn't mean she had any particular interest in Luke Dakota.

He was just a nice guy who was doing her a big favor. Well, maybe he was an awfully nice guy doing her a huge favor. But that was hardly relevant, because she knew it was going to take time to adjust to the idea of noticing men again. And by then, Luke would be long gone.

THE PHONE RANG. While Caitlin answered it, Luke, sitting next to her, looked out over the swimming pool, wondering how he could be feeling so at home when he'd arrived only yesterday.

Maybe it had been helping out around the place, giving Caitlin a hand with a few things she'd been letting slide because she couldn't manage them on her own. Or maybe it had been playing with the baby in the pool.

Whatever, he was starting to feel almost like one of the family—the baby fast asleep in his crib, he and Caitlin just relaxing in the twilight.

Since they'd finished dinner, a deep purple had painted over the dry tans and whites of the desert. The sun had dipped below the mountainous backdrop of the Santa Ritas, and the temperature had been dropping, dissolving the scorching day into a gorgeous evening.

He glanced at Caitlin and she shrugged, indicating that she really *was* trying to get off the phone.

He'd already gathered that. It was pretty well impossible not to eavesdrop when she and her cordless were only three feet away.

"Grandma," she was saying, "I didn't avoid phoning you because I was trying to keep it a secret. I was busy. Luke helped me replace that rotted wood in the carport, and he gave me a hand with a couple of other things, too.

"Yes," she went on after a minute, "I'm sure it's going to work out just fine. I told you, he and Mike were friends. The baby's named after him, for heaven's sakes. And he's very nice."

She gave Luke another shrug as she said that—an embarrassed-looking one, this time.

It made him grin. He hadn't needed to hear more than her side of the conversation to know how concerned Grandma was about a stranger moving into the house.

Culpepper was obviously a small town with an extremely efficient grapevine. From the sound of things, Grandma had heard most of the details, both about his arrival and Billy-Bob's departure, long before she'd phoned.

"Yes, your great-grandson *does* like him," Caitlin said. "So does Sam."

Sam lifted his head and looked at her, then let it flop back onto the deck.

"No, Grandma, I don't know if anybody warned him we have monsoons in July."

That got Luke's full attention.

"But he's from Florida," Caitlin went on, "and they get hurricanes there, so I'm sure he'll cope. Look, Grandma, I've got to go, okay? We can talk about this on the way to Tucson. Yes...yes, I'll be there before seven for sure. Bye now."

She put down the phone and turned to Luke. "My grandmother has an eight o'clock dentist's appointment in Tucson tomorrow. She doesn't drive, and my grandfather's blood pressure shoots up if he has to drive in rush hour traffic, so I said I'd take her."

"Ahh...and what about those monsoons I heard you mention? That was a joke, right?"

"No, not at all. We get incredibly fierce thunderstorms. Didn't you notice any of the signs on the roads warning about flash floods?"

"No...I must have missed them," he said, still not sure she wasn't joking. He liked her sense of humor, but it was very subtle at times.

"Maybe I should have asked about danger pay," he said, still trying to decide if she was serious. "Sky Knights doesn't fly during monsoons, does it?"

She smiled. "Monsoon season doesn't usually start until mid-July. And this is only what? The ninth, isn't it? So we might have a week or so yet. And even when the storms start, the mornings are always clear enough to fly. The thunderclouds don't roll in until the afternoon."

"Then it's not really a problem."

"No, not for Sky Knights. My grandmother was just hoping to scare you off because...well, you heard enough to realize she's not exactly thrilled about your being here."

"She's worried I'm the big bad wolf."

His remark made Caitlin laugh. "Actually, I think her imagination's running more along the lines of an ax murderer. She's probably been after my grandfather to bring her out from the moment she heard about you. But don't take it personally. I went through this when I said Billy-Bob could stay here, too."

"I can see why. The place is pretty isolated."

"That makes my grandmother a lot more nervous than it does me. I've got Sam as an early-warning system, and Mike always insisted we have a handgun in the house. And you've probably noticed the rifles in the family room."

"Yeah, I wondered if you could shoot."

"Pretty well. Well enough to blast a rattler that almost got Sam once. But my grandmother...well, she and my grandfather raised me, so she's had years of practice worrying about me. And she has absolutely no intention of letting all that practice go to waste."

Luke smiled, then waited, thinking she'd elaborate on her upbringing. When she didn't, he asked about it.

"Ahh...if it's none of my business," he added when she hesitated, "just say so."

"No, it doesn't really matter. Everybody in town knows the story. If I don't tell you, somebody else would be sure to dredge it up. You see, my mother was my grandparents' eldest child. They have a son, Jack, and another daughter, Mary, but my mother...I think she was always a little special because she was the first. And when she got older she turned out to be...apparently, she was really beautiful. Does that sound conceited for me to be saying? Because I'm her daughter, I mean?"

"No, I don't think so. Not if you're just stating a fact."

"Well, I don't remember her at all, but from the pictures my grandparents have, it seems to be true."

"And do you look like her?" In the dim light he wasn't sure, but he thought the question made Caitlin blush.

She brushed back her hair, and said, "Mary always tells me I do, but I know she just means there's a resemblance. Anyway, my mother won some local beauty contests when she was a teenager, and she was the high school prom queen—things that mattered thirty years ago. Mattered to her, at least, because she wanted to be a movie star."

"Don't all teenagers? I remember my sister Sarah did."

"Well, I guess a lot of girls have fantasies about it, but my mother was serious. Her problem, though, was that there wasn't exactly a swarm of casting directors in Culpepper. She took off for Hollywood right after graduation.''

''And then?'' Luke prompted.

''And then, about fifteen months later, she came home with a baby in her arms.''

''You?''

''Right. She wouldn't even tell my grandparents my father's name. She just said it didn't matter because she wasn't going to marry him. At any rate, she brought me here. But by Christmas she was gone again—and I wasn't.''

''Oh.'' Luke looked out over the pool once more, wishing he hadn't been so nosy.

''It's okay,'' Caitlin said quietly. ''My grandparents are terrific, and I was a lot better off living with them. Jack and Mary always treated me like their little sister rather than their niece and...and as it turned out my mother ended up dead when I was only seven.''

Luke shifted uncomfortably in his chair, wishing even more that he hadn't asked.

''It was a long time ago,'' Caitlin murmured. ''She was a victim of life in the fast lane, I gather, although I don't know the details. I think my grandparents were too brokenhearted to ask many questions. So, how about some coffee?'' she asked, bringing her story to an abrupt end.

''Sure. Can I help?''

''No, it's no trouble.''

Luke watched her walk across the deck, past the two sliding glass doors that opened into the family room and dining room, then in through the one that led to the kitchen.

She had on jeans and a shirt, now, but he could still visualize how she looked in that black bikini she'd worn in the pool. It was enough to make him drool, but it also made him kind of uncomfortable.

Mike had been his best buddy during Desert Storm. And even though the Gulf conflict had been over in a matter of months, there was something about serving in a war that forged fast and deep friendships. So he was having trouble reconciling his attraction to Caitlin with the fact she was Mike's widow.

Because she was, he'd expected to feel...he wasn't sure exactly how he'd expected to feel toward her. Brotherly came close, but like so much about Arizona, reality wasn't falling in line with his expectations.

In the back of his mind, Caitlin was the widow of a friend. But in the front of his mind she was an attractive woman. It was a strange mixture of feelings...as if by being attracted to her he was being disloyal to Mike.

Not that he thought the feelings were particularly logical. Any normal man would find Caitlin a desirable woman—whether he'd been a friend of Mike's or not. She had the kind of body that made a man's fingers itchy with wanting to touch it.

Absently, Luke ran his fingers through his hair. The more time he spent with Caitlin, the more desirable he was finding her. And there was definitely nothing brotherly about the way looking at those long tanned legs of hers affected him.

He sat back in his chair and gazed up at the stars, telling himself that his feelings weren't worth worrying about because he had absolutely no intention of making a move on her.

She'd told him she hadn't even looked at another man since Mike's death. And the first time she did... Hell, it didn't take a degree in psychology to know she'd be extremely vulnerable the first time. Which meant he'd be a total jerk even to think about coming on to her when he was merely passing through her life.

He pushed himself up from the chair and wandered across the deck. She was still in the kitchen, waiting for the coffee to finish brewing. He watched her through the glass for a minute, thinking about the story she'd just told him.

It had to be hard, never knowing either of your parents. Even for little Luke Michael Alexander, never knowing his father was going to be rough. But with a mother like Caitlin, the baby would make out just fine.

In no time, Luke had seen enough to know she was a far better mother than her own had been. It was impossible to imagine her handing her baby over to someone else, no matter how tough things got.

Maybe *that's* why he'd offered to help out at Sky Knights. Maybe he'd wanted to help keep things from getting tough at all.

WHEN THE COFFEEMAKER sputtered a final time and was done, Caitlin simply stood gazing at it, still trying to psyche herself up.

She was over Mike's death. She never broke into tears anymore without reason. And the unexpected ripples of thoughts about him, that always used to bring sadness, were now usually just simple remembrances.

But she still found it difficult to talk about the way he'd died. And when she went back outside she was going to have to tell Luke the details. She'd been putting it off all day, but he was flying his first mission for Sky Knights in the morning, so she had to tell him before he left. And if she kept putting it off until breakfast, she'd spend half the night worrying about it.

She poured the coffee, her hands trembling just a little, then headed outside again.

The moon had risen high enough to cast a glow onto the deck and turn the water in the pool to shimmering silver. Luke was a shadowy figure in the pale light—standing on the far side of the deck, looking off toward the dark, rolling shapes of the foothills.

Seeing him there brought a lump to her throat. How many times had she seen Mike gazing into the darkness like that?

"It's really peaceful out here at night," Luke said, turning as she started across with the coffee.

As if to contradict him, a coyote howled, its wail splitting the silence. Sam was on his feet like a shot, his nose twitching in the air.

"Sam, don't you dare!" Caitlin told him, but he was already charging off the deck.

"That's the hound part in action," she explained as he vanished into the night. "When his nose goes on alert, his ears shut off."

Luke laughed. "As I was saying, it's really peaceful out here at night, except for the coyotes."

"Yes . . . this was one of Mike's favorite places."

Luke didn't say a word. He just took his coffee from her and waited, as if he could tell that there was something she wanted to discuss.

Lord, she *didn't* want to discuss it, though. But she had no choice. She leaned against the railing beside him, took a sip of coffee, then began her story. "I...Luke, when I told you about my mother, I said that if *I* didn't tell you the story, somebody else would."

"Uh-huh," he said quietly.

Taking a deep breath, she continued. "That's because Culpepper is like most small towns. There aren't many secrets. And there's something else you're going to hear about that I'd rather you heard from me."

"All right. I'm listening."

Caitlin paused again, and in the moonlight Luke could see she was close to tears. When she put her coffee on the railing he put his down, too. When she still didn't go on, he said, "Look...if you don't want to talk about whatever this is..."

She shook her head. "Before Mike died he'd been sick for quite a while. He'd come down with the Gulf syndrome."

"Oh, God," Luke murmured. When tens of thousands of Desert Storm veterans had ended up sick—or dead—their illness had long ago been dubbed the Persian Gulf syndrome. But hadn't Caitlin's letter said Mike's death was unexpected?

"Do you know much about it?" she asked.

"Uh-huh. Aside from what's been in the news, I'm still in the navy, remember? I hear all kinds of stories." Stories about veterans who'd served in the Gulf developing a baffling array of symptoms—everything from severe fatigue, to pains in their joints, to cancer.

And the official Pentagon line might be that there was no conclusive evidence proving Iraq had used chemical and biological weapons, but when all those people had taken ill in the years since the fighting...

He looked at Caitlin again, wondering just how much she knew about the syndrome. Whether she knew there'd been a steadily growing number of wives and children getting sick. That some veterans might have been exposed to weird germs and brought them home to their families.

"You're positive it was the syndrome?" he asked at last.

"Nobody seemed to have any doubts."

He nodded, although the notion seemed a little strange. It was almost exclusively ground troops who'd ended up sick. Not guys based on aircraft carriers. Not guys like him and Mike. And then it struck him.

"That night he was in Al Jubayl?" he asked.

"Yes, we thought it had to be. An amazing number of troops stationed there have had problems."

Luke turned toward the railing and stood staring at nothing, thinking that it was only a damn fluke *he* hadn't been the one sent to Al Jubayl instead of Mike.

When the ground war had finally begun, after all those months of embargoes and the weeks of air attacks, General Schwarzkopf's aides had organized a morale-building tour. They'd wanted a few officers, ones who'd been on active duty in the Gulf from early on, to visit American bases in Saudi Arabia and talk to the troops.

And hell, for him and Mike, who'd spent almost all their time sitting off the coast aboard the *Saratoga*, the prospect of getting a look at what was happening on shore had been awfully inviting. So they'd both volunteered, and had both been sent to visit a few bases.

But it was Mike who'd ended up in the desert near Al Jubayl. And while he'd been there, in the early morning hours of January 20, there'd been two explosions—so loud they'd jolted people from their bunks.

The sky, Mike had recounted later, was lit up with bright flashes, and a command to go to full Mopp-4 had been given, ordering everyone into full chemical gear.

Mike had left for the next stop on his tour the following day, unsure whether or not that command had only been precautionary.

Caitlin was right, though. An incredible number of troops stationed at Al Jubayl had subsequently developed the syndrome.

Luke turned from the railing and looked at her. She was quietly watching him. In the moonlight, she looked almost ethereal. But sad, so sad.

"So that's what Mike died of," he said gently. "I'd wondered."

She shook her head. "No. He was sick, but that's not how he died."

CHAPTER FOUR

WHEN LUKE SIMPLY WAITED, Caitlin continued.

"I don't think I'd have told you this if you hadn't decided to stay in Culpepper for a while because... because Mike is dead and that's what matters. But somebody's bound to say something, and I don't want it coming as a surprise to you. Luke...they say Mike killed himself."

"Oh, God," he whispered.

Caitlin had begun to cry quietly, so he stepped closer and put his arms around her. That enticing meadows-in-moonlight fragrance she wore gently assailed his senses, and she felt soft and fragile against him.

Soft and fragile and so desperately in need. But he didn't know what to do—except hold her.

For a moment, Caitlin tried to ignore the way being in the warm shelter of Luke's arms made her feel. But some things were impossible to ignore, and his solid male body pressed against hers was one of them.

It had been such a long, long time since a man had held her. And it felt so good to have someone care enough to comfort her. She hadn't known just how much she'd missed that.

She rested her cheek against Luke's chest. And just as they had yesterday, her thoughts drifted to things people had told her in the months after she'd lost Mike.

When they'd said the day would come that she'd feel comfortable in another man's arms, she'd never really quite believed them. But Luke Dakota made it easier to see that was possible.

And even though she knew there'd never be anything between them, his holding her like this made her wonder what might have happened if they'd met under different circumstances.

But they hadn't. He'd only come through Culpepper because he'd been curious about his namesake. And he'd only offered to stay and help her out because Mike had been his friend. And he'd be gone again in no time. So she'd be foolish to dwell on what might possibly have been *if*...

Finally, reluctantly, she eased away a little, murmuring, "I'm all right now. I'm over it, you know. I really am. I'll never forget Mike, and part of me will never stop loving him, but I've accepted the fact that he's gone. It's just...sometimes it's still hard to talk about how he died."

"It's okay." Luke hesitated, knowing this wasn't a good time to ask for details. But he wanted the whole story, and she'd told him she'd rather he heard it from her.

"You said," he added, "they *say* Mike killed himself."

"That's what the sheriff decided. Mike was working late one night and...and he shot himself...if the sheriff was right."

"You don't think he was?"

Caitlin slowly shook her head. "Luke, I just don't know. But I think Mike might have been murdered."

CAITLIN SAT WATCHING Luke, not at all sure revealing her suspicions had been the right thing to do. She'd meant to simply say the official verdict had been suicide, and she'd just wanted to be the one who told him.

But her doubts made it hard to say suicide straight out, as if it were an indisputable fact. And the impression she'd formed of Luke told her she could be forthright with him—that he'd listen with an open mind.

There was no guarantee, though, that his conclusion would be different from everybody else's. And everyone in Culpepper was certain Mike had killed himself—everyone but her, at least.

"I probably shouldn't have said that," she murmured when Luke finally looked at her again. "I'm the only one who thinks it might not have been suicide, so... I guess that makes me seem a little crazy, doesn't it?"

"No." He pulled a chair around and sat down facing her. "You don't seem crazy at all. But you kind of came at me from left field with this. Tell me the details."

She'd been right. He was going to listen. She took a deep breath, then began.

"There really aren't many details to tell. It was the first week in January, and there'd been a few break-ins at airport buildings over Christmas. Nothing serious, just teenagers stealing cigarettes from vending machines and that sort of thing. But Rayland... Rayland Skoda is the sheriff."

Luke nodded.

"Well, because of the problems, Rayland took to driving around the airport more often than usual.

And that night he noticed a light on in the Sky Knights hangar, so he went in to check. And . . . and he found Mike. He'd been killed with his own gun. It was lying beside his body. And he'd died from a single shot . . . and . . ."

"Could it have been a botched break-in?" Luke asked gently. "Teenagers after more than cigarettes?"

She shook her head. "His wallet was still in his pocket, and there was no sign anyone else had been there. And Rayland said that if someone had come in, if someone had found Mike there and there'd been a confrontation . . . well, Rayland said the guy would have taken off the second Mike was shot, in case anyone had heard the noise. He'd never have wasted time trying to make it look like suicide."

"So you're saying that if somebody else was there . . . you think he checked beforehand to be sure the place was empty? No one around to hear a shot? That he went there *planning* to kill Mike?"

"I think . . . oh, Luke, I know how unlikely this sounds, but someone else *could* have shot him, then made it look . . . but both Rayland's report and the medical examiner's said there was no doubt Mike killed himself."

"You read the reports?"

"No. Rayland told me what was in them, and there didn't seem to be any point in reading them. It . . . I knew it would upset me. And knowing Rayland, if there was anything about Mike's death that didn't quite fit in with his suicide theory he'd have simply omitted it."

"That's this Rayland's approach to things?"

She shrugged. "Rayland likes to be right. He wouldn't want to leave himself open to questions about a case."

"But you said there's a medical examiner's report, too. So we're talking about *two* experts who both—"

"No, not really. The medical examiner drinks. Heavily. Late at night, he'd have done well to realize Mike had been shot, let alone notice if anything seemed peculiar. So he'd have just gone along with whatever Rayland said, the way he always does. And looking at his report would just be looking at a copy of Rayland's, with a few medical terms added in."

"He's a yes-man as well as a drunk."

"Uh-huh. That's something else Rayland likes— being surrounded by yes-men. He wants to be the one calling the shots."

"That's why he's a small-town sheriff?"

"Exactly. He grew up in Culpepper, then spent ten or twelve years on the Tucson police force. But when the Culpepper County sheriff retired a couple of years ago... well, Rayland's happier being a big fish in a little pond. And this county's pretty small, so there's only him and a couple of deputies—who both do whatever he tells them to."

"Okay, then it's only Rayland's opinion that matters. But it's certainly possible to cover up a murder by making it look like suicide. So why was he so positive Mike killed himself? Did he figure there was a reason?"

When Caitlin left Luke's question hanging for a few seconds, he reached over and took her hand.

"Sorry," he said quietly. "If you don't want to talk about it any more now, we don't have to."

"No. Thanks, but I'll be okay in a second."

"All right." He leaned back once more, removing his hand.

She wished he hadn't. She needed all the reassurance she could get. "Rayland assumed," she made herself continue, "that Mike just couldn't cope with being sick any longer. I guess that's what everyone assumed."

SICK. IT TOOK Luke a minute to bring himself up to speed on that. Once they'd started in on the question of suicide versus murder, he'd forgotten about Mike having come down with the Gulf syndrome.

"At first," Caitlin went on, "he was sure he'd be well again in no time. But when he wasn't, when he just kept deteriorating, he got more and more depressed. He...people he knew were dying of it, Luke. He got involved with some veterans who were suffering from it. People from all over the country who filed a class action to get compensation. And every time he heard that another one of them had died... well, it would have been surprising if he *hadn't* been depressed."

Luke waited, wanting to let her tell this her own way. But she'd said the gun had been Mike's. And if he'd been sick and depressed...hell, everything she'd said so far seemed to indicate suicide. So why did she believe it might have been murder?

"Mike and I didn't know what would happen," she finally said. "With his illness, I mean. But the doctors certainly hadn't given up on him. And when we found out I was pregnant he was thrilled. For the first time in months, he was looking forward to the future."

"So you're saying the timing was hard to believe. But aside from that, is there any real evidence it might not have been suicide?"

"Oh, Luke," she murmured. "You knew Mike. Do *you* think he'd have killed himself?"

Luke looked out into the darkness once more, memories from the months he'd spent with Mike drifting through his mind. The answer to Caitlin's question was no. The man he'd known in the Gulf wouldn't have killed himself. But the war had been years ago. And things had changed for Mike after that. Changed for the worse.

"A few months after he died," Caitlin said quietly, "I joined a bereavement group in Tucson. And one of the things I learned was that denial is a normal reaction to a suicide. You can't stand to believe someone you love would choose to leave you. Especially not that way."

"But?" Luke said, hearing the word she hadn't said aloud.

She gave him a wan smile. "But I still don't think my doubts are only denial at work. There are a couple of things...not what anyone would call evidence, but things I've just never been able to come to terms with."

He waited again, wishing he were better in this sort of situation. There had to be something he could do or say, but he didn't know what.

"What things?" he said at last.

"Well, there was no note. And it's so hard to believe Mike wouldn't have left me some sort of explanation. And there's another thing. When he left the navy, he took out a good life insurance policy. And several times after he got sick, he mentioned how glad he was he'd done that, which just doesn't add up with..."

"With what?"

"With the fact there was a clause in the policy saying no death benefits would be paid on a suicide."

Luke exhaled slowly. "Is there any chance he wasn't aware of that?"

"No. Only a few weeks before he died the insurance agent was here—checking on something to do with the property insurance. And Mike had some questions about his personal policy, so the three of us sat and went over it very carefully. We both knew exactly what the terms were."

"That *does* put a different light on things, then, doesn't it?"

Caitlin gazed at him for a moment. "I thought so," she murmured at last.

"What about that class action suit you mentioned? Will you be getting anything from that?"

"I doubt it. I haven't really kept up with what's happening, but I can't imagine it's likely now."

So Caitlin was losing out on all sides. And suddenly, what she was saying didn't seem to be indicating suicide at all.

"And the sheriff?" Luke said at last. "Did you raise all this with him?"

"Eventually. At first I wasn't functioning very well. But later, I told Rayland it didn't add up."

"And he said?"

"He just brushed it off. He said people don't always think straight when they're depressed."

"I guess that's true," Luke said slowly. On the other hand, once the sheriff had labeled Mike's death a suicide, he probably wouldn't have liked anyone suggesting it wasn't.

"Is this Rayland competent?" he finally asked. "I mean, if Mike didn't kill himself, if somebody did try to make it look like suicide, what are the odds Rayland might have just taken a quick look and been fooled?"

"I don't know. People seem to think he does a good job, but it's got to be possible he simply missed something. Either that or..."

"Or what?"

"I...Luke, I'm not trying to say Rayland's as crooked as a dog's hind leg or anything like that. But if...if one of his buddies was the murderer..."

"Sheriff Skoda is another one of the good ol' boys?"

She nodded. "And if one of his friends had anything to do with what happened, I can't help thinking Rayland might have gone along with a cover-up."

"Even though it meant Mike's killer going free?"

"Rayland...well, *hated* would be too strong, but Mike was never Rayland's favorite person."

"Oh?"

"I went out with Rayland for a little while once. It was a long time ago and only...oh, half a dozen times, maybe. Then I realized I just wasn't that crazy about him. But I started seeing Mike right afterward, and I think Rayland always figured Mike took me away from him. It wasn't true, but...oh, the baby's awake."

Caitlin rose. "I won't be long. He's probably just wet."

Watching her disappear into the house, Luke started thinking about that insurance policy clause again. It sure did make the idea of suicide a lot harder to swallow. Hell, no matter how depressed Mike had been, surely he wouldn't have left his wife pregnant and facing financial disaster.

And even if he had decided to kill himself, wouldn't he have at least tried to make it look like an accident? So there'd have been doubt, and Caitlin might have gotten the money?

Luke sat staring at the moonlight on the pool, wondering if it was possible someone really had murdered Mike. Had Rayland Skoda missed something? Or had he played a role in a cover-up?

CAITLIN FINISHED changing the baby's diaper and settled him back into his crib. "You sleep through till morning now, Chief," she whispered, kissing his cheek.

"Ghaaa," he murmured, but it was a tired sound that said he was already halfway back to dreamland.

She tucked his teddy in beside him and switched off the light. His bedroom was at the back of the house, and through the window she could see partway along the dimly lit deck—far enough to see that Luke was still sitting where she'd left him.

He looked lost in thought. She knew what he had to be thinking about, but she didn't know which way his thoughts were running.

She was certain, though, that he was a far more objective thinker than any of Culpepper's good ol' boys had ever been. So, if he said he couldn't see that her suspicions added up to much, it might be time to put her doubts to rest. But if he thought there was a chance those suspicions could be valid...

If he did, she knew he was the kind of man who'd offer to help her follow up on them. And that prospect was half encouraging, half terrifying.

She'd never been able to gather enough courage to challenge the whole town's beliefs. Not on her own, and not just on the basis of a couple of things that didn't seem right to her. But if Luke figured they were significant, and he offered to help, she was going to take him up on it. Because if Mike had been murdered she wanted the killer caught. Even though trying to make that happen was bound to tear her life apart.

Feeling as if Luke was about to pronounce final judgment on her, she turned and headed from the baby's room into the hall. But just as she made it back to the deck a flash of headlights down the side of the house told her someone had arrived.

"Someone's parking out front," she said when Luke looked over.

He glanced at his watch, then back at her. "It's past ten-thirty."

She managed a smile. But whoever was here couldn't have chosen a worse moment. Now she was going to have to wait to hear what Luke had to say, and she'd be on tenterhooks until she knew what he thought.

"I'll bet it's my grandparents," she told him. "My grandmother probably wore my grandfather down and they're here to inspect you. They'll realize we're out back," she added, starting toward the far side of the deck.

Following along, Luke hoped he looked trustworthy enough to pass her grandparents' inspection. But it wasn't anyone's grandparents who appeared around the corner of the house. It was Lonnie McDougall and a woman about Caitlin's age.

Lonnie was wearing an extremely self-satisfied grin. The woman, a good-looking redhead, had a Sky Knights jacket draped over her shoulders.

Luke glanced at Caitlin in time to catch a puzzled expression cross her face. She quickly replaced it with a smile that didn't strike him as quite genuine. Then she hugged the woman, saying, "Well, this is a surprise."

"So, Dakota," Lonnie said, "you get settled in here all right?"

"Yeah...fine." But he doubted Lonnie had dropped by just to check that he was happy with the accommodations.

"What are you two doing here?" Caitlin asked.

"Oh, we just thought we'd pay you a little visit." The woman gave Luke the once-over.

Caitlin caught her looking at him and laughed. "You mean you just thought you'd come and check out Sky Knights' temporary pilot. Well, here he is. Luke, this is Peggy-Sue Curtis, my best friend."

Peggy-Sue smiled at him. "Wait, please don't ask. I've already been asked a million times in my life, and yes, my mother *was* a big Buddy Holly fan." She turned to Caitlin once more, and dangled her left hand in front of her face.

"Oh, my," Caitlin whispered.

When she started hugging Peggy-Sue again, Luke glanced at Lonnie, hoping somebody would clue him in soon.

Lonnie was grinning even more broadly. "We just got engaged," he explained.

"Let me have a closer look!" Caitlin reached for Peggy-Sue's hand, inspected her diamond and declared it gorgeous. "Have you set the date?"

"Not yet. We're thinking maybe between Thanksgiving and Christmas. Can you spare a day in there to be my matron of honor?"

"You think I'd miss being part of your wedding? Not for the world! But how did...I mean, I thought that job in Minneapolis was a done deal."

"It was, but I decided I didn't want to leave Arizona after all. I—"

"The real story," Lonnie interrupted, "is that she finally realized she just can't live without me."

Peggy-Sue rolled her eyes at Caitlin. "I'll tell you the real story some other time."

Luke was watching Caitlin out of the corner of his eye. This seemed to have taken her completely by surprise. But if Peggy-Sue was her best friend, surely it shouldn't have been that big a shock.

"But...oh," she finally said, "this is just so unexpected I can't think straight. What on earth did your parents say?"

"The same thing you're saying," Peggy-Sue told her. "Although I don't know why it's throwing everyone. How many times have Lonnie and I broken up and gotten back together?"

"A million and twelve?"

"Very funny, Caitlin," Lonnie muttered, firmly wrapping his arm around Peggy-Sue's waist. "Only this time we're back together permanently."

Caitlin turned her attention to him. "And what did your folks say?"

He shrugged. "We haven't been by the house yet. But the old man will probably say he hopes we don't expect a wedding present—he's got too many shaky loans out to be throwing any money around.''

"Oh, Lonnie, don't be like that," Peggy-Sue murmured.

"Does your dad know Billy-Bob left?" Caitlin asked him.

"Does a bear live in the woods? Billy-Bob stopped by the bank on his way out of town. To close his account. And I hear the old man was on him like fleas on a dog. Then he called the hangar to tear a strip off me—like it was my fault Billy-Bob packed it in.''

Caitlin glanced at Luke. "I mentioned Lonnie's father is president of Culpepper's local bank, didn't I? And that he loaned us money to help start Sky Knights?"

"And there hasn't been a day since that he doesn't remind me about it," Lonnie muttered. "Mr. Quentin 'Big Financier' McDougall. Thinks because we owe him money he can tell us how to run the business.''

"But he was okay once you explained about Luke," Peggy-Sue said.

Lonnie grinned again, glancing at Caitlin. "Yeah, you should have heard him reverse gears when I said we already had a pilot to replace Billy-Bob. It really shot him down in flames.''

Luke didn't bother reminding Lonnie that their replacement couldn't hang around for much more than a couple of weeks. It wasn't the sort of fact that had likely slipped the guy's mind.

"Well let's get back to more important things," Caitlin said. "We should be toasting your engagement with champagne, but I don't have any. There's some wine, though. And beer.''

"It's okay," Peggy-Sue told her. "We can't stay. We've got to get over to Lonnie's parents' before they hear about this from somebody else."

"Yeah," Lonnie agreed, sounding decidedly unenthusiastic. "Well, see you for the morning mission, huh, Dakota?"

"You're just going to start him right in like that?" Peggy-Sue asked. "Doesn't he need a few practice flights or anything? Before he takes up a customer?"

"Honey, I told you, he's a flight instructor. And he flew real missions in the Gulf. He sure as hell doesn't need any practice to fly pretend dogfights. So," he added to Luke, "I'll see you about eight, then. And listen, thanks again, huh? Both Caitlin and I really appreciate your helping out."

Luke nodded. Despite telling Caitlin he wanted to fly mock combat because he'd heard it was fun, he'd been having trouble actually believing he'd have much fun with Lonnie around. But maybe it wouldn't be too bad, after all. Getting engaged to Peggy-Sue seemed to have improved the guy's attitude considerably.

LUKE AND CAITLIN stood watching until the rear lights of Lonnie's pickup disappeared into the night, then they started back along the side of the house.

As tempted as he was to ask why Peggy-Sue's engagement had come as such a surprise, he merely said, "Your friend seems like fun."

"She is. She's great. Her parents live only two doors from my grandparents, and we've been friends for as long as I can remember. I just... I just hope she's doing the right thing."

"Marrying Lonnie, you mean?"

"Uh-huh. I thought . . . well, saying they'd broken up and gotten back together a million and twelve times was being facetious. But it's happened so many times I've lost count. And I thought, this last time, it was really over."

"Ahh. I wondered why you seemed so surprised."

"Well . . . she had this terrific opportunity lined up in Minneapolis. She's an interior designer, and right now she works for a department store in Tucson. But this new job was with a top design firm. And she was really excited about it. So to throw away the chance and get back together with Lonnie . . ."

"You don't figure things will work out for them?"

Caitlin shrugged. "They don't have a very good track record. Peg started going out with Lonnie when she and I were in high school, and their relationship was bumpy right from the start. Then, a while after he joined the air force, he suddenly dumped her and married a girl from Tucson."

"Oh. I guess that would have made for a major bump in their relationship, wouldn't it?"

Caitlin gave a weak smile, but it was a far cry from the one she sometimes gave him. The one that said she liked him . . . the one that started the little itching sensation in his groin that he'd been doing his best to ignore.

"At any rate," she was saying, "when Lonnie's marriage didn't last, he and Peggy-Sue got back together. But it's been on and off ever since. And it's been months now since they last broke up, so I thought she'd really decided it was time to find somebody new."

"His temper's one of the problems?"

"I don't know if it really is or not. Peg seems to have learned to ignore it. I think for the last while, the problem was more that she'd like to get married and have kids, while Lonnie's pretty gun-shy about commitment now. They've never even tried living together."

"They're both right in Culpepper, though?"

"Uh-huh. Peg rents a little house, and Lonnie has an apartment."

They reached the back of the house and started across the deck.

"But I really thought," Caitlin added as they reached the kitchen door, "that Peg would be leaving—given this new job offer and all. Apparently I thought wrong.

"I guess we'd better turn in," she said, changing the subject as Luke slid the door open. "You'll be heading for Sky Knights pretty early, and I've got that drive into Tucson with my grandmother."

He followed her inside and watched her lock up behind them, thinking he had to be reading things wrong. She couldn't *possibly* be intending to leave their conversation about Mike hanging fire all night.

She didn't say another word about it, though, just added, "I guess the baby and I will be gone before you're ready for breakfast in the morning, but there's bacon and eggs in the fridge."

She flicked off the kitchen light, then paused in the soft moonlight. "You know where everything is by now, so just make whatever looks good."

"Caitlin?" He leaned against the counter. "I'm not really tired, so let's get back to what we were talking about before. If you figure someone might have killed Mike, and the sheriff is sure there was no intruder in his office, do you have any idea who could have been there? Any idea who might have wanted Mike dead?"

She pushed back her hair and stood gazing at him. He thought she looked incredibly beautiful in the silvery light. But also incredibly anxious.

"I . . . mmmm . . . he didn't have any real enemies, Luke. So when I get to possible motives, that's where I kind of come up against a brick wall. Sometimes it's enough to make me think everybody else must be right about what happened and I must be wrong."

She must be wrong? He hesitated, not sure what the hell the deal was. Half an hour ago, she'd been telling him she just couldn't buy the idea of suicide. So why the abrupt about-face?

"Maybe," he said at last, "there was a motive you don't know about. Because that clause in the insurance policy really bothers me."

"I know. It really bothers me, too."

"So . . . if you have any idea at all, I'd like to help you look into it. Mike was the best friend I had in the Gulf, Caitlin. And if somebody murdered him . . ."

"Thanks. He'd have been glad to hear you say that. But . . . let's talk some more tomorrow, okay? It really *is* getting late."

"All right," he agreed slowly. "I guess if it's waited eighteen months, it can wait a few more hours."

Caitlin forced a smile, then seized her opportunity to escape and started off ahead of Luke through the house. Once she made it to her bedroom, she'd be safe from his questions for a while.

She paused to take a peek in at the baby, and when she turned back into the hall Luke was standing in the doorway of the room she'd given him—the one directly across from the Chief's.

His presence seemed to make the hallway seem smaller. And the even way he was watching her made her intensely aware of that blatant masculinity he radiated.

The same fluttering sensation she'd felt before started again, but this time she told herself it was just a symptom of her uneasiness. She was certain Luke thought she was playing games with him, and she wished he didn't. She hadn't known him long, but she already owed him a lot…and already liked him a lot.

As much as she wanted to be straight with him, though, she couldn't be. At least, not before she'd had a chance to reconsider the situation. "Well, good night, Luke," she finally said.

"'Night, Caitlin."

She felt his eyes still on her as she walked the rest of the way down the hall, but she didn't look back. She simply closed the door of her room and quickly slipped out of her clothes and into a nightshirt.

After she'd finished in the ensuite bathroom she crawled between the cool sheets, her mind still racing. What was she going to do tomorrow, when Luke started in with those questions again? What was she going to say?

Lying in the darkness, she listened to the quiet sounds of him getting ready for bed, wondering if fate had taken a hand in things tonight, if that's what had made Peggy-Sue and Lonnie arrive when they had.

If they hadn't appeared, she and Luke would have finished their conversation. He'd already know the rest of the facts, and it would be too late to consider keeping them from him.

Restlessly, she rolled onto her side. She had only one idea about who might have killed Mike. And that's all it was. Just a suspicion, not a shred of evidence. And saying anything about it would be like poking at a hornets' nest with a sharp stick. She'd be certain to get stung. The only question would be how badly.

Despite that, though, if Luke had asked her his questions earlier, she'd have shared what little there was to go on with him. But could she do that now?

She could live with alienating Lonnie forever, but she wasn't sure she could live with losing her best friend. So could she still tell Luke her suspicions about Lonnie, now that he was engaged to Peggy-Sue?

CHAPTER FIVE

THE ARIZONA MORNING SKY was an endless cornflower blue. High, cloudless and peaceful. But inside Luke's cockpit, it was anything but peaceful.

"Chief! Chief!" Harry hollered into the intercom—so loud Luke's earphones practically blew off his ears.

Then Harry glanced over his shoulder, obviously wanting to make sure Luke had heard, even though he'd have to be stone deaf to have missed it.

"Head back up and come at him from behind again!" Harry yelled.

Luke was tempted to reach forward and snap off the boom mike attached to Harry's headset. Instead he just said, "Sure thing, Mad Dog," and pulled back on the stick, muttering a few choice obscenities under his breath.

The first thing Lonnie had done during preflight had been to assign their two amateur pilots call signs. And he'd sure picked the right one for this character.

Harry "Mad Dog" McCluskey was a real lunatic who'd probably be happy if they flew straight into Lonnie's plane. It would make a better story for the folks down home in Boise, Idaho.

Mad Dog's only saving grace was that he didn't care about trying to do any of the flying. Learning that had made Luke feel a lot better. Since it was his first time playing this game, he liked being in complete control. And he figured he could live with Mad Dog screaming instructions and shooting up the sky whenever they got anywhere close to the enemy.

"Okay! Okay!" he yelled as Luke started turning toward Lonnie's bird. "I'm gonna kill that 'Ricochet' guy for sure this time."

Mad Dog began firing away, his finger locked on the trigger even though there wasn't a hope in hell he could make a kill from where they were.

When they'd finished the premission briefing and actually gotten into the cockpit, Lonnie had carefully explained how to operate the gun sight, saying that the target should be within the thirty-degree cone. But Mad Dog apparently had no concept of how narrow a thirty-degree arc was.

If his machine gun had been loaded with real ammunition instead of laser bullets, he'd have been out of ammo long ago—without scoring a single kill. Nobody could hit the broadside of the Goodyear blimp, never mind a plane, by shooting at the angles Mad Dog was attempting.

Luke glanced at his watch. Lonnie had said they'd stay up about an hour, and they were getting close. He'd also said to make sure Mad Dog got at least one real good hit, so he'd go home a happy camper.

"Mad Dog!" Luke said over the sound of the gun. "Mad Dog, stop shooting for a minute and hold on to your helmet. We're going to rock and roll."

With Mad Dog giving him a thumbs-up from the front seat, Luke whipped the plane up and left in a half roll that got them directly over Lonnie and Ricochet.

"Look! Look!" Mad Dog screamed, peering down at them. "They don't know where we've gone!"

Luke grinned, ignoring the ringing Mad Dog's shouting had started in his ears. Beneath them, in the front seat, Ricochet was looking from right to left, trying to find them. The bubble canopy gave him unlimited visibility, so if he just looked up he'd spot them, but he didn't think of that.

Behind him, Lonnie was studiously staring at his instruments, knowing full well what was going on but pretending he didn't—letting Mad Dog have his big chance.

"Okay," Luke said. "Now, hold off on the trigger until I tell you. We're going in for the kill."

Mad Dog let out some kind of crazy war whoop while Luke rolled right and down—thinking that if any of his students tried some of the maneuvers he'd pulled this morning he'd wash them out so fast their heads would spin.

"Okay! Now! Take the bounce!" he ordered as they dropped directly behind the other plane.

Mad Dog's guns blazed away and the billowing smoke around the other bird told them they'd hit it.

"I did it!" Mad Dog screamed. "I did it! I told you I'd get him this time!"

"Good shooting, ace. That was a kill. You were dead center on his fuselage." Luke started into a roll away, adding, "Now let's disengage, before Ricochet gets his sights on us."

"Mad Dog and Chief," Lonnie said as the smoke cleared, "this is Squadron Commander 'Terminator' McDougall."

It was the first time he'd broken radio silence since they'd taken off, and Luke could see why he'd maintained it until now. It immediately destroyed the illusion that Lonnie and Ricochet were Mad Dog's mortal enemies.

"You shot us up pretty bad, Mad Dog," he continued, "so we'd better take 'em down now. See you on the deck for debriefing. Over and out."

"Roger. Ten-four." Luke eased the throttle back and started a gradual descent. Then he pushed the transmit button, overriding the intercom, and contacted the tower as they headed back for the Culpepper City Airport.

After that, Mad Dog started going on about how great the flight had been.

"Yeah." Luke grinned. "It's the most fun you can have with your clothes on."

"Damn right! Damn right it is," Mad Dog agreed, proceeding to review every minute of the adventure for Luke, as if he hadn't even been there, let alone been flying the plane.

Luke shut out Mad Dog's words and concentrated on his landing, then taxied over to park in front of the Sky Knights hangar, where Lonnie and Ricochet were already down and waiting for them. Ricochet had his helmet tucked tightly under his arm and it looked as if he was hoping they'd let him take it home.

"Hey, you were great up there!" Lonnie told Mad Dog as he climbed out of the plane. "You and Ricochet can go up with us again anytime."

Luke laughed to himself. Lonnie might be a hothead, but he was good with the customers. So good they probably forgot about how much money they'd forked out for their morning of excitement. And he had to admit, it *had* been fun to let loose, instead of having to do everything by the navy's books.

"Hey, Dakota." Lonnie clapped Luke on the back and fell into step with him behind Mad Dog and Ricochet. "You're really a honcho up there. Now that I know you can hold your own, I won't worry about taking it easy next time."

"Don't worry on my account."

As they headed into the hangar for the debriefing, Luke wondered if Lonnie actually figured he *had* been taking things easy on that mission.

The truth was, he'd come just a little too close for comfort a few times. And after Billy-Bob Wiggins's remark about him being a maniac in the air...

But hell, the guy was obviously a good flier. And every pilot alive knew that a midair could ruin your whole day.

ON THE DRIVE INTO TUCSON, Caitlin and her grandmother had talked almost nonstop. Betty Chastain had asked at least a hundred more questions about Luke. And when she'd finally been satisfied that he didn't have rape, looting and pillage on his mind, Caitlin had told her about Peggy-Sue and Lonnie's engagement—which, miraculously, Betty hadn't already heard about via the grapevine. On the trip home, though, they'd both fallen into silence.

Caitlin glanced into the back of the van at the baby, sitting quietly in his car seat, and her eyes lingered on him for a second. He looked so sweet and innocent her heart filled with love.

When she turned her attention back to the highway, they were just passing a sign that told her they were halfway to Culpepper. So if she was going to ask her grandmother for advice, it was time to get asking.

She seldom did that anymore. It seemed childish when she was an adult—a twenty-eight-, almost twenty-nine-year-old woman with a child.

Sometimes, though, she still felt like a child herself, whereas Betty Chastain had seventy-three years of life experience to draw on. And more common sense than any other ten women put together.

"Caitlin?" Betty said, breaking the silence. "Is there something wrong? You've seemed awfully distant since we started home."

"You're a mind reader, you know that?" Caitlin smiled at her.

Her grandmother smiled back. "That's what bringing up children did for me. What's the problem?"

"Well...it's about Peggy-Sue and Lonnie. Partly about them, at least. And...and it's about Mike."

"Oh," Betty said quietly. "Their engagement got you feeling blue about him?"

"Not exactly." She stared ahead at the highway for a moment, then glanced across the van again. "Remember back after Mike died? When we talked about...how it happened...about what I kept wondering...about Lonnie?"

"Oh, Caitlin, you aren't still having those awful doubts, are you, dear? Not after all this time."

She looked straight ahead again. Her grandmother had never thought those doubts could have any basis in reality. After Mike had died, she'd given Caitlin all the sympathy in the world and all the help possible. But she'd been certain the doubts were only grief talking.

"Grandma," she continued at last, "Luke Dakota and I discussed it some last night and—"

"Darling, you didn't tell him you suspected Lonnie had anything to do with it, did you? The man's a perfect stranger and—"

"Grandma, he's *not* a stranger. He was Mike's friend and I thought he should know the details. So I told him about Rayland's report, and that I wasn't sure his conclusion was right. And Luke said . . . he said if I really thought there was a chance Mike was murdered, he wanted to help me get to the bottom of it. But just when I was going to tell him about Lonnie, he and Peggy-Sue showed up and . . . and now I'm not sure what to do."

She waited, but her grandmother remained quiet. "Well?" she finally asked.

"Caitlin, by getting to the bottom of it, do you mean asking questions? Maybe even pointing fingers?"

"I . . . yes. I mean I don't know about the pointing fingers part. I guess that would depend on what we found out."

"And you really do think there might be something to find out?"

"I'm honestly not sure," Caitlin admitted slowly. "But it's not being sure of what actually happened that . . . Grandma, I just want to *know*."

Betty gazed out the window for a minute, then looked at Caitlin once more. "Darling, I thought you'd worked this all through with that bereavement group of yours. I realize there's a stigma attached to suicide, but—"

"Grandma, it's not that I care what people think. And I have worked it all through. But I just can't make myself say, 'Oh, well,' and forget about it. If Mike didn't kill himself, I want to know."

"And if you ask your questions, and the answers make you decide he *did* kill himself? Then what?"

"Then I guess I'd have to live with it. But at least I'd know for sure."

"Caitlin...I don't mean to sound critical, but don't you think you've gotten a little obsessive about this? It's been over a year and a half now and—"

"It's not just for me, Grandma. It's for the baby, too. You know what he's going to think when he's old enough to understand? He's going to think his father didn't even want to stick around long enough to see him born."

"Oh, I can't imagine him ever—"

"No, it's not just some fantasy I'm making up. It's something we discussed in my group—how a parent's suicide affects children. And you know what else I learned from those people? That a parent who commits suicide is giving his child a deadly message—that when things get rough there's an easy way out."

"Oh, Caitlin, it sounds as if you're just looking for things to worry about."

"I know. I'm not out of touch with reality—I know exactly what it sounds like. But I also know that when he's older and has a problem, I'll always worry about what thoughts are going through his mind. And if I could only prove Mike *didn't* kill himself..."

"At what cost?" Betty said quietly. "There's absolutely nothing you can do that will bring Mike back."

"I know, but—"

"And there would be an awfully high cost in trying to prove Rayland was wrong."

Caitlin shrugged, but she had a pretty good idea how high the cost would be.

"I hardly have to remind you," Betty went on, "that Lonnie is your business partner. Do you really think you could keep on working with him if you accused him of murdering Mike?"

She didn't answer. What was there to say? She had to keep on working with Lonnie. If Sky Knights failed, she'd lose everything. It was as simple as that. So she and Lonnie were going to sink or swim together. But even if it was only a nagging possibility, the fear that she just might be trying to swim with Mike's killer was eating away at her.

"And what about Peggy-Sue?" Betty pressed. "How do you think she'd react if she thought you were trying to make people think her fiancé was a murderer?"

"I . . . she wouldn't be happy, Grandma, I know that, but—"

"And what do you think things would be like for you around here if you voiced your suspicions about Lonnie? You know what a powerful family the McDougalls are."

Focusing on the road ahead, Caitlin silently admitted her grandmother was right on all counts.

"Caitlin . . . you could end up ruining your life in Culpepper."

"I know," she murmured. And if she did, pulling up stakes and leaving wouldn't be an option. Not as long as the bank had both Sky Knights and her property tied up. Her share of the company and her ranch were all the security she had in the world. So she had to stay right where she was and make sure those debts got paid off.

"Darling, just think hard on what the outcome will be before you say anything more to Luke Dakota. Because it might end up hurting you a lot more than it would help. Why is he so eager to help you, anyway?"

"He's not exactly eager. He just offered. I guess because he was Mike's friend."

"Oh."

Caitlin shot her grandmother a sharp look. She knew there was a lot of meaning in that *oh.* "Oh, what?"

"Nothing. It was just that you were talking away about him the whole drive into Tucson. And you did say he was an attractive man."

"I was talking about him because you kept grilling me. And I told you he was attractive because you asked me point-blank. Did you want me to lie?"

"Of course not. It's just that the way you were talking about him made me wonder if there might be something happening between the two of you."

"Grandma, Luke Dakota only arrived a few days ago. Aside from anything else, there's been no time for something to be happening."

"Sometimes it takes no time at all, Caitlin. Sometimes all it takes is a single look."

"Well this isn't one of those times. Luke is staying to fly for Sky Knights for a week or two. That's all there is to it."

"To fly for you . . . and to help you ask questions that could ruin your life."

"Grandma—"

"Darling, all I'm saying is consider the consequences. Weigh them against how strongly you feel you need to dig for a different answer than the one you've already got. All right?''

"All right," she murmured.

"Good, then let's change the subject. Why don't you leave the baby with me for the afternoon? You said you were behind with your books, and that would give you a chance to get caught up.''

"Well..."

"Your grandfather and I can bring him out to the ranch later.''

And that, Caitlin thought, would give them a chance to meet Luke—which she suspected was the whole point of the suggestion. When she glanced over, Betty was wearing her best innocent look. That confirmed the suspicion.

"Your grandfather was just saying it's been at least a week since he's seen you," she pressed.

"Well...sure, thanks. I could use a few free hours." And one way or another, her grandmother was going to check Luke out, so it really didn't matter whether that happened today or a few days down the line.

They'd reached the outskirts of Culpepper, and Caitlin eased up on the gas. Driving along Main Street, she was still mulling over the advice her grandmother had given her.

It had been sensible, just as she'd expected it would. But she'd already considered the consequences and weighed the options. She'd lain awake all last night doing exactly that. And deep down, she knew she'd decided what she had to do before this conversation had even begun.

Luke's offering to help had given her the courage she needed. So now, despite the cost, she was going to tell him everything. As soon as he got back from Sky Knights they'd sit down and talk. Because, regardless of the potential fallout, she had to find out the truth—both for herself and for her son.

EACH OF THE SKY KNIGHTS planes was equipped with a video system—its cameras mounted in the cockpit, tail and wings—that was programmed to record the entire hour of flight on video for the customers to take with them.

The classroom debriefing, Luke discovered, consisted mainly of reviewing the mission's videos for Mad Dog and Ricochet—tossing around some terminology they could use to impress the folks back in Boise. Since this was Luke's first time through, Lonnie was doing most of the talking.

At the moment, he had the video frozen and was explaining the split S Luke had used to disengage when Lonnie and Ricochet hadn't kept enough nose-tail separation. Half listening, Luke let his mind wander back to last night, still trying to figure out what had happened.

This morning, Caitlin and the baby had been on their way out the door by the time he'd finished his shower, so he'd barely said hello, let alone gotten back to talking about Mike. And last night...

He mentally shook his head, not able to make sense of that. Before Lonnie and Peggy-Sue had arrived, Caitlin had been doing her best to convince him Mike had been murdered. Then, after they left, she'd sounded as if she thought it was a remote possibility—at best.

Glancing over at Lonnie, he wondered if either he or Peggy-Sue had said something that had gone straight over his head but that Caitlin had caught. As far as he could recall, though, no one had even mentioned Mike's name.

"Well," Lonnie was saying to Mad Dog and Ricochet, wrapping up the debriefing, "tell all your friends in Boise about us. And y'all be sure you come back and see us again. A few more missions and we'll turn you both into real aces."

Luke and Lonnie waited while the other two men stripped off their flight suits, then all four of them headed through the hangar and shook hands out front.

"We'll be back," Mad Dog promised. He gave them a mock salute with his video, then followed his buddy to their car.

"Think they really will?" Luke asked.

Lonnie shrugged. "It's a long drive from Idaho, but you never know. We've got people who just can't get enough of it." He looked over to where Trout was checking one of the planes and called, "Trout? You eating out today?"

The mechanic shook his head. "Na, Sally-Mae packed me somethin'. Just damn rabbit food I'll bet, though." He patted his beer belly. "She says there's gettin' to be way too much of me. So I asked her how there could be way too much of such a good thing."

Lonnie laughed, then turned back to Luke. "How about you? You want to grab something? The snack bar in the terminal isn't bad."

Luke hesitated. Lonnie was giving a couple of lessons in the afternoon, but there were no more combat customers booked until tomorrow morning. So he'd figured on heading straight home to Caitlin's when the debriefing was through and get back to that question she'd wiggled out of answering last night. His question about who she thought might have wanted Mike dead. But maybe...

"Sure, lunch sounds good," he said, deciding it wouldn't hurt to stay and talk to Lonnie. After all, he'd been Mike's cousin as well as his partner. And even though Caitlin said she was the only one who suspected Mike's death hadn't been a suicide, he'd like to hear firsthand what a few other people thought.

They'd just reached the terminal when a Culpepper County sheriff's car pulled into a no-standing zone in front and stopped. The door opened and a tall, burly man in a tan sheriff's uniform got out.

Luke tried to get a look at his badge, not sure if this was Rayland Skoda or one of his deputies.

"Hey, Rayland," Lonnie greeted him, giving Luke the information he needed.

"Hey, Lonnie," he said, his glance flickering over Luke. "Y'all catching some lunch?"

Lonnie nodded, then introduced Luke.

The sheriff turned out to be one of those guys who used his handshake to impress people. Luke pretended he didn't notice the bone-crushing pressure, then sized up Rayland as they headed into the terminal and across to the snack bar.

He was younger than the mental picture Luke had formed of him—probably only about thirty-three or thirty-four. But now that he thought about it, a dozen years on the Tucson police force and a couple of years in charge here would add up just about right. And Caitlin had said she'd dated him for a while, so he couldn't be that much older than her.

Luke eyed him, wondering what she'd seen in him...then wondering why it bothered him that she'd seen anything at all.

Rayland had brown hair, brown eyes, even features, and wasn't bad-looking—although the toothpick sticking out of the corner of his mouth was hardly a class act.

Caitlin had mentioned he was one of Culpepper's good ol' boys, and given his build he'd probably played high school football with Lonnie and Trout. So maybe he'd been a star athlete or something. Maybe that sort of thing had impressed her way back when.

"Hey, Conchita," Lonnie called as they reached the snack bar.

The Mexican girl behind it couldn't be more than eighteen. She greeted Lonnie as if he was a regular, but when she glanced at Rayland, her *"Buenas tardes,* Sheriff" was decidedly cool.

Luke wondered if Rayland was a lousy tipper or if she had some other reason for not liking him.

"This here's Luke Dakota," Lonnie told her. "He's flying with me for a spell, so I want you to take good care of him. You like chicken and chili tacos?" he asked, glancing back at Luke.

"Sure."

"Two of your specials, then," Lonnie told her. "And put whatever Rayland wants on my tab, too."

"A taco sounds good," Rayland said.

The snack bar had six stools, plus four small tables set up a few feet away. After Conchita had served their tacos and coffee, they headed over to sit at one of them.

"I heard the name Conchita means saucy," Rayland muttered as they sat down. "But I could do with that one being a little less saucy and a little more friendly. Doesn't she know she's lucky to be in this country?"

"She's legal," Lonnie said. "Rayland," he added to Luke, "has a real burr under his saddle about Mexicans who come across the border illegally."

"Well, what the hell," Rayland said. "They take jobs they've got no right to. But hey, I hear Billy-Bob left kinda sudden," he added, changing the subject.

"Kinda," Lonnie said. "We were lucky Dakota here was around to fill in."

Rayland nodded, then fixed Luke with a cop stare. After all his years in the navy, it didn't strike Luke as particularly intimidating. He gave Rayland a military stare back. So far, he wasn't finding any of Culpepper's good ol' boys easy to like right off.

"Staying out at Caitlin's place, huh?" Rayland said at last.

"Uh-huh. Mike and I were friends," he added, although he had a feeling Rayland already knew the details.

"You could give her a message for me, then. Tell her we're having trouble with the saguaros again. She should keep an eye out."

"Sure," Luke said, although he couldn't imagine what the hell kind of trouble people could have with a cactus—unless they walked into one or something.

"So, how long you here for?" Rayland asked.

"Depends."

The sheriff clearly didn't like that answer, but before he could ask for a more specific one Lonnie said,

"I'm looking for someone permanent, but Luke'll probably be here for a couple of weeks."

"You're navy, huh?" Rayland said. "On leave from Pensacola?"

"That's right." The sheriff *definitely* already knew the details.

"So... you come all this way just to visit Caitlin?"

"Hey, Rayland," Lonnie said. "You sound like you're interrogating a suspect."

Rayland grinned and told Luke he was sorry. Luke didn't believe it for a second. He took a bite of his taco, trying to figure out a way of easing into the subject of Mike's death. Finally, he decided he might as well just plunge right in.

"Caitlin mentioned you were the one who found Mike's body," he said to Rayland.

"Yeah. Nasty business, that Gulf syndrome. Causin' grief for so many people. You and Caitlin hear anything new about your claim?" he added, looking at Lonnie.

When Lonnie simply shook his head, Luke said, "What claim?" He couldn't see he had anything to lose by being nosy.

"Oh, Caitlin didn't tell you about that?" Rayland asked.

Lonnie shot the sheriff a look that told him to shut up. Luke saw it and grew even more curious, but either Rayland had missed the message or he was intentionally ignoring it.

"I figured she'd have said something," he went on. "She and Lonnie've got the makings of a landmark case."

"Oh?" Luke pressed, eyeing Lonnie.

The other man shrugged. "Mike and I couldn't get any partnership insurance when we started Sky Knights. The insurance companies thought mock combat was too dangerous. So when Mike killed himself, the business got no insurance benefits, but I suddenly had a lot of extra expenses. I had to hire a pilot. Plus pay people to do stuff Mike had been doing, as well as things Caitlin had been doing—the books, promotion, stuff like that. She just wasn't coping too well for a while. Then she had the baby and all."

"So what's this landmark case?" Luke pressed when Lonnie seemed through talking.

"They've got a crack lawyer in Tucson working on it," Rayland offered. "Applied to both the Veterans Admin and the Department of Defense for compensation for business losses."

"But if Mike committed suicide...?" Luke said uncertainly.

Rayland wiped his mouth with the back of his hand. "Mike killed himself because he had the Gulf syndrome. Only reason that makes sense."

"The legal argument," Lonnie explained, "is that Mike would still be alive if he hadn't been depressed. And the only reason he was depressed was because he was sick. So the lawyer advised us to file for compensation for what his death cost the business."

"Ahh," Luke said. "And what's happened with the claim?"

"They've been stonewalling. Don't want to set a precedent by paying up. So we just have to wait and see what the lawyer can do."

Luke nodded, then looked over at Rayland. If there was any subtle way of asking he hadn't thought of it, so he came straight out with the question. "You're absolutely sure Mike's death was a suicide?"

"Caitlin tell you she thought I might be wrong? Both me *and* the medical examiner?"

"Uh-huh, as a matter of fact she did. And you know, I knew Mike pretty well, and I have trouble believing he'd kill himself, too."

"Yeah? Well you weren't the one who found the body, were you. Hell, Luke, it's my job to know the difference between homicide and suicide. And like Lonnie was just saying, Caitlin wasn't coping too well for a while back then. So, when she found out she wasn't going to get that insurance money and came to me saying... well, I can't really blame her."

"It had to be worth a try," Lonnie put in. "I don't know how much she's told you, but Mike left her with a pile of financial troubles."

"That's right," Rayland agreed. "And if she could have convinced me to change my tune, she might have had a chance with the insurance company."

Luke's gut clenched. "You're implying," he said slowly, "that she never *really* doubted it was suicide?"

Rayland shot Lonnie a look Luke couldn't read. "As I recall," he said, glancing back at Luke, "Caitlin told me that policy of Mike's was worth two hundred thousand bucks. So if she could have made the insurance folks believe somebody else killed him, she'd be sitting real pretty right now."

CHAPTER SIX

TURNING OFF AIRPORT ROAD in the direction of Caitlin's place, Luke switched on the cruise control to keep himself from speeding. He'd lay odds that Rayland and his deputies just loved handing out speeding tickets, and getting one sure wouldn't improve his mood. Especially not when he was already steamed.

Until a few minutes ago, the thought that Caitlin might be trying to use him hadn't even crossed his mind. But listening to Rayland, that's sure the way things had started adding up.

She'd had no success, on her own, trying to convince anyone that Mike might not have committed suicide. So had all that talk last night been aimed at getting him to play white knight? Try to somehow help her get her hands on that two hundred thousand dollars?

He doubted Rayland Skoda was the type to ever change his tune, as he'd put it. But maybe Caitlin figured, with someone helping her, she could convince the medical examiner to say that murder was at least a possibility. Then the insurance company would be forced to reconsider.

Staring ahead through the windshield, he wondered if she really had any doubts about how Mike had died. Or did she just figure she still had a chance at that money? And that Luke Dakota was enough of a sucker to try and help her get it?

He flicked on his turn signal as he came to the side road leading to her place, not at all sure what was fact and what was fiction. He'd never have taken Caitlin for the type who'd try to play him for a fool, but he'd been wrong about women before.

Hell, he'd *frequently* been wrong about women before. Starting with the girl he'd have married way back when, if she hadn't dumped him, and continuing on with every woman he'd ever thought might be Ms. Right.

When he reached Caitlin's property and neared the house, he could see the minivan in the carport, so she was obviously back from Tucson.

He parked his Mustang, then just sat staring at the house. He wanted answers, yet he was almost afraid to go in and ask for them.

Maybe he'd been wrong about women before, but for some reason he'd hate to learn he'd been wrong about Caitlin.

SINCE SHE'D GOTTEN HOME all Caitlin had been thinking about was her grandmother's warnings—about the Pandora's box she'd open by asking questions about Mike's death.

But now, seeing Luke through the kitchen window, her thoughts shifted to him. She watched him climb out of his Mustang with a strong sense of déjà vu.

She'd been standing in exactly the same spot when she'd seen him for the first time…only days ago…not nearly long enough for anything to be happening. So why wouldn't her grandmother's words leave her alone?

"Sometimes," she'd said, "it takes no time at all. Sometimes all it takes is a single look."

The primitive sexual tug Caitlin felt, just seeing Luke again, confirmed that in spades. And deep down, she knew that telling her grandmother nothing was happening had only been part of the game of self-deception she'd been playing.

Since the first moment she'd laid eyes on Luke, she'd been trying to convince herself he was merely a man who'd been Mike's friend... an attractive man who'd been Mike's friend.

But despite her sense that she wasn't ready to feel anything for another man, Luke's chiseled good looks, easy smile, and that sexy cleft in his chin were definitely making her feel things.

Outside, Sam ambled over from his favorite patch of shade. Luke bent to give the dog a pat. As he moved, his T-shirt and jeans pulled tightly across his body, molding themselves to his lean muscles.

Caitlin's eyes lingered on him. She didn't even bother pretending he wasn't a darned fine specimen of a man. And when he straightened up once more, she let her gaze drift across his broad chest and down the length of his legs, even though she knew gazing at him like that wasn't wise.

Maybe that meant she'd given up on trying to convince herself there was nothing between them. But there was no way she intended to let anything more happen. He'd been Mike's friend. She'd been Mike's wife. And that made her feelings extremely confusing.

She turned from the window and headed to the front door. When she opened it, Sam scuttled into the house first and made a beeline for the kitchen—where he often slept through the heat of the afternoon.

"So," she said to Luke, quickly reclosing the door against the scorching day, "how did your first mission go?"

"Fine."

She waited for him to tell her about it, but he didn't. He simply stood looking at her...making her pulse race. But the gray-blue of his eyes seemed a shade cooler than usual.

"Did you have lunch?" she asked at last. "I could fix something."

"Thanks, but I ate with Lonnie. And Rayland Skoda. He showed up just as we were heading for the snack bar."

"He probably wanted to check you out. He likes to be up on everything that's happening in town."

"Yeah, I gathered that."

When Luke fell silent again, she told him the baby was at her grandparents, but he barely seemed to be listening.

"Look," he said at last, "there's something I want to talk to you about."

"Sure." She led the way into the living room and sat down on the couch, wondering what on earth was wrong.

"I talked to Rayland about Mike's death," Luke said, sinking into one of the chairs across from her.

"Oh?" The even way he was eyeing her was beginning to make her more uncomfortable by the second.

"He asked if you'd told me you thought he was wrong about the suicide."

"And you said I had?"

"Uh-huh. Then he mentioned you hadn't said a word about your doubts until *after* you found out you weren't going to get the insurance money."

That told her where Luke was going with this. It also sent an icy trickle of sweat slithering down her back. She knew some people thought she'd only questioned Rayland's conclusion because she was after the money, not because she was after the truth. But she didn't want Luke to be one of those people.

"I told you last night," she reminded him, "that I didn't say anything to Rayland right away. I just accepted it was suicide at first. It was later that I started wondering if he might be wrong. But asking him about it had nothing to do with finding out I wasn't going to get the money."

She waited for Luke to say something. "The way Rayland put it," she went on when he was silent, "it must have sounded as if that suicide clause came as a big surprise to me, but it didn't. Don't you remember? I told you Mike and I went over the policy with the insurance agent. We both knew the terms."

Luke nodded slowly. Earlier, he hadn't recalled that, but now that she'd jogged his memory he did. It didn't prove, though, that last night hadn't been a performance, an attempt to drag him into some scheme to help her out of what Lonnie had called "her pile of financial troubles."

"Well, regardless of whether you knew the terms," he finally said, "the way I read Rayland, he figures you never really doubted it was suicide. That you just wanted to convince him to say it could have been murder—so you'd be in line for the money."

Caitlin gazed at him for a long moment, not even a flicker of guilt in her big brown eyes. "And what do you think, Luke?" she asked at last. "Do *you* think that's all I care about? The money?"

"I don't know." It wasn't what he wanted to think, but that wasn't the point. "I guess . . . well, then they got talking about how you and Lonnie have a legal action going for business compensation. So I guess that tells me money's not exactly unimportant to you."

She silently gazed at him for another minute, then said, "Excuse me, I think I hear Sam scratching at his water bowl. It must be empty."

Luke didn't hear a damn thing except the hum of the air-conditioning, but a second later Caitlin was on her way to the kitchen.

He sat watching until she disappeared, feeling like total pond scum. He'd expected . . . hell, he didn't know what he'd expected. Maybe that she'd launch into a self-righteous defense. Or maybe that she'd lash out about Rayland.

He certainly hadn't expected the reaction he'd gotten—the way she'd simply asked what *he* thought, as if she figured he'd never have questioned her about this if he'd just relied on his instincts.

And she was right, dammit. His instincts had told him she'd been completely honest with him. So why the hell had he bought right into Rayland Skoda's version of things? Was it his talent for being wrong about women that always made him quick to assume he was doing it again?

He knew that was probably it. But Caitlin wasn't like any of the women in his past. Caitlin wasn't like any other woman he'd ever known.

Shoving himself off the couch, he headed into the kitchen after her. Sam was lying under the table, dead to the world, and Caitlin was standing at the window with her back to him.

For a moment he just gazed at her. She was wearing shorts again, and those long slender legs of hers really got to him. "Caitlin?" he finally said.

When she didn't respond he hesitated, then strode across the room and rested his hands on her shoulders. She felt incredibly tense...but she smelled incredibly good. Fleetingly, he wondered if a man could grow addicted to her meadows-in-moonlight scent...if *he* was growing addicted to it.

"Caitlin?" he said again.

"What?" she whispered.

"I'm sorry. I didn't mean to sound as if I thought Rayland was right. I was just telling you what he figures."

She swung abruptly around to face him, shrugging off his touch. "I *know* what Rayland figures, Luke. I know what half the town figures. It just didn't occur to me that's what *you* would figure."

Her eyes were luminous with unshed tears threatening to spill over, and seeing that made him want to take her in his arms and hold her. But the tears didn't hide the anger in her eyes, and that made him doubt she'd welcome a hug—not from him, at any rate.

He tried to think of something to say. Before he could, the quiet of the afternoon was shattered by a blast of gunfire.

FOR AN INSTANT everything seemed frozen in time. Then Sam was charging across the kitchen at full roar and Caitlin snapped, "Damn! That's coming from over toward the foothills. On my land, from the sound of it.''

"Get down!" Luke ordered, reaching for her. He came up empty. She was already heading for the dining room at a dead run, ignoring the danger of stray bullets.

"Don't let Sam out," she shouted over her shoulder, "or they'll shoot at *him.*"

Luke took off after her, trying to listen to the sound of the gunshots through the sound of Sam's frantic barking. He'd guess there were two guns. Semiautomatics. The noise wasn't single blasts but round after round, coming from a quarter to half a mile away.

He caught up with Caitlin in the family room, where she had the gun case open and was taking the two rifles from it. A box of shells was already sitting on the chair next to the case.

"What the hell do you think you're doing?" he demanded.

"I'm defending whatever's getting shot at on my property! I assume you can handle one of these?"

When he nodded she thrust one of the rifles at him, then started running again, this time for the front door.

He followed on her heels, not liking what was happening one bit. But he clearly wasn't going to stop her unless he wanted to wrestle her to the ground. He seriously considered that for a couple of steps, but was damn sure she wouldn't take kindly to it.

With Sam still in the kitchen, wailing like the Hound of the Baskervilles, they raced out of the house. ''You want to drive or ride shotgun?'' Caitlin demanded.

Nice choice, he thought. But all he said was, "We'll take the Mustang." At least that way he had control over how close they got to whoever was out there in the desert.

The afternoon was a scorcher, and the interior of the car was sweltering. He started the engine while they rolled down the windows. Then Caitlin took his rifle, as well as holding her own, and he roared down the drive—certain his hands were getting second-degree burns from the steering wheel.

When he turned onto the road he could make out the shape of a pickup, parked on the shoulder in the distance.

"What do you figure they're shooting at?" he said, stepping on the gas.

"At night it would be coyotes. But this time of day it's more likely saguaros."

Cactuses! People shooting at some damn cactuses, and they were riding to the rescue? Hell, he was liking this less by the minute. They were liable to get themselves killed over a little vegetation.

It dawned on him that must be what Rayland had been talking about. The *trouble* they were having with the saguaros. He'd forgotten all about it, and it was a little late to be passing on the message now—with the sound of the shooting getting ever louder as they drew closer to the pickup. Then the noise abruptly ceased.

"Over there!" Caitlin said, pointing past him.

Sure enough, there were a couple of guys a hundred yards or so across the arid land, semiautomatics in their hands. They'd spotted the Mustang and were watching it. Off behind them stood a saguaro that had to be fifty feet high.

When Luke started to slow the car, Caitlin said, "What are you doing?"

"I'm going to park. What do you want me to do? Drive straight over to them?"

"Yes, that's exactly what I want you to do."

He thought about it for half a second and decided she was right. They'd be safer in the car.

Swerving off the road, he sped across the baked clay and stopped in a swirl of dust about ten feet in front of the shooters. They were a couple of young guys, maybe twenty and twenty-three.

"Here." Caitlin handed Luke his rifle.

"Stay in the car and cover me," he said, opening his door.

She gave him a look that said "no way," and opened *her* door.

He climbed out, hoping to hell these guys weren't high on something. Even without any added complications, he didn't much like the odds when they had semiautomatics and he and Caitlin didn't.

The dust had cleared enough that he could see the huge saguaro behind the two was riddled with bullets. The main column was oozing liquid where one of its chubby arms had been blown away, and pieces of shattered pulp lay on the ground all around it.

"This is my property," Caitlin said evenly.

The two guys looked at each other, then back at her. One of them shrugged.

"And that's my cactus you're using for target practice."

"Look, lady—"

"What the *lady* is saying," Luke interrupted, "is she wants you off her land. And she doesn't want you on it again. Got it?"

They seemed ready to argue, so he leveled his rifle at them, hoping to hell they wouldn't call his bluff. The navy frowned on its officers shooting civilians— even officers who were on leave. But if these guys forced the issue...

"Hey," the older one said, manufacturing a grin. "No big deal. We was just havin' a little fun."

"Well go find a shooting range to have your fun on," Luke told him.

This time they both shrugged, but they turned and started for the pickup.

"Damn punks," Caitlin muttered, staring after them. "That cactus has probably been standing there for more than two hundred years, and a couple of damn punks come along and shoot the hell out of it. It makes me want to cry."

Luke glanced at it again, then at her. "Will it die?"

"You can't tell right away. It has an internal skeleton, just like a person, and if that's not badly damaged it'll heal. At least we gave it a chance." She paused and smiled at him. "Thanks for the help."

He merely shrugged, but her smile made him glad they'd come chasing out here—even if it *had* been a damn fool thing to do.

When she went back to following the shooters with her eyes, he wiped his brow. He was drenched in sweat—partly from the relentless heat of the day, partly from the fear he'd felt before he'd been sure those guys were backing down.

He wondered if Caitlin had been afraid. If she had, it certainly hadn't showed. Glancing at her again, he had that same crazy feeling of pride in her he'd had when she'd stood up to Lonnie about Billy-Bob.

She seemed so vulnerable a lot of the time, yet she could be as fierce as a tiger. And if she was that protective of a cactus, what would she be like if a person she cared about was in trouble? Hell, she was definitely someone he wanted on his side in a fight.

Or maybe she was someone he wanted *at* his side—for the long run.

The thought hit him like the proverbial ton of bricks. He didn't have time to dwell on it, though, because the pickup was starting off down the road and Caitlin was saying they should head back to the house before they got sunstroke.

THIS TIME, WHEN THEY WENT into the living room, Luke sat down on the couch beside Caitlin rather than in a chair.

She wasn't certain whether she liked that or not. It wasn't that she was still angry with him. It was hard to stay mad at a man while he was helping you drive off a couple of guys with semiautomatics.

The problem was, since she'd given in and accepted the fact that she was attracted to him, his being close was making her feel at risk of melting inside.

That made her extremely nervous, and she'd been nervous enough *before* he sat down, because she hadn't changed her mind. She still intended to tell him the whole story surrounding Mike's death. And once she did that, her life could well turn upside down.

Luke drank a little of the beer he'd grabbed from the fridge, then smiled at her. That made her even more nervous. And when she tried to smile back it felt all wrong.

"So where were we?" he asked. "Before Billy the Kid and his buddy interrupted?"

"Well, as I recall, we were standing in the kitchen and I was mad as hell at you. But let's forget about that, and pick up where we left off last night."

Luke nodded, his expression serious now.

"First, though, I want to explain about that compensation claim Lonnie mentioned." It seemed the least-threatening place to begin. From there, she could ease into the rest.

"It's okay," Luke was saying, "he already told me the basic details and—"

"No, that's not what I mean. I don't want...that remark you made about thinking I was only after money, I—"

"Caitlin, I said I was sorry." And he'd meant it. He should have taken everything Rayland and Lonnie had to say with a grain of salt. "I can understand that—"

"Wait, just let me explain, all right?"

Luke leaned back and took another swig of his beer. He liked to get straight to the heart of things, but Caitlin was obviously happier if she could cover the whys and wherefores first.

"I don't know exactly what Lonnie told you," she said, "but filing that action was *his* doing. I'm not trying to tell you I didn't go along with it, but it isn't something I'd have thought of on my own. I didn't even know he'd seen a lawyer until they had the claim ready to file. Then Lonnie showed up here with the forms and told me to sign them."

"And you did?" That didn't sound like the Caitlin he was starting to know.

She shrugged. "I just did what was easiest. I didn't have much energy to argue at the time. It was...it was only a couple of weeks after Mike's funeral."

"A couple of weeks after the funeral," Luke repeated, feeling his jaw clench. Caitlin had barely been functioning back then. She'd told him that, and so had Rayland and Lonnie. So for a guy to push her into doing something under those circumstances . . .

Hell, for someone who could seem like a real regular guy when he wanted to, Lonnie sure was a son of a bitch.

"He was just doing what he figured was best for the business," Caitlin said as if she could hear Luke's thoughts. "And as I said, I *did* go along with it. Now, though . . . now I wish I hadn't. You wouldn't believe how many people have been here from the Department of Defense and the Veteran's Admin. All asking a million questions and none of them wanting to pay us a cent. I'm just so sick of it, and they've practically made me paranoid. I even thought . . ."

"What?"

"Well, there's something about you that told me you were military. I knew it the very first moment I saw you. And it made me think you were another one of them, arriving out of uniform to throw me off guard. That really *is* paranoid, isn't it."

She gave him a sad little smile, and he could barely stop himself from reaching for her. He did, though. He might have had a sudden crazy thought out in the desert, about wanting her for the long run, but a crazy thought was all it had been—probably brought on by the heat and the adrenaline he'd been pumping.

Since that first time, when he'd been too young to know better, he'd never seriously considered a long-term relationship with any woman. No promises, no strings.

And he hadn't forgotten that Caitlin was Mike's widow. It was still very much on his mind. He also hadn't forgotten that he was only passing through her life. Or that getting involved with her while he was here would make him a total jerk.

"I just wanted you to know the whole story behind the claim," she said quietly. "To know I don't really care much about money."

"Okay. Now I know, so let's forget I ever made that remark."

Caitlin nodded, feeling better...except that now she had to start in on the hard part. She sat trying to psyche herself up, but it was awfully difficult.

"You said we were going to get back to last night," Luke reminded her. "You're going to answer my question about who you think might have killed Mike?"

"Yes," she made herself say. "I'd have told you then if Peggy-Sue and Lonnie hadn't arrived. But after they did, after I found out Peggy-Sue was engaged to him, I wasn't sure if it was best just to keep quiet. Because if Mike *was* murdered, I think Lonnie might have been the one who killed him."

Luke leaned forward. Without taking his eyes off her, he set his beer bottle carefully on the coffee table.

"I...I feel guilty even saying that, because it's nothing more than speculation. I'm not convinced Lonnie did it, and I don't want him to have been the killer."

"But?" Luke said when she paused.

"But I keep coming back to the basic problem—if Mike didn't commit suicide, then *somebody* murdered him. And Lonnie's the only one I know who might have had a reason.''

''Which was?''

''He wanted control of Sky Knights. He wanted to buy Mike out, but Mike wouldn't sell.''

''Lonnie had enough money to do that? From the way he was talking about his father, I assumed he was as much in debt to Mr. Quentin 'Big Financier' McDougall as you are.''

The perfect way Luke mimicked Lonnie made Caitlin smile a little. ''He is,'' she said. ''Lonnie owes the bank a bundle, too. Or he owes his father, whichever way you want to put it. But that's another part of the story, and it might be simpler if I leave the money bit for later.''

''All right, then tell me the other part.''

''Well, for months before Mike died, he and Lonnie had been arguing about how the company should be run. Lonnie wanted to expand—lease more planes and hire more pilots.''

''How? I mean, I guess I'm asking about the money part of the story again, but where was it supposed to come from?''

''Lonnie figured they could convince Quentin to increase their line of credit. But Mike thought they should take things slowly and not get even further into debt. So, finally, Lonnie said he was tired of fighting about it and asked Mike to sell out to him.''

''But Mike said no.''

''Right. He was sick, don't forget. He was still forcing himself to fly mock combat, but it was a real effort. He couldn't have worked for somebody else. And he figured Sky Knights would eventually do well, so he didn't want to lose out in the future...or he didn't want me to lose out if he wasn't still around."

Caitlin paused again, but not because she felt overwhelmed by sadness. People were right about time helping to heal. It was easier to talk about this now than it had been a few months ago.

"At any rate," she concluded, "Lonnie and Mike had been at a stalemate about it before Mike died."

"But...I think I'm missing something here. Where would killing Mike get Lonnie, when *you* were Mike's beneficiary? He must have known."

"He did, but...if he did kill Mike, if he did have a plan, it involved getting me to sell where Mike wouldn't."

Luke rubbed his jaw, eyeing her skeptically.

"I know that sounds as if I figure Lonnie is Machiavelli or somebody," she went on. "But even though I wasn't thinking too well at the time, it seemed suspicious—as if maybe he did have everything planned out in advance. We'd barely filed that stupid compensation claim before he was back with *more* legal papers. He'd had an agreement of sale drawn up, saying that he'd figured with Mike gone I'd want completely out of Sky Knights, so he was making me an offer."

"But you're still his partner, so you obviously turned him down."

"No, I said fine. Sky Knights was Mike's dream, not mine. Lonnie was right. With Mike gone, I didn't want any part of it."

"So what happened?"

Caitlin shook her head, remembering what a horrible time that had been. "What didn't happen would be a better question. I was still in shock over Mike's death, I was getting bigger by the day with the baby, and I felt as if I was in the middle of a tug-of-war. Lonnie was on one side, badgering me to sign the papers. And my grandparents were on the other side, having fits because they thought his offer was way too low. They kept telling me he was trying to take advantage of me.''

"And was he?''

"Well . . .'' The fact that Lonnie could be a bastard didn't mean he'd killed Mike, but she worried that might have influenced her thinking in all this.

"His offer *was* low,'' she admitted at last. "But to his way of looking at things, he wasn't trying to take advantage of me. It would just have been getting himself a good deal.''

"Nice way to treat your cousin's widow,'' Luke muttered. "So why didn't you end up selling? Your grandparents convinced you not to?''

"No, I really wanted out, and I knew the only offer I'd get was Lonnie's. But when we got right down to completing the deal we hit a snag.''

"Which was?''

"Quentin McDougall. Lonnie had been assuming his father would lend him the money, but Quentin turned him down. That's why Lonnie sounds so resentful when he talks about his father. Quentin is the reason our deal fell through.''

"His own father cut him off at the knees?'' Luke shook his head. "Old Quentin sounds like an even nicer guy than his son.''

Caitlin waited, but when Luke didn't say anything more she finally murmured, "Well, that's the story . . . and it's not really much, is it. Just a possibility that Mike was murdered and just a possibility

Lonnie figured owning a hundred percent of Sky Knights was enough motivation to..."

"To murder his own cousin," Luke quietly finished her sentence.

She nodded, already starting to regret having told him. Going over her theory aloud made it seem even weaker than it had the thousand times she'd gone over it in her head. Luke must think she was completely absurd.

"It isn't much to go on," he said at last.

"I know." She stared at the floor, feeling like such a fool she couldn't meet his gaze.

"Just because Lonnie was fighting with Mike... well, that's a long way from murdering him. But you know, there's something you said..."

"What?" She forced herself to look Luke in the eyes—and saw sympathy. It made her throat ache. She wanted him to tell her he didn't think she was absurd, not feel sorry for her because he thought she was.

"Well, there are two different issues here," he said. "The possibility that Mike was murdered, and the chance that Lonnie did it. So maybe the first thing we have to decide is whether we believe Mike killed himself. And if we do, then we let this go. But if we don't... well, I guess *then* we'll have to worry about whether the killer was Lonnie or somebody else."

She hesitated, not sure Luke wasn't simply trying to humor her. "What do you think we should believe?" she finally asked. "I've spent the last eighteen months trying to decide and I'm still not sure. So what do *you* think?"

CHAPTER SEVEN

LUKE PUSHED HIMSELF up and paced across the room. If he sat beside Caitlin for two seconds longer he was bound to do something he didn't want to do.

No, that wasn't accurate. He very much wanted to do it, even though he knew he shouldn't. He just couldn't breathe that intoxicating scent of hers, couldn't look into her gorgeous sad eyes, without wanting to do a whole lot more touching than looking. And he was starting to wonder how the hell he'd ever make it through the rest of his leave here *without* touching her.

"What I think," he said at last, "is that when it comes to Lonnie you're only speculating. But when it comes down to whether Mike killed himself or not, your doubts seem legitimate."

"You honestly think so?"

He nodded. "If it was suicide, then why *didn't* he leave you a note? I just haven't been able to come up with an answer for that. And the timing... with the baby on the way. And that damn suicide clause in his insurance policy bothers me most of all."

"So what do you think we should do?" she whispered.

"I don't know, Caitlin. This is your town. When I'm back in Florida, you'll still be here. And if we stir things up, you're the one who's going to be left facing the music."

"Oh, Luke, that's exactly what my grandmother said just this morning. She told me I'd get so many people upset that..."

"They might decide to ride you out of town on a rail?"

Caitlin gave him a rueful smile. "I'd have to shoot them before I let them do that. My family is here, and my friends...or I guess I should say whatever friends I'd have left if I started talking about my suspicions. And everything I have is tied up in the ranch and Sky Knights. There's no way I could leave Culpepper. Not in the foreseeable future, at least."

"And that's why *you* have to decide what we're going to do—whether you want to try poking around and see what we can find out, or let it alone."

She pressed her fingers to her mouth, as if she was afraid of the words that might come out. "If Mike didn't kill himself," she said at last, "there's a murderer walking around in Culpepper. My husband's murderer."

"That's right. There is."

"I just don't know," she murmured. "If that's the case, don't I owe it to Mike to...? Oh, Lord, Luke, it's like I'm being haunted by an unanswered question. And I want to answer it for so many reasons. I need to be sure what really happened."

"Despite the music you'll have to face?"

"I think so. Mike would have wanted someone to find out the truth. And...and I want to do it for him."

"Okay, then we'll go for it." If that was what she wanted to do, he'd help her any way he could.

Mike had been his friend, so he wanted to know the truth, the same as she did. But even if he'd never met Mike he knew he'd have no choice about helping Caitlin. He could practically see his feelings for her growing by the hour—even though he was still having trouble believing it was happening. It just wasn't like him to fall fast and hard for a woman—any woman, let alone the widow of one of his best friends.

Still, wasn't his sister always telling him that someday the right woman would come along? He stood gazing over at Caitlin, thinking that his sister knew a bit more than he gave her credit for.

That thought he'd had in the desert might have seemed sudden and crazy at first. And Caitlin *had* just finished telling him she'd never be able to leave Culpepper in the foreseeable future. Yet the idea of a long run for the two of them wouldn't quit playing around in the back of his mind. And the more it played, the more he was wondering if it could somehow be a possibility.

His thoughts were interrupted by the ringing of the phone. Caitlin glanced at her watch. "It's after four, so that's probably my grandmother, letting me know what time they'll be bringing the baby home."

The phone was sitting on the coffee table, and she bent over and picked it up. "Oh, hi, Grandma." She shot Luke a tiny smile to say she'd been right.

Then her smile faded, and he stood watching uncertainly as she listened, her face growing pale and her hands starting to tremble.

"Oh, God, Grandma," she said at last. "Yes, *you* phone his doctor. It'll save time. And I'll be there just as fast as I can."

"What?" he demanded as she put the phone down.

"It's the Chief," she whispered. "There's something wrong with my baby."

LUKE TURNED ONTO the main highway in the direction of Culpepper, then glanced at Caitlin again.

Her hands were still clasped in her lap—so tightly her knuckles were white. She'd almost been hyperventilating when they'd first gotten into the car, but at least now her breathing seemed a little more normal. So maybe this was the time to ask about the Chief.

He searched for words and finally said, "You know, it might not be nearly as bad as you're thinking. Maybe your grandmother just—"

"No, you didn't hear her voice. She said she's never seen anything like this before. And she sounded scared to death."

"What *exactly* did she say?"

Caitlin looked at him, clearly still fighting for control. The rigid little lines around her mouth were a dead giveaway.

"She said the Chief fell when he was trying to walk into the kitchen. Her first thought was that he's just not too steady on his feet yet. But then it happened again, and she realized he seemed almost faint. And then he started crying and throwing up and he has a fever and..."

"And?" Luke said gently. Caitlin's grandmother couldn't possibly have sounded as scared to death as she did.

"And she said he seems like someone strung out on drugs. He doesn't even know her or my grandfather."

"Well, we'll get him to the doctor right away, and—"

"Oh, Luke, I wish we could get him there in two seconds, but his doctor's in Tucson. At this time of day, right away is going to take well over an hour."

"There isn't a doctor in Culpepper?"

"Yes, but not one I'd trust with this. It could be something he wouldn't know how to deal with. It could be...have you heard anything about children of Gulf veterans coming down with strange diseases?"

"Ahh...yeah, I've heard the odd story." So she *did* know that had been happening. When she'd first told him Mike had the syndrome, he'd wondered.

"Well, because of the chance Mike might have passed some germs along, the pediatrician said if anything unusual ever happened, I was to get the baby to *him* as fast as I could."

"Then I'll drive like a bat out of hell." Luke accelerated to show her he meant it—even though he was already going well above the limit—and reached over to take her hand. "He'll be okay, Caitlin."

She nodded, but when she turned toward the side window he suspected it was to keep him from seeing her tears.

They made the rest of the trip in virtual silence, Caitlin only speaking to give him directions to her grandparents' house.

It proved to be a modest cream-colored bungalow. When he pulled up in front Caitlin was out of the car before he even cut the engine. He climbed out and headed up the walk after her.

As they neared the front door a gray-haired woman hurried out. She wrapped her arms around Caitlin and murmured, "He's going to be all right, dear. I'm sure he is. Your grandfather's bringing him."

Despite her words, Luke thought she looked every bit as frightened as her granddaughter.

"What did Dr. Peterson say?" Caitlin asked. "You got hold of him?"

"Yes, and he's going to be waiting for us at the Children's Hospital."

"The hospital? Not his office? He thought it sounded that serious?"

"He...he just said it sounded unusual, dear. He didn't want to take any chances—not given the circumstances. Here's your grandfather now," she added. "We're both going with you."

As she said that, a man who put Luke in mind of a taller and younger version of George Burns appeared. He had a diaper bag slung over one shoulder, a big baby shawl over the other, and the baby in his arms.

Caitlin reached for her son and burst into tears at the same moment.

Luke swallowed hard. The little guy didn't even seem to recognize his mother. He was wearing only a diaper, and his skin was blotchy. His head was kind of lolling to one side as if he couldn't hold it up.

Caitlin's grandfather handed him over to her, then glanced at Luke. "You Luke Dakota?"

He nodded.

"Harry Chastain," he introduced himself. Then he looked anxiously back at Caitlin and the baby.

"I've been sponging him down, trying to reduce the fever," her grandmother told her. "And there's a bottle of water for him in the bag. You drove Caitlin here?'' she asked, glancing at Luke, acknowledging him for the first time.

He nodded. "I'll drive us to Tucson, too."

"I can take them," Harry said.

"No, Grandpa, let's all go with Luke," Caitlin whispered, cradling the baby in her arms. "And let's get going now."

They hurried to the Mustang, her grandparents scrambling into the back, Caitlin carefully climbing into the front with the baby.

"Luke?" she murmured as he started the engine.

He looked at her. Her cheeks were damp, her eyes dark with tears and huge with fear. He started praying the baby really *was* going to be all right.

"Don't forget what you said," she whispered. "Like a bat out of hell."

THE EMERGENCY WARD was busy, with the sights of childhood tragedies, sounds of pain and the smells of antiseptic and illness that made Luke hate hospitals. As promised, though, the pediatrician was there when they arrived—a short, balding man in his early fifties who whisked the baby and Caitlin straight into an examining room.

Betty and Harry Chastain had been quiet in the car, but once the three of them settled into chairs in a back corner of the waiting area, Betty began talking a blue streak.

Luke assumed she was trying to keep them all from worrying about the baby, but he'd rather have just sat and quietly worried. She'd obviously realized he was attracted to her granddaughter and was taking the opportunity to give him a not-very-subtle grilling.

Just as he was expecting her to come right out and ask what his intentions were, Harry told her to stop sounding as if she were planning the next Spanish Inquisition, and began telling Luke a little about them.

Betty had spent her entire adult life as a wife and mother. Harry had retired, ten years ago, from the Cactus Square Bank of Culpepper. And it turned out he was none too fond of the bank's president—Lonnie's father, Quentin McDougall.

"He's a hard man," Harry was saying. "When people need money from a bank, a lot of the time it's because they've got a problem. And it always seemed to me a banker should pay some mind to that, not just look at numbers. Especially in a small town. But Quentin only cares about the bottom line. He just doesn't consider people's feelings."

Luke nodded. "Caitlin mentioned he got Lonnie pretty upset—squelching the deal to buy her out of Sky Knights."

"He sure as hell did," Harry said. "And you know why he wouldn't let Lonnie have the money?"

"No, I don't think she said."

"Well, I'll tell you, Luke, he—"

"Harry?" Betty interrupted. "Caitlin might not like you talking about her personal business."

"To Luke, here? Why, from what I've gathered, he already knows most of the story."

When Betty simply shrugged, Harry looked at Luke again. "Caitlin tell you that Quentin holds the mortgage on her place?"

"Uh-huh. She said something about it."

"And she tell you she signed a personal guarantee on the business loan Mike got for Sky Knights? That Quentin insisted *she* sign, as well as Mike?"

"Yeah, I think she said something about that, too."

"See?" Harry glanced at his wife. "Luke *does* know the story. All Caitlin didn't tell him was *why* Quentin kept Lonnie from buying her out."

Luke leaned forward a little in his chair, waiting for Harry to explain.

"You see," Harry said, turning to him again, "if Lonnie had bought Caitlin's share of Sky Knights, she'd have been out of debt to the bank. She'd have paid off both the mortgage on the ranch and the business loan she and Mike guaranteed."

"So," Betty put in, "even though Lonnie would have bought her out by borrowing from his father, Quentin wouldn't have been out much more money overall. It just would have meant Lonnie owing it all, instead of Caitlin owing half."

"Yes, dear," Harry said, "I'm sure Luke was following me just fine. And, of course," he continued, "if Caitlin's debts had been paid off, Quentin wouldn't have her property as collateral. So, if anything major had gone wrong at Sky Knights, if it failed with only Lonnie owing Quentin all the money...well, hell, knowing that boy, he'd have just laughed in his father's face and ridden off into the sunset."

"But you don't know for certain that's what Quentin was thinking," Betty said.

"Sure I do. It was Quentin who was in charge for the last ten years I was at the bank. I'm *damn* certain that's what he was thinking."

Harry looked back at Luke. "Mike was Quentin's own sister's boy, which makes the baby Quentin's great-nephew or something. But if Sky Knights fails he'll foreclose on Caitlin before you can say *treasury bonds*. The McDougalls aren't a family that holds with blood being thicker than water."

Luke just shook his head. The more he heard about the McDougalls, the more he wished Caitlin had nothing to do with any of them.

"Oh, there she is," Betty suddenly said.

When Luke glanced toward the front of the waiting area, Caitlin was standing there, gazing straight at him. Seeing her started his heart pounding. She wasn't in tears, which had to mean the news was good. Didn't it?

He was on his feet and heading for her before he remembered that *he* wasn't her family. Betty and Harry were. Reluctantly, he waited for them to hurry past him, then followed along in their wake, wondering if he'd only imagined that it was *him*, not them, she'd been gazing at.

"Well?" Betty demanded, hugging her granddaughter.

"Well...we don't know anything much yet. They've given him something to bring the fever down, and they've got him on an IV drip and—"

"Oh, no, the poor darling," Betty murmured.

Caitlin took her hands. "I know. He cried and cried when they were trying to find one of his little veins. But they're just making sure there won't be any problem with dehydration. And...and now they're going to do some tests. But being so late in the day, they won't know all the results until tomorrow."

"Tomorrow," Harry said. "You mean we've got to go home not knowing?"

Caitlin looked, Luke thought, like a frightened little girl doing her best to put on a brave front. It made

him want to wrap his arms around her and let her cry
if that's what she felt like doing. But Betty was still
holding on tightly to her hands, so he didn't move.

"I'm going to stay here overnight," she said.
"There's a lounge parents can use and...I was hoping they'd let me spend the night right in the Chief's
room with him, but...but because of the risk that it's
some kind of Gulf disease, they're going to keep him
isolated until they know for sure."

A tear trickled down her cheek as she said that. It
made Luke feel helpless as hell.

He hated what Desert Storm had done to so many
people. He especially hated what it was doing to
Caitlin right now. Even if the baby didn't have some
weird sickness, courtesy of a bug Mike had brought
back from the Middle East, Caitlin had to be thinking that he did. And she had to be terrified.

He opened his mouth to say he'd stay overnight
with her, then remembered they'd all come in the
Mustang. He'd have to drive the Chastains back to
Culpepper.

"Why don't we stay here, too?" Betty asked Harry.

Luke felt like hugging her. The last thing in the
world he wanted to do was leave Caitlin alone with
her worries.

But she was already shaking her head. "No, I'll be
okay. You two go home and sleep in your own bed.
Really," she insisted, when nobody moved. "They
told me the lounge isn't very big, so I don't think
they'd like all of us staying. And I'll be fine on my
own."

"You'll call if you hear anything," Betty said,
clearly reluctant to leave. "Anything at all. And any
time at all."

"Of course I will. They said there are phones right in the lounge."

"Well...all right then, dear. I'll call Mary and Jack as soon as we get home, and let them know what's happened."

"That's our daughter and son," Harry explained to Luke.

He nodded. Caitlin had mentioned her mother had been the eldest of three children.

"And we'll be back first thing in the morning," Betty said.

Caitlin hugged her, then Harry. "Not *too* early in the morning," she told him. "I don't want the traffic doing evil things to your blood pressure."

Watching the little farewell scene made Luke feel like a complete outsider. He didn't like the feeling.

Since he'd started thinking about a future with Caitlin, the idea hadn't left his mind for even a minute. And the longer he spent with her, the more he kept imagining what it would be like to be part of her life. The problem was, he didn't know if his imagination was being remotely realistic.

She walked them all to the front door of the emergency wing and hugged her grandparents again. This time, though, she turned and hugged Luke, as well.

He held her as tightly as he dared, breathing in her intoxicating scent, wishing he never had to let her go.

"Thanks, Luke," she murmured against his neck. "I don't know what I'd have done without you."

The whisper of her breath on his skin, the soft warmth of her body pressed to his, sent a shiver of desire through him.

He nuzzled the top of her head, unable to resist, and pretended what she'd said was that she didn't know what she *would* do without him. God, his imagination was running completely wild on him.

When he finally forced his arms from around her, she clung to him for a few more seconds...or was that his imagination, as well?

"Look," he said, "do you want me to come back in the morning? I could call Lonnie tonight and tell him he'll have to cancel that morning mission."

For a second he thought she was going to say yes, then she shook her head. "No, it's a really important one. You're taking up a couple of fellows who operate some kind of an adventure booking agency in Phoenix. They're coming down to see if they like what we're doing. If they start sending people to us it could go a long way to keeping Sky Knights solvent."

"Well...at least phone me first thing, then. You won't get much sleep with all the hospital noises, so call me before I have to leave and let me know if you've heard anything."

"Okay, and you'll feed Sam for me?"

"Sure."

"And don't let him stay out all night."

Behind them, Harry cleared his throat.

"And *you* try not to worry too much," Luke whispered. Then he turned and headed out into the early evening with Harry and Betty.

When he looked back, from halfway down the sidewalk, Caitlin was still gazing after them. He gave her a quick wave, and this time her sad smile was heartbreaking. It was all he could do to turn away again and keep walking toward the parking lot.

THE TRIP BACK to the Chastain's bungalow was somber, the atmosphere in the car heavy with unspoken fears.

As they reached the house Betty asked Luke if he'd like to stay for dinner, but it was clearly a half-hearted invitation. He knew she and Harry didn't feel any more like eating than he did. When he said he'd better just get going neither of them pressed.

"Another time, then," Betty said. "Next week, maybe... as long as everything's all right."

He hadn't noticed it until then, but he could suddenly see a resemblance to Caitlin in Betty's worried face. He could also see how much she loved her granddaughter and the baby. "I'm sure everything will be fine," he said quietly.

As he drove back through town, dusk was beginning to gather. He passed a field where a peewee baseball game was just wrapping up, and his gaze lingered on the small boys. He couldn't help wondering if his namesake would be playing baseball on that diamond one day, or if...

He shook off the thought, speeding up when he reached the highway. Twilight was falling fast by the time he passed Airport Road. A few more minutes and he flicked on his signal, slowing as he neared the turnoff for the road to Caitlin's place. Just beyond it was a sign telling him Tucson was forty-two miles ahead.

He hesitated, tempted to switch the turn signal back off and press his foot down on the accelerator. Then he remembered he had to feed Sam, and made his turn.

When he pulled up in front of the house the dog appeared from nowhere and played out a canine melodrama that said he'd have died of starvation if Luke had been one minute later.

"You're a faker, Sam," he told him, starting for the house, the dog dancing at his side.

In the kitchen, the light was flashing on Caitlin's answering machine. For half a second, he wondered if listening to messages on someone else's machine was an invasion of privacy. Then he pushed the play button.

Hell, for all he knew, the message was for him. Maybe the morning customers had canceled and Lonnie had called to say the mission had been scrubbed.

Luke started scooping kibble from the bag into the dog's bowl while the tape rewound, then stopped what he was doing when the message started. It wasn't Lonnie. It was Sheriff Rayland Skoda.

"Cait, sugar," he said, "it's Rayland."

Cait, sugar? Luke stood staring at the machine.

"I don't know if your boarder mentioned it, sugar," the sheriff went on, "but I was talking to him out at the airport today."

Your boarder? Luke was liking Rayland less by the word, and he hadn't liked him much to start with.

"Any rate, Luke was saying you're still worrying about how Mike died. So I thought the two of us could get together some night and talk about it. Maybe drive into Tucson...have dinner someplace...be just like old times."

Dinner? Luke felt a surge of pure, unadulterated jealousy.

He told himself he was being ridiculous. Caitlin had said she'd only dated Rayland half a dozen times.

It had been a long time ago, and she'd never been all that taken with him.

Hell, even if she had liked him, who was Luke to be jealous? He hadn't so much as kissed Caitlin... although that sure wasn't because he hadn't wanted to... more than a few times. And ridiculous or not, the thought of her having dinner with Rayland Skoda had started a slow burn.

"So why don't you figure out a good night?" Rayland's voice was saying. "I should be in my office most of the day tomorrow, so you give me a call, huh? Or else I'll get back to you tomorrow night. See you, Cait."

The machine beeped to say the message was finished. Sam echoed the beep with a bark that said he was getting tired of waiting for his food.

Luke put the bowl on the floor, then pushed the replay button and listened to the message a second time. It didn't sound much like the guy he'd met. At lunch, Rayland hadn't exactly been overly friendly, whereas the voice on the tape was dripping honey.

He stood watching Sam wolf down his food, wondering what Rayland really had in mind with his "just like old times" line and his familiar tone. Luke didn't like either of them a damn bit.

But, hell, even though he'd barely started to trust his instincts about Caitlin, he really believed he could. And they were telling him loud and strong that those old times were entirely dead and buried as far as she was concerned. Which meant the last thing she needed was Rayland Skoda coming on to her. So maybe he'd just see what he could do about that before it became a problem for her.

Sam finished his dinner and hustled over to the sliding door, then took off like a shot when Luke opened it.

"Damn," he muttered, realizing he'd made a mistake. Sam was undoubtedly gone for the night—off after the coyotes. So here he was, all alone in the middle of Arizona, without even the dog for company. And there was Caitlin, all alone in the damn hospital. That just didn't sit right with him.

He stood gazing toward the dark shapes of the foothills for a minute, then turned and started back through the house to the front door.

BY THE TIME Luke reached the Children's Hospital again, Tucson was cloaked in darkness and the air had grown chilly.

It made him realize he should have brought along some clothes for Caitlin. She'd been wearing only shorts and a T-shirt, and by now she was probably freezing in the hospital's air-conditioned lounge.

Popping the Mustang's trunk, he dug out the bag that held the Remember the Alamo sweatshirts he'd picked up on his way through San Antonio. He took out the adult ones he'd bought for his sister and her husband, then grabbed the smallest of the three for their boys, as well—deciding he could easily stop for replacements on the drive back through Texas. Tugging the extra-large one on over his T-shirt, he draped the other two over his arm and headed into the hospital.

The parents' lounge turned out to be at one end of the third floor. Adjacent to it was a door marked Chapel, and seeing that made his gut clench. Some of the children who were brought into this building never left it again. If little Luke Michael Alexander was one of those...

He paused, wondering how the Chief could have become so important to him in such a short time. The Chief *and* his mother.

He had no idea how. He only knew they had.

Finally he started forward again, then stopped in the doorway of the lounge. Its calming blues and grays made it far more inviting than the waiting area on the main floor. But not a soul in the room, mainly women with worried faces, looked glad to be there.

He stood gazing across at Caitlin—curled up asleep in one of the chairs, a child-sized blanket tucked around her bare legs. Then he quietly crossed the room, still thinking how amazing it was that his feelings for her had become so strong, so fast.

Too fast, he warned himself. And too complicated, as well—because of Mike, because Florida was so far from Arizona, and because Caitlin might turn out to be just another woman he eventually realized he was wrong about.

Looking down at her, though, it was hard to make himself believe that could happen. He was absolutely dying to kiss that tantalizing mouth of hers. To kiss those long lashes and high, exotic cheekbones. And he just couldn't help imagining her dark tangle of hair spread out on a snowy white pillowcase. Hell, everything about her was so damn beautiful it made him ache with need.

But there was more than that. Something about her made him want to keep all the evils of the world away and make everything right for her. He wanted the baby to be well, her financial problems solved, and all her unanswered questions answered.

And with that final part, at least, he was going to do his damnedest to help her.

CHAPTER EIGHT

CAITLIN WAS STILL half asleep, but she sensed Luke's presence without his saying a word.

She opened her eyes, certain she'd only dreamed he'd come back, but there he was. And he was a more welcome sight than anything she could possibly have dreamed up—despite his silly sweatshirt that told her to Remember the Alamo.

When he wordlessly reached down and pulled her into his arms, it seemed the perfect place to be. Her blanket slipped to the floor, but Luke's embrace made her a hundred times warmer than the blanket had.

She wanted to tell him she'd heard good news about the baby, but just for a minute she wanted to simply enjoy the way he was making her feel. She let herself melt against the solidness of his body, resting her cheek on the soft cotton of his sweatshirt and drinking in his sea-breeze male scent.

The thudding of his heart was reassuring. His arms around her made her feel protected and ...

Her heart skipped a beat, but she forced her mind to stop that line of thought right where it was. She was attracted to Luke. The idea of acting on that, though ...

Nobody had been able to tell her exactly how you knew when it was time to move on. "You'll just know," they'd said.

But she didn't know. She still had all those lingering feelings about Mike and . . . and she just couldn't do anything about Luke. She couldn't risk that. Not when one day soon she'd blink and he'd be gone. She knew only too well how much it hurt to love and lose.

So letting anything develop with Luke Dakota would be all wrong. The timing, the circumstances, the geography, everything was wrong. But if that was true, why did being in his arms feel like coming home?

She couldn't manage to find an answer to that—at least, not while he was holding her. Finally, she drew away a fraction of an inch and looked up at him, murmuring, "What are you doing back here?"

He smiled at her. Lord, she adored that smile. And the sexy cleft in his chin. It was all she could do to resist the urge to trace it with her fingers.

"I wanted to know if you'd heard anything more from the doctor, and I couldn't find a phone."

"Ahh. They all went into hiding?"

"Guess so."

"They do that a lot in Arizona. I think they have an abnormal fear of cactuses or something. But, yes, I did hear a little news."

Luke was still smiling at her, and it filled her with joy. But . . . but if she didn't want to let anything develop with him, why on earth was it filling her with joy?

Lord, after she'd dozed off, her brain and her emotions must have declared open warfare on each other. She needed time to think. Time alone, without Luke holding her, without his smile reminding her how easily he could make her laugh—even when the past few days hadn't been the best of times.

She didn't *want* to be alone, though. She wanted to be with him. But wanting to be with him and not wanting anything more just didn't seem to add up right.

"The doctor?" he reminded her. "You *are* going to tell me what you heard, aren't you?"

She nodded. "I didn't actually hear anything from Dr. Peterson, but a nurse stopped by to let me know the Chief's fever is gone."

"That's good."

"And all his signs are stable...whatever that means, exactly."

"It's good, too...whatever it means."

"The nurse didn't actually offer an opinion about what's wrong with him. I guess they have to be pretty careful what they say. But you know what she said?"

"No. What?"

"That she's a mother, too. So she knew how much better I'd feel if someone told me the Chief was looking good. *Really good,* were her precise words. And the way she said it, I just knew she was telling me *she* thought he'd be all right."

"That's better than good. That's great."

Luke hadn't stopped looking at her for a single second. And the gray-blue of his eyes was so warm it was making her feel hot inside.

"I had another reason for coming back," he said, giving her a teasing smile. "I haven't eaten, and I had a sudden, overwhelming craving for hospital food. And this was the only hospital I knew how to get to."

Caitlin laughed. A few hours ago, she'd been a million years away from laughing, but not now. "Nobody gets a craving for hospital food."

"Well, I don't mean just any old hospital food. Not the kind that gets cold while they're wheeling it around to the rooms. I mean the stuff in hospital cafeterias that's been drying out under heat lamps since noon. And coffee that's been on the burner for twelve hours or so."

"Coffee isn't food," she pointed out, trying not to smile. But suddenly she couldn't help it. The nurse thought her baby was looking good, and Luke Dakota had come back to be with her.

At the moment, the battle between her brain and her emotions seemed almost decided. Her emotions were winning hands down. And it felt so good to be happy that she decided to stop worrying about what her brain was telling her for a while.

"Coffee's not food?" Luke was saying as if he couldn't believe she'd said that. "Well, let's go see what they've got that is food, huh? Oh, and I brought you something."

She hadn't noticed until then, but there was a twin of his silly sweatshirt draped over his arm.

"And one for the baby," he added, moving the big one to reveal a miniature.

She stared at the little one, her throat filling with tears. The sweatshirt wouldn't fit the Chief for another two years, but she was inexplicably touched. "That's . . . very sweet," she murmured.

"How sweet?" Luke asked, leaning so close that his breath kissed her lips.

It turned her liquid. She gave in and let her fingers trace the cleft in his chin. "This sweet," she whispered. And then she kissed him.

It was a hot, melting kiss... and oh *so* sweet. Rough and tender, gentle and hard, sweet and sexy—all at once.

It was a kiss that sent shivers to her toes and started heat licking deep inside her belly. A kiss that was a tall cool drink after a trip across the desert and hot mulled wine after a hard day's skiing. It was a kiss she wished would never end.

When it finally did, she was so weak-kneed that she still clung to Luke. Then she remembered where they were and realized the other people in the lounge were staring. And she felt guilty that she was luckier than most of them.

They were all worried about children they loved. But the nurse thought *her* child was going to be just fine. And the combination of that and being in Luke's arms made everything seem wonderful in her little corner of the world.

She pulled on her new sweatshirt, then tried to tidy her hair with her fingers.

"Leave it," Luke said. "It looks great."

She smiled. Lord, everything the man said made her smile. And after that kiss, not letting things go any further with him was going to be quite a feat.

"Well, let's go look for the cafeteria," she suggested. "All your talk about how great hospital food is has got me starving."

"We don't have to look for it. I scooped it out before I came up. I knew you wouldn't be able to resist the lure of well-aged coffee."

"How could I? I hear it ranks right up there with well-aged Scotch."

THE CAFETERIA PROVED to be on a lower level that could most kindly be described as semibasement. And the food proved to be every bit as *wonderful* as Luke had promised—except that Caitlin suspected it had been under the heat lamps since breakfast, not noon.

It had been a long time since she'd eaten, though, so she forced down a greasy burger and some shriveled fries covered with a congealed brown glop that was advertised as gravy.

Then, from nowhere, Dr. Peterson was standing beside their table. "Caitlin? I'd like to speak with you for a minute."

He looked so serious a ring of fear formed around her heart and the food turned to a solid lump in her stomach. Suddenly, she didn't feel nearly as confident that everything would be okay.

"Dr. Peterson," she managed to say as evenly as she could, "this is Luke Dakota. He was a friend of the baby's father."

"John Peterson," he said, nodding to Luke. "I'm going home now," he added, turning to Caitlin again. "And I just wanted to let you know it'll be tomorrow afternoon before most of the test results are in."

"But he's going to be all right," she said anxiously.

"Well, we got the fever down with just acetaminophen, and he's recovered from that episode he had. But until we know for sure what caused it we can't really predict what to expect."

"Can't predict," she repeated, the ring of fear tightening. She wanted that nurse back again, telling her the Chief was looking good.

Instead, Dr. Peterson continued, "We've drawn blood samples and taken some cultures. Those will tell us whether we're dealing with bacteria or with a viral infection of some kind.''

''Some kind ... you mean a common kind?'' She held her breath, praying he'd say yes.

''I really don't know. He doesn't have the obvious physical signs we see with some of the more common childhood illnesses.''

Definitely *not* a yes. Luke reached across the table and took her hand, but she barely noticed. Nothing was going to make her feel better except Dr. Peterson sounding a lot more optimistic than he was sounding right now.

''We can't definitely rule out anything yet,'' he went on. ''Not until we've got the blood and culture results. And since we don't know exactly what the problem is, I haven't put him on any medication. It's better to wait and see.''

''But ... while we're waiting ... what if ... ?''

''He's sleeping quietly, Caitlin, and there'll be a nurse checking on him all night long. I'm sure he's fine for the moment. In fact, I suggest you go home and get some sleep yourself. Even if he wakes up, you can't do anything for him when he's in isolation. I'll be back here around two tomorrow. I'll have a look at the lab reports and stop by the parents' lounge after that. In the meantime, try not to worry too much, okay?''

When she nodded, the doctor said good-night and headed off. She watched him walk across the cafeteria, as if by keeping her eyes on him she could make him come back and start their conversation over again, this time sounding as reassuring as that nurse had been.

It didn't work, of course. He kept right on walking until he was gone.

She looked across the little table at Luke. He gave her a smile, but it wasn't the easy one she'd grown used to. This one seemed forced, and his expression was so worried that she didn't want to see it. When she looked down at the remnants of her food, though, she felt nauseous.

"Let's get out of here," Luke said, shoving back his chair and reaching for her hand.

"Bacteria or a viral infection of some kind," she murmured as they headed for the door. "And no signs that it's a common illness. What if—"

"Shh." They'd reached the empty corridor and he stopped her—gently pressing his fingers to her lips. "What he said was there aren't *obvious* signs. It could still be something as common as sand on a beach. Your Dr. Peterson's probably just on the conservative side. He doesn't want to tell you he thinks it's one thing and have it turn out to be something else."

"But...oh, Luke, all those rumors Mike heard from other veterans. About Iraq using chemical warfare and germ warfare and...and families back home getting sick years later and...what if it *is* some crazy virus from the other side of the world? One that nobody here has ever seen, let alone knows how to treat? What then?"

"Hey." He tucked his fingers under her chin and captured her gaze in the depth of his. "Don't worry about things that might never happen. Come tomorrow, odds are those test results will tell them it's illness X or Y or Z, and they'll know exactly how to treat it."

She nodded, but it was her baby's life they were talking about. Which meant that even if the odds they wouldn't know how to treat it were only one in a million, they were too high.

"So what do you think about going home?" Luke asked.

"I . . . I don't think I can."

"All right then, I'll stay here."

"You don't have to do that," she murmured, even though she desperately wanted him to.

"I know I don't have to. But I like the idea of curling up with you on one of those little love seats for the night."

She more than liked the idea, but an inner voice was reminding her that she wasn't thinking straight, so she should be insisting Luke not stay.

She suspected the voice was right. But she was so worried about the baby, and so filled with happiness that Luke was with her, that she really didn't care what was right. Luke was here—that was enough.

"Do you want to change your mind about me phoning Lonnie?" Luke asked. "I'd rather stay with you in the morning than fly that mission."

Reluctantly, she shook her head. "You're taking up those fellows from that adventure tour place, remember? A lot of future Sky Knights' business is riding on them deciding we're reliable. Lonnie would have twenty fits if you weren't there."

"Caitlin, I wouldn't really care if Lonnie had a thousand fits. To get there from here for an eight o'clock mission, I'd have to leave well before seven. Which would mean you'd be sitting on your own for hours."

"No, I'll be fine. I called Peggy-Sue, and...I mentioned last night that she works in Tucson, didn't I?"

"Uh-huh."

"Well, she said she'll drive in early tomorrow and bring me some clean clothes. And after that my grandparents will be here, so I won't be on my own for very long at all."

Luke simply gazed at her for a minute, then wrapped an arm around her shoulders, and they headed back to the lounge.

LOST HALF IN DREAMS, half in thoughts, Caitlin kept drifting in and out of sleep.

Each time she woke it took a second to realize she wasn't still dreaming—that she really *was* curled up in the parents' lounge with Luke Dakota, that his arms were wrapped reassuringly around her, and she was cuddled against the solid breadth of his chest.

She snuggled a little more closely to his warmth, so her ear was resting just over his heart. Above its rhythm, though, she could still hear the sleeping sounds of strangers in the room with them. And all the hospital smells and noises in the night were sneaking through the darkness, shrouding her with a sense of unease.

Everything felt strange and unfamiliar—everything except being in Luke's arms. That felt so right it frightened her. But did it also mean she was ready to move on?

Just thinking about that brought tears to her eyes. She closed them to the darkness, a confusion of emotions flooding her. Even though a part of her had died with Mike, there was nothing she could do about the fact he was dead.

And even though she'd expected she'd be living the rest of her life simply trying to get through the day, the feeling had gradually died, just as people had told her it would.

So... well, perhaps they'd been right about other things as well. They'd said she'd reach the point where she'd healed enough to love again. And maybe she had. Maybe Luke Dakota was the man they'd told her about, the one who would eventually come along and make her feel alive once more.

The way he was holding her, it seemed as if he were part of her life. And he was, for the moment, at least. He was so solid, so dependable, that she'd begun relying on him with barely a second thought. Relying on him and wanting to be with him.

He was just so comfortable to be around. She loved the easy way he had with the baby, the way he listened to her and cared about her problems. And being in his arms made her feel so wonderful, she was tempted to try ignoring the hopelessness of their situation.

But she knew she couldn't do that. Falling in love with Luke would be asking for heartache further down the line. And the closer she let him get, the worse the heartache would be. So instead of letting herself fall, she needed to keep in mind he'd soon be going home, without her. There was no way she could leave Culpepper.

She had to do a far better job of remembering all that. But just for tonight... just for a little while, she needed his strength too much to worry about what would happen in the future. Even if it was the not-very-distant future.

"JEEZ!" BANDIT SHOUTED into his microphone. "You guys are madmen!"

His yelling jolted Luke back to the moment. He realized Lonnie's bird was heading straight at them and went pure vertical, his heart pounding.

In the front seat, Bandit had begun whispering something to himself. Luke suspected it was a prayer that they'd make it through the mission alive.

It had been obvious from takeoff that Lonnie was really out to impress these tour guys, but if any aviation safety types happened to be watching, Sky Knights would be up to its corporate ass in alligators.

Once he'd leveled off he glanced around for Lonnie and discovered him closing in from the side. Luke spiraled away, which got Bandit excited all over again.

"Jeez," he shouted once more. "You sure you haven't ever killed anybody playing these games?"

"Not a one," Luke said calmly into his mike. He started to pull up again, adding, "Worst we've ever done is made people airsick."

He might not be able to make that claim for long, though. Not if he didn't start keeping his mind on what he was doing. The midst of a dogfight was definitely not the time to let his thoughts wander. But when he wasn't thinking about Caitlin, he was wondering if the madman flying the other plane was a murderer.

"Don't you know the old aviation maxim?" he asked Bandit, forcing himself back to the job at hand. "Ninety-nine percent of all accidents happen on contact with the ground."

"Very funny," Bandit muttered. "I tell you, Chief, I'm not booking any customers for you unless they swear they've had their hearts checked recently. You two are . . . jeez, he's come up after us again!"

Glancing to his left, Luke saw that, sure enough, Lonnie was close aboard. They were wing tip to wing tip, maybe thirty feet apart.

"Hold tight!" he ordered, going into a rollover, then pushing down his nose and heading into a steep dive.

"That killer ground's getting damn close!" Bandit hollered after a minute.

Luke grinned. They were still above two thousand feet, and there was nothing you could be doing there that you couldn't safely recover from.

"Jeez, this is a damn roller coaster ride!" Bandit yelled as Luke yanked the nose up and did a five-G pullout from the dive. When he started to level off, at about 6,500 feet, Lonnie was still right with him.

Luke checked the panel clock and decided the mission had to be a wrap. They'd been up for an hour, and both Bandit and his partner from the tour company had scored half a dozen hits. If they weren't impressed by now, they never would be. Besides, he had things to do on the ground.

Lonnie S'ed a couple of times, trying to get behind them for another kill, but Luke stayed out of his way, then suddenly cut the throttle to lose a bit of headway and managed to roll back behind the other plane.

"Go for it, Bandit," he shouted.

Bandit hit the trigger and smoke blasted from Lonnie's bird.

"Good shooting! Now, let's get the hell out of here!" Luke went into another dive, turning in the direction of the airport as he began leveling off.

"Falcon and Terminator," he said, breaking the radio silence, "this is Bandit and Chief. You hit our fuel tank a while back and we're running low. Got to get her home, so we'll see you on the deck. Over and out."

"Roger," Lonnie "Terminator" McDougall radioed back. "Hope you make it down in one piece. Ten-four."

Bandit had turned around in his seat and was staring anxiously at Luke.

"Relax," he said, unable to keep from laughing. "That was a joke. We've got enough fuel to make it to California and back."

"Some joke," Bandit muttered.

WHEN LUKE SUGGESTED he skip the debriefing Lonnie turned purple, so he hung in—reminding himself Caitlin wanted the business these guys could send Sky Knights as much as Lonnie did. After they were finally done, he and Lonnie walked the other two out of the hangar.

"I tell you," Bandit said, "you guys are really something up there. I've never been so scared in my life."

Lonnie shrugged, the picture of nonchalance, but Luke could tell he was pleased with himself.

"Well," he said, "I did my air force training at Nellis, and the motto there was Every Man a Tiger."

The other two laughed and Luke managed a grin. But a motto like that had to cause some aggressive, unsafe flying. And he bet some deaths, too.

He glanced at Lonnie again, unable to stop wondering if *he'd* caused any deaths. And he wasn't thinking about in the air force.

Hell, if he was going to help Caitlin out, he had to start asking questions, instead of wandering around with only her speculations to chew on. And he was going to help her out. He hadn't wavered from that decision.

Last night, in the hospital, he hadn't slept much. Mostly, he'd just cuddled her in his arms, thinking about various things she'd said about Mike's death.

She felt she owed it to him to learn the truth. She needed to know how he'd died—for a whole lot of reasons.

It didn't really matter to Luke what those reasons were, but it was obvious that being certain about what happened was important to her. And if was important to her, it was important to him.

Forcing his attention back to the others, he tuned in as Lonnie was saying, "Well, tell all your customers up in Phoenix about us. And y'all be sure you come back and see us again yourselves. A few more missions and we'll turn you both into real aces."

Luke manufactured another grin. This was only his second mission, and Lonnie's script was already starting to wear thin.

"You catching lunch today?" Lonnie asked as the guys from Phoenix climbed into their car.

"Uh-uh. I told Caitlin I'd head for Tucson right after the mission. The baby took sick yesterday, and he's in the hospital up there."

"Sick? With what?"

"They aren't sure yet."

"Well, shoot, I hope it's nothing serious. Does Peggy-Sue know?"

"Yeah, Caitlin said they were having breakfast together this morning."

"Oh, good. Well, tell her I hope the little guy's all right, huh? And that if she needs anything, she should call."

Luke nodded, wondering if Lonnie's concern was as sincere as it sounded. If it was, it made it tougher to write him off as a complete son of a bitch.

"And tell her I've already had a couple of inquiries about our ad in the *Star,* so we just might be getting ourselves a new pilot quicker than she figured. In fact, tell her one guy's coming to see me this afternoon."

"Really?"

"Uh-huh. And he could start almost right away, so if he turns out to be a winner we'll be all set. I guess that would be good news for you, too, huh? You'd probably like to get out of here before you end up spending your entire leave in Culpepper."

Lonnie turned and started back to the hangar, leaving Luke feeling as if the rules had just been changed in the middle of the game.

The longer he spent with Caitlin, the more he *wanted* to spend the rest of his leave in Culpepper. And he'd just been assuming he would. But if Lonnie got another pilot fast...

Hell, if that happened he didn't know whether Caitlin would ask him to stay on or not. Maybe she'd decide—

"So how'd it go?" Trout asked, interrupting Luke's thoughts. He'd wandered over from the planes, a wrench in his hand. "With those two from

Phoenix, I mean. You figure they'll send some business our way?"

"Yeah, I think they were impressed."

"Good. I kinda wondered, 'cuz that one you took up looked a little green around the gills when you landed."

"Just nerves, I think." Luke hesitated, but now that he might not have the luxury of time, he couldn't beat around the bush trying to be subtle. It looked as if he'd just have to get started and come straight out with some questions. And where better to start a fishing expedition than with a guy called Trout?

"Say," he ventured, "okay if I ask you about something that's got me curious?"

"Sure."

"What do you figure is the true story about Mike? Do *you* buy the idea that he killed himself?"

Trout rubbed the wrench against his coveralls, suddenly looking extremely uneasy. "The idea? It ain't no idea, Luke, it's what happened."

"According to Rayland."

"Uh-huh. And it's Rayland's job to know, right?"

"Yeah . . . yeah, I guess."

Trout hesitated, then said, "I heard Caitlin told you she's not sure Mike killed himself . . . heard you asked Rayland about it."

"Yeah, I did." Briefly, Luke wondered which was more efficient—Culpepper's regular grapevine or its good ol' boys network. Between the two of them, the town sure wasn't a place for keeping secrets.

"Don't be listenin' to her too much, Luke," Trout was saying, "'cuz she's ridin' the wrong horse on this. She just don't want to believe the truth, but . . ." He paused, looking around.

Luke took a quick glance around, too, saw there was no one else within fifty yards of them, and looked back at the mechanic.

"I'll tell you something Caitlin don't know," Trout said quietly.

CHAPTER NINE

"WHAT DOESN'T CAITLIN know?" Luke wiped the sweat off his brow and waited curiously, wishing they weren't having this conversation out on the tarmac, under the blazing sun.

Trout checked again that there was nobody else around, then said, "Before Mike died, he took a real likin' to bourbon. And a lotta the time, when Caitlin thought he was here workin' late, he was really just sittin' in his office, drinkin'."

"You're sure about that? He didn't drink much when we were in the Gulf. The odd beer, but not usually anything else."

"Well, like I said, he took a likin' to it. After he got sick he...well, he could see things startin' to fall apart for him. And sometimes I'd stick my head in the office to say good-night, and he'd already have a bottle of Old Grand-Dad on the desk. He had one out the last time I saw him alive, when I was leaving to go home after work, the night he died."

Luke nodded, but he was having a problem with this. Surely Mike couldn't have been drinking as much as Trout was intimating without Caitlin knowing about it—regardless of where he'd been doing it.

He'd have been coming home drunk. So wouldn't she have mentioned that when they'd talked about him being sick? And about his death? She'd been open about everything else, so was Trout just feeding him a line for some reason?

"And the night it happened," the mechanic went on, "the medical examiner told me an' Lonnie that if you're depressed, drinkin' makes things look even worse. So it was...what the heck did he call it? Oh, yeah, a contributing factor, that was it."

"Wait a minute. You and Lonnie were talking to the medical examiner the night it happened?"

"Yeah...yeah, but don't ask me about what all we said because I don't remember much of it. All I remember's how gruesome it was, with Mike lying there in a pool of blood and all."

"Whoa." Luke held up his hands. "You're losing me. You and Lonnie were right here that night?" But hadn't Trout just said he'd gone home after work? And, according to Caitlin, Mike had been alone in the hangar.

"*After* it happened," Trout was already explaining. "When Rayland found the body, he called me an' Lonnie to get out here. And he called the medical examiner to come, too, o' course. That's when we were talkin' to him."

"But why did Rayland call you and Lonnie?"

Trout rubbed his palms up and down on his coveralls, looking decidedly uncomfortable. "He wanted to ask us some questions."

"So you came out here. And who arrived first? You or Lonnie?"

"I...why? What difference does it make?"

Luke shrugged, trying to look casual. He didn't know if *anything* he was asking made any difference or not, but maybe something would give him a clue as to what had really gone on that night.

"I don't remember who got here first," Trout finally answered. "I think maybe I did, but I'm not sure. Seeing Mike dead like that just...all I really remember is the four of us standing around in the office."

"You were right *in* the office? I thought you meant you saw Mike's body through the glass."

"Uh-uh. We were in there while the medical examiner was doing his...whatever he does, exactly. And Rayland was askin' me an' Lonnie questions and makin' notes about stuff. But, look, I gotta get back to work. There's a noise in one of the engines I don't like."

"Okay, just give me another minute." Luke rubbed his jaw, trying to decide what else to ask while he had the chance. He might not be a detective, but he'd read a lot of murder mysteries. And unless all the authors had it wrong, Rayland should never have had Lonnie and Trout in that office.

It had been a crime scene—regardless of whether the crime had been murder or suicide. And a crime scene was supposed to be completely checked for evidence before *any* civilians were allowed near it. Hell, that's why they used that yellow police tape.

"Luke, look, I really gotta—"

"Wait, just tell me one more thing. You said Caitlin didn't know Mike had taken to drinking. And the fact he'd been drinking the night he died...nobody ever mentioned it to her?"

Trout shrugged. "I didn't. So unless somebody else changed his mind...see, that night...I can't remember who's idea it was, but somebody said we should just keep quiet about the booze."

"Why?"

"'Cuz we figured tellin' Caitlin that Mike had been liquored up would only make her feel worse. So we agreed not to."

"But what about Rayland's report? Does it say Mike had been drinking?"

"Don't know. Never saw Rayland's report."

"Well...thanks for telling me all this, Trout. It puts a different perspective on things."

"Hey, no problem," he said.

He was saying no problem, but Luke noticed he was sweating like a pig—and doubted it was entirely because of the heat.

Trout turned away, but instead of starting back to the planes he walked rapidly toward the hangar.

Luke watched him for a minute, thinking it had been a long time since he'd seen anybody as nervous as Trout had just been. But why? Did any of the good ol' boys know something more about what had happened that night than they'd let on?

And what the hell was with Rayland calling Lonnie and Trout out here after he found Mike's body? That seemed awfully peculiar. And now, after being so anxious to get back to work on the planes, why was Trout heading for the hangar?

Did he want to tell Lonnie what he'd said, so they could keep their stories straight? Or was it just that Trout thought Lonnie should be told their temporary pilot was asking questions?

Hell, at this point the only thing Luke was sure about was that he'd been dreaming if he'd really thought he could ask anything on the quiet.

By tonight, the whole damn town would know he was nosing around about Mike's death. So there wasn't much point worrying about what else he asked from here on in.

DESPITE THE HEAT, Luke waited right where he was until Trout disappeared into the hangar, rethinking the idea of leaving for Tucson right away. Even though he wanted to get back to the hospital, he had a feeling he'd better pay the sheriff a visit first.

Once Trout told Lonnie about their conversation, it wouldn't be any surprise if the next person to hear about it was Rayland Skoda. Hell, it would be more of a surprise if they *didn't* call Rayland.

And since Luke wanted a look at that report on Mike's death—before it had a chance to mysteriously go missing or anything—he'd sooner the sheriff didn't have advance warning.

After a quick glance at his watch, he looked over at the hangar again, knowing he should call Caitlin and tell her he'd be delayed. But he didn't really want to use the phone in the office, where Lonnie and Trout would be breathing down his neck. One of the pay phones in the terminal would be better.

Starting off across the sweltering tarmac, he dug out a credit card to make the call to Tucson. Once inside, he told himself to forget about his conversation with Trout for a few minutes. Caitlin had enough on her mind, without hearing about it right now.

He dialed the hospital's number and was put through to the parents' lounge. An anxious-sounding woman answered on the first ring. A minute later, Caitlin was on the line.

"Hi," he said, "everything okay? Your grandparents made it there all right?"

"Yes, and Peggy-Sue said she's coming back at lunch to drag me out to a deli."

"Good. Have you had any word about the baby?"

"Not really," she murmured. "I talked to an intern, but she was falling all over herself being circumspect."

Caitlin sounded so worried he began thinking maybe he'd better head straight to the hospital, after all.

But if Lonnie was already starting to interview pilots... Hell, the pressure was on now. And that message Rayland had left at the house last night had said he'd be in his office most of the day, so this had to be a good time to catch him.

"The only thing she'd tell me," Caitlin said, "was that the Chief doesn't seem any worse."

"Well, hey, if she was being circumspect, maybe no worse actually meant better."

"Maybe... I just don't want to get my hopes up in case..."

"He's going to be fine, Caitlin. Which reminds me, Lonnie said to give you his best. And he said he's already had a couple of responses to his ad in the *Star*. He's even interviewing a guy this afternoon."

There was a small silence at Caitlin's end of the line. "Oh," she finally said. "So he really might get somebody right away."

Luke waited, willing her to say something more. Something like she didn't want him to leave Culpepper until he had to get back to Pensacola—even if Lonnie *did* hire another pilot.

"Well," she said at last, "that would be good, wouldn't it. You'd end up with time to go and see your buddies in San Diego, after all."

He swore to himself, wishing he'd waited to talk to her about this face-to-face. Over the phone, he couldn't tell whether she meant *she'd* want him to be on his way or that she was assuming *he'd* want to leave.

"I'm not in any hurry to head for San Diego," he finally said.

"Good," she murmured. "I'm glad. I...Luke, someone else desperately wants to use this phone. So I'll see you soon?"

"Yeah, I just...I'm going to drop by and talk to Rayland before I drive up there."

"About Mike?"

"Uh-huh."

When she didn't ask anything more, Luke assumed it was because whoever wanted to use the phone was standing right beside her.

He asked her where Rayland's office was, then said, "I'll try to get to the hospital before the doctor arrives."

"Good," she murmured again. "That would be good."

"Okay, I'll see you in a while." He hung up, hating Alexander Graham Bell. How could anyone have invented something as impersonal as the telephone?

As he glanced across the terminal toward the snack bar, it occurred to him that his choice for lunch was probably between it and the cafeteria at the Children's Hospital. There was no real choice, so he decided to grab something here and eat it on his way into town.

The Mexican girl behind the counter—whose badge reminded him her name was Conchita—greeted him with a smile and a friendly, *"Momentito, por favor."*

He waited impatiently on one of the stools while she finished serving another customer, then asked her for a take-out ham and swiss on rye.

"You were a friend of Mike Alexander's, *sí?*" she said as she began making the sandwich.

"Yeah. How did you know that?"

"Oh, from the Trout. His wife, she has put him on the diet, so he comes to me when the planes are flying and I make him the hamburger. *Una hamburguesa y cerveza,* that is what the Trout likes best."

Luke grinned. Trout was sure going to lose weight on a diet of hamburgers and beer.

Conchita took his money and made change, flashing him a smile when he left a dollar bill on the counter. She slipped his sandwich into a bag, but instead of handing it to him right away, she leaned closer and quietly said, "Your friend Mike Alexander was a good man. I had a problem and he was trying to help me with it. And I wonder...when he died..." Her gaze flickered past Luke and her words trailed off.

He swiveled around on the stool. Lonnie was ambling across the terminal, headed for the snack bar.

"Hey, Dakota," he called, "I thought you were passing on lunch."

"I will tell you about this another time," Conchita whispered.

LUKE SPENT THE FIRST few minutes between the airport and Culpepper eating his sandwich and trying to figure out what Conchita had been about to tell him.

When he died, she'd said. But had she been going to tell him something about Mike's death, or was it just that Mike had been in the middle of trying to help her with whatever her problem was when he'd died?

She hadn't said enough for that to be clear, so he put their conversation on the back burner for the time being and spent the rest of the drive trying to figure out the best way of handling Rayland.

He was pretty sure the public had a right to see the sheriff's reports. But Caitlin had said that Rayland liked to call the shots, so marching in and demanding to see them would just get the guy's back up.

Before he had time to decide on an approach he really liked, he reached his destination. The sheriff's office, along with what he figured had to be the local hoosegow—given the bars on the windows—were housed in an ancient two-story brick building on Main Street.

There was a vacant parking space right out front, so he pulled into it, then opened the Mustang's door to the heat—thinking that when those monsoons Caitlin had mentioned arrived, they'd at least offer a break from the blistering sun. In that respect, he'd welcome them.

Assuming, that was, he'd still be here by then. Assuming that when Lonnie hired his new pilot, Caitlin wouldn't expect her current *boarder* to hit the road right away.

Hell, he was going to have to have a long talk with her and establish exactly where things stood between the two of them. But he knew that would have to wait until after they were sure the baby was going to be okay. Until then, he could only guess what she was feeling.

He locked the car and headed across the sidewalk, telling himself that after the way Caitlin had kissed him last night there wasn't much doubt she felt *something* for him. Unless…maybe she'd just needed someone to hold her.

No, he firmly reassured himself. That didn't explain her kiss. It hadn't just been needing someone, it had been the kiss of the century.

Still, hoping whatever she felt might be even half as strong as what he was feeling for her might be hoping for too much. Or maybe he was crazy to be hoping at all. His feelings about this whole situation were totally confused. He wanted to stay in Culpepper as long as he could. But maybe, if he had the chance to leave, he'd be smart to take it.

When he walked into the building, Rayland was standing just outside the office marked Sheriff, talking to a young deputy sitting at one of the two desks in the outer office. They both looked over at him— the younger man curiously, Rayland with an expression that fell somewhere between suspicious and hostile. It made Luke wonder if Trout or Lonnie had already been on the phone, warning the sheriff that Luke Dakota might be looking to cause trouble.

"Hey, Luke," he finally said, shifting the toothpick he was chewing to the other corner of his mouth. "What can I do for you?"

"Can I talk to you in your office for a minute?"

Rayland nodded and ushered him inside. Shutting the door behind them, the sheriff leaned against his desk and gestured Luke to the chair in front of it.

Sitting in it would have left Rayland staring down at him, so he said, "Thanks, but between the car and the plane, I've been sitting all day." He wandered over to the window, took a quick look out, then turned back to Rayland. "I need a favor."

"Uh-huh?"

"I'd like to look at your report on Mike Alexander's suicide."

"Oh? And why's that, Luke?"

He rubbed his jaw, trying to look sincere. "Well, I was thinking about what you said at lunch yesterday. About it being your job to know the difference between homicide and suicide."

"Uh-huh," Rayland said with barely a hint of interest.

"And ... well, when Caitlin first told me she had trouble believing Mike killed himself, I guess I wanted to believe she might be right. But after you and I talked, I realized this idea she has is nothing more than that. Just an idea. But you know how sometimes people latch on to something and don't want to let go?"

"Uh-huh." Rayland worked his toothpick to the other side of his mouth again.

"Well, it seems to me that's what's happened here. And I think it would help set her mind at ease if someone she trusted looked at the report and assured her the details all added up."

"Someone like you."

Luke shrugged. "I was a friend of Mike's. She has no reason not to trust me."

"You saying she *doesn't* trust me?"

"No, I'm not saying that at all."

"But she asked you to come here."

"No, this was entirely my idea."

"Well, why is it she never asked to see the report herself? You think to ask her that?"

"As a matter of fact, she mentioned why—said she knew reading it would upset her."

"Yeah? Well, I guess it just might, because it would sure as hell throw cold water on her *fantasy* about somebody murdering Mike."

Luke could feel his anger rising and tried to suppress it. He was tempted to tell Rayland that Caitlin suspected his report might be a whitewash, so she hadn't thought it would be worth reading. But antagonizing the sheriff would hardly be productive.

"I guess that could be it, Rayland," he said at last. "Maybe she just never wanted to see the truth written down in black and white. I'm no psychologist, but I know it's harder to deny something when you're looking the facts in the face."

"So you figure *you* should look at them, then tell her they're all in order?"

"As I said, I think it might go a long way to helping her put her doubts to rest."

Rayland shifted his weight on the edge of the desk, eyeing Luke evenly. "Well," he finally muttered, "I sure as hell wouldn't want to be accused of not helping Caitlin out."

He shoved himself up and dug a file folder from his cabinet. "Here you are, Luke. There's an interview room just along the hall. So you take this on down there and read to your heart's content. Then give it to my deputy when you're done. I'm just on my way out."

Rayland grabbed his sheriff's hat off the top of the filing cabinet, handed Luke the folder and walked out of his office without a backward glance.

LUKE TOOK THE STAIRS up to the parents' lounge, hoping Caitlin's thoughts would be so focused on the baby that she wouldn't ask about his visit with Rayland right away. Because there'd been nothing in the sheriff's report to support her theory, nothing at all.

Not that Luke was thinking her suspicions were off target. Not after that conversation with Trout. There was too much about his story that just didn't seem to add up right.

But this wasn't the time or place to start telling Caitlin about everything Trout had said. He'd save that for later. But if she *did* ask about the report...well, she wasn't going to like hearing about it.

Basically, it said exactly what she'd been told. There were only two real differences. The first was that it contained a lot more detail than Caitlin had recounted the other night.

It specified the precise time Rayland had discovered the body—just before midnight on January 4, 1994. It also stated that the medical examiner's estimate as to time of death was from two to four hours earlier.

It described where Mike had been lying on the floor, where the gun had fallen, the angle the shot had entered and exited his head.

And just as Rayland had told Caitlin, way back when, the report said there'd been no sign of an attempted theft or a scuffle—no evidence that someone else might have been in the office.

There were a whole lot of other details, but the bottom line was Rayland's conclusion—that Mike had been alone in his office and that he'd killed himself with a single bullet from the Smith & Wesson he'd kept there.

There was also a bit that said "friends and associates of the deceased reported that he'd been depressed due to illness." So maybe Rayland had called Trout and Lonnie out in the middle of the night because he'd wanted to ask them about a possible motive for suicide.

At any rate, aside from the amount of detail, the only other difference between Caitlin's version and the report, itself, was that it *did* state that Mike had been drinking before he died.

It was just as Trout had said. According to Rayland's report, there'd been an almost empty bottle of Old Grand-Dad on Mike's desk, along with a single glass. And a blood sample had shown there'd been a significant amount of alcohol in his bloodstream.

That was definitely not something that lent any credibility to Caitlin's murder theory. In fact, it made it a lot easier to believe Mike had killed himself. As the medical examiner had told Trout, drinking could have been a contributing factor in Mike's death.

But aside from what Luke had read in that report, everything else he'd learned today only made him more suspicious that Rayland's conclusion of suicide wasn't the whole truth.

He reached the third floor and headed out of the stairwell toward the parents' lounge. When he turned down the corridor that led to it, Caitlin was standing right there in the hallway.

She was wearing jeans, now, instead of shorts. Peggy-Sue had obviously brought the fresh clothes she'd promised. But she was still wearing her Remember the Alamo sweatshirt, and seeing that gave him a warm feeling.

When she spotted him, she smiled a weary smile and started along the hall. A second later she was in his arms and he was breathing that meadows-in-moonlight scent he'd come to love.

He simply held her for a minute, loving the feel of her against him even more than that scent. "Have you heard anything yet?" he finally asked.

"Not yet," she murmured against his chest. "But it's after two. The doctor should be here any time now."

She drew back a little, and Luke reluctantly lowered his arms to his sides. She looked incredibly tired. Overnight, little lines had appeared around her eyes.

Seeing her so worried made him ache for her. He wanted to kiss those lines away. Instead, he asked if her grandparents were in the lounge.

"No, they went down to the cafeteria a few minutes ago. They didn't want to go out to the deli with Peggy-Sue and me. My grandfather says delis should all have stayed in New York. But he takes a pill at noon—at least he's *supposed* to take it right at noon, and he has to have food with it. So my grandmother finally dragged him downstairs to get something. But they'll probably just grab a sandwich and bring it back."

Luke nodded, reaching for her hands. He just couldn't seem to keep from touching her.

Then Dr. Peterson suddenly rounded the corner and was walking toward them.

CHAPTER TEN

CAITLIN'S HEART BEGAN hammering with fear. Dr. Peterson was carrying a fat file folder, and he looked so serious that her breath caught in her throat. She clutched Luke's hands so tightly her fingers hurt.

"Relax," he whispered, taking both her hands in one of his and wrapping his arm around her shoulders.

"Caitlin," Dr. Peterson said. And then he smiled.

She felt like laughing and crying at the same time. That one little smile was all it took. "He's going to be all right?" she whispered.

"Yes, I think it's safe to say he's going to be just fine."

She closed her eyes and offered up a silent prayer of thanks. Luke gave her shoulders a gentle squeeze, and when she opened her eyes again he was grinning at her.

"Your smile's as big as the Cheshire cat's," he murmured.

"Only *that* big?" she murmured back.

Dr. Peterson began speaking again, but she felt so relieved and happy it was hard to concentrate on the rest of what he had to tell her.

"It's not what we were afraid of," he was saying. "Nothing strange and exotic from the Gulf. What little Luke has is something called labyrinthitis."

"Labyrinthitis," she repeated. It was a totally foreign word on her tongue.

Dr. Peterson nodded. "Also known as otitis interna. It's sometimes a little tricky to diagnose because it manifests itself as a viral infection, but it's not."

"What is it?" Luke said.

"Basically, it's an inner ear condition, an inflammation of the semicircular canals. And that causes dizziness, which was what had him falling yesterday. The nausea he had is another symptom, and one of the others is disorientation. That's why he didn't seem to recognize anybody."

"But it won't cause any permanent damage," Caitlin said, suddenly afraid she was letting herself feel too relieved before she'd heard everything.

"Well ... the only possible danger is the infection could spread to the meninges, the membranes covering the inner brain. But I can't see that happening in this case. We've diagnosed it quickly and I've already prescribed antibiotics. Aside from that, it's really just a question of keeping him quiet—a few days of bed rest."

"He's a pretty active little guy," she said anxiously.

"Well, he won't be for the next couple of days. I expect he's going to want to sleep for most of today and tomorrow. He won't feel up to doing much until he's better, but he should be back to normal in less than a week."

"Thank heavens," she whispered. "Can I see him?"

"Absolutely. We've moved him out of isolation and he's in room 614. When I left him he was asleep, but if he's awake when you get there just be careful not to get him excited. Are your grandparents here again today?''

She nodded.

"Well, I know they'll want to see him, too, but keep it brief. He should be getting as much sleep as possible."

"I can stay with him, though?"

The doctor nodded. "You can stay for the rest of the afternoon, and feed him his dinner. After that, though, I want you to go home and get a good night's sleep yourself."

"Can't I stay all night and—"

"Caitlin, I want you to go home. We'd like to keep an eye on him overnight, but we'll probably release him tomorrow morning and—"

"Tomorrow morning? So soon?" That was so good to hear she could barely believe it.

"Yes, and I don't want you dead tired when you get him home. So don't argue with me, okay?"

"Okay." She'd still like to have stayed with the Chief all night, but after the news this man had just given her she'd jump out the window if he asked her.

Glancing down the corridor toward the elevators, she wondered how much longer her grandparents would be. She wanted to get up to room 614, but she could hardly have them come back and find her gone.

"Want me to wait here for them?" Luke said, reading her thoughts.

"You wouldn't mind?"

"No We'll come up as soon as they get back."

She smiled at him. "You know, you're an awfully nice guy, Luke Dakota."

He smiled back. "I try."

Caitlin hurried down to the elevators and rode anxiously up to the sixth floor. Despite the doctor's encouraging words, she had to see for herself that the Chief was really all right.

When she reached 614, she paused in the doorway, almost afraid of what she might see inside. But it proved to be the most beautiful sight in the world.

Her son was lying asleep in a crib beside the window. And aside from being a little pale, he looked perfectly healthy. There were no IV tubes hanging beside the crib, no needles taped into any of his tiny veins.

She simply stayed where she was at first, unable to take her eyes off him, her own personal miracle, while the sight of his sturdy little body gradually convinced her he really *was* all right.

The room was quiet, the other three cribs empty. It was only her and the Chief—the way it had been since the day he was born.

Finally, she slipped across the room and stood gazing down at him, her eyes detailing the bruise on his hand where the IV had been and the tiny bandage on his inner arm. That, she assumed, was where they'd drawn blood.

She wanted to take him in her arms and hold him close, but she made herself do with just watching him breathe and thinking how lucky she was he hadn't had something really serious. If she ever lost little Luke Michael Alexander, she'd die.

After she'd been with him for a few minutes he wiggled around in the crib, then sleepily opened his eyes and saw her standing beside him.

His face brightened with a tired smile, and he waved his little fists, gurgling, "Ma-ma."

Her heart felt so full of love she almost began to cry. "Right, darling," she murmured, "Ma-ma's here with you, and you're going to be well again in no time. Everything's all right. Everything's just fine now." She leaned over him, crooning endearments, then kissed him gently on the forehead.

He caught one of her hands with his chubby fingers and she stroked his hair with the other, savoring the smell of the baby powder and his own clean baby scent.

She didn't know what was going to happen in the next little while. But right this minute everything seemed pretty wonderful again, in her little corner of the world.

OUTSIDE THE CHILDREN'S Hospital dusk was rapidly giving way to darkness. Inside, the Chief's room had grown dim—lit only by stray light drifting in from the corridor.

When Caitlin got up to tuck the baby's blanket carefully around him again, Luke leaned back in his chair and closed his eyes for a minute. They'd been sitting here for hours, but as Dr. Peterson had predicted, the Chief had slept most of the day. So Luke and Caitlin had spent the time quietly talking.

As soon as her grandparents headed back to Culpepper, she'd asked about his visit to Rayland. And he'd hedged, telling her there'd really been nothing in the report she hadn't already known.

He *did* intend to tell her Mike had been drinking that night. And about his conversation with Trout, of course. But she was still so exhausted from worrying about the baby that it just hadn't seemed like a good time.

So, instead, he'd tried to keep things light, and they'd talked mainly about their childhoods and growing up, things they'd done over the years, and what they liked and what they hated.

In one afternoon, he'd learned more about Caitlin than he'd learned in years about most people he knew. And he'd probably told her more about himself than he'd ever told anyone else.

She was just so damn easy to talk to, so damn great to be with, that a hundred times he'd wanted to ask her how she felt about him. But he'd never been the best guy in the world with words, and he hadn't been able to come up with the right ones this time, either.

Or maybe this wasn't the right place to discuss it. Maybe later, when they were back at the ranch...just the two of them. God, it only took the thought of that to get him aroused.

"You're tired of sitting here," Caitlin said, bringing him back to the moment. "We'd better get going."

When he glanced over she was standing beside the crib smiling at him. It made her mouth look extremely kissable.

"It's okay," he told her. He'd sit here with her all night if that's what she wanted.

"No, it's not okay, Luke. I know I've been taking advantage of you."

"Don't be silly."

"Right," she murmured. "I'll bet that you've always been dying to spend a leave in Culpepper, Arizona. And you must have loved being out there in the hot sun the other day, helping me fix the carport. Not to mention being dragged out to chase cactus killers armed with semiautomatics."

"Hey, I've never had more fun in my life than I've been having here."

"Sure. You've probably really enjoyed playing taxi driver, too."

"Well...I've got to admit the tips haven't been the greatest."

That made Caitlin laugh. And her laugh made him think of silver bells.

"And today," she said, "I suppose there's no place in the world you'd rather have been than in this hospital room." With a final smile, she turned and bent to kiss the baby goodbye.

Luke pushed himself out of the chair, tempted to tell her she was right. There *was* no place in the world he'd rather have been—no place he'd rather have been since the day they met—than wherever she was.

But his feelings for her had hit him so damn fast that if he told her about them...hell, she might think he was being ridiculous...or that he was just handing her a line, or... Damn. He felt like a tongue-tied schoolboy, instead of a thirty-three-year-old man.

"Come on, let's go now," she said.

"You're sure?"

She nodded. "It looks as if the Chief's asleep for the night, and you look as if you're ready for bed."

That line almost made him groan. He managed to stifle it and looked down into the crib. The little guy really did seem fine now.

"He's just so sweet, isn't he," Caitlin murmured.

Luke nodded, still gazing down at his namesake. He gently rested his fingers against the soft baby cheek, stood listening to the gentle baby breathing. And he couldn't help wondering how such a simple thing as sharing his name with the little guy could make him feel so strongly connected.

He glanced at Caitlin, thinking that if the baby hadn't been named after him she might never have written him that letter. She might have just assumed he'd heard about Mike's death some other way. And if she hadn't written, he'd never have met her.

"What?" she said.

"Do you believe in fate?"

She gazed at him uncertainly. "Yes ... I guess I believe some things are inevitable. Why?"

He shrugged. His sister was the philosopher in the family, not him. He'd always just taken things as they came, never wondered much if there was any *reason* behind them. But right now he was wondering if fate had anything to do with Caitlin sending him that letter. Or with his spur-of-the-moment decision to come to Culpepper.

The letter had arrived more than a year and a half after Mike died. And only days before his leave began.

If it had come a week later, he'd have been gone. He wouldn't have even known about the Chief, let alone be here. And if the letter had arrived months earlier, if he'd had time to give the idea of making the trip more thought, he'd probably have decided it wasn't worth it, driving across the country, during the hottest month of the year, just to see a baby.

"Why did you ask about fate?" Caitlin said.

Now what did he tell her? The truth? That he was thinking they'd been predestined to meet? He couldn't say that. He just wasn't the kind of guy to say something that might have come straight out of an old late-night movie.

"I'll tell you about it some other time," he said at last. "Maybe when we get home."

THEY STOPPED for a quick dinner at Carlos Murphy's, a Mexican restaurant Caitlin had always liked, then left the lights of Tucson behind and sped south through the darkness. Glancing at Luke's even profile, Caitlin couldn't help thinking how lucky she was he'd been with her the past few days.

Yesterday, when she'd told him she didn't know what she'd have done without him, she'd meant it. When her grandmother had phoned to say the Chief was sick, she'd have been in such a panic she doubted she could have driven. But with a man like Luke to lean on . . .

She forced her eyes away from him and stared ahead into the night. She couldn't let herself get used to his being there to lean on. Because one day soon she'd turn around and he'd be gone. Maybe even sooner than she'd first thought, if Lonnie did find a new pilot right away.

Her gaze strayed across the car again. The faint light from the dash was painting the angles and planes of Luke's face with sexy hollows and shadows. He looked so virile her pulse began to race.

Despite all her good intentions, she'd been letting herself sink deeper and deeper. The better she got to know him, the nearer her heart was coming to being his for the asking. And she just couldn't deny that she wanted him—in her heart and in her bed.

But that would be foolish, wouldn't it? When she knew he'd be leaving soon?

He glanced at her, smiled that easy smile she loved, and asked what she was thinking about.

"Nothing," she lied, then went right back to thinking about him. Thinking that maybe it wasn't so foolish. Maybe it would be more foolish not to take what she wanted—without worrying about tomorrow.

You couldn't count on the future. That had been driven home to her when Mike died.

Mike. Her thoughts turned to him, and she wondered what he'd think about the way she was feeling. Would he want her to lock her emotions away for the rest of her life? Or would he want her to get on with things, to start to feel alive again with a good man— a man like Luke.

Tears stung her eyes and she wiped them away. If she had been the one to die, rather than Mike, she'd want him to be happy—to pick up the pieces and make a new life for himself. And she knew that's what he'd want for her.

She wiped her eyes again. Putting the past behind you was hard. But it had to be done. You had to live in the present. And the present was tonight. Not sometime down the line when Luke would be gone...when it would be too late to share the present with him.

She sat lost in thought as the miles slid by, and in no time they were turning off the highway and heading down the road to the ranch.

"Sam's going to be glad to see us," she said. "Did you think to let him out this morning? When you stopped by the house before your mission?"

Luke gave her a sheepish look. "Actually, I let him *in* this morning. He got away on me last night. Guess I forgot to mention it."

It was so obvious he'd intentionally not mentioned it that she laughed.

"What?" he said.

"You didn't really forget."

"No." He glanced at her again, grinning this time. "No, I didn't tell you because I felt like an idiot for letting a dog outsmart me."

"Well . . . he *is* a pretty smart dog."

A moment later they were turning in at her place. Ahead, at the end of the drive, the living-room lights were welcoming them—courtesy of her timer.

As they got closer to the house, though, the headlights revealed the not-so-welcoming sight of a parked car. A Culpepper County sheriff's car.

"You've got company," Luke said.

She nodded, wondering if it was Rayland or one of his deputies, and wondering why *any* of them would have come here in the first place. She could hear Sam barking inside, and when their headlights captured the dark figure standing at the front door, she saw it was Rayland—out of uniform.

"Mmm . . . looks like the sheriff's paying a social visit," Luke said, pulling to a stop.

"Looks like." She'd taken off her Remember the Alamo sweatshirt when they'd left the air-conditioned hospital, and now she draped it and the one for the Chief over her arm.

"Hey, Cait, sugar," Rayland said when she got out of the car.

The *sugar* made her grit her teeth, and reminded her why she'd never been overly crazy about Rayland, even when she'd gone out with him.

"Good timing," he said as she and Luke headed over to the house. "I was figuring you had to be home because your van was here and the lights were on. But when nobody answered I was just about to leave.''

Behind her, Luke muttered something that was obviously meant only for her. She wasn't certain she caught it right, but it sounded like, ''We should have stayed at Carlos Murphy's for dessert.'' Then he said hello to Rayland—rather coolly, she thought.

''Oh, yeah, hi, Luke.'' Rayland gave him a nod and turned his attention back to Caitlin. ''I was out to the airport earlier, and I heard the baby was in the hospital. So...is he okay?''

''I think he's going to be fine, thanks. The doctor said they'll be releasing him tomorrow.''

''Oh, good. Well, I figured that was why you didn't call me back, and I thought if there was anything I could do...''

''Call you back?'' she said uncertainly.

Luke cleared his throat. ''Sorry, I guess I forgot to tell you. There was a message from Rayland on your machine last night.''

''Oh?'' Suddenly, Luke seemed to have become very forgetful. She briefly wondered if there was anything else he'd forgotten to tell her.

''I really *did* just forget that one,'' he whispered, practically into her ear.

''So you never got my message?'' Rayland was saying on her other side.

''No.'' She glanced at him in time to catch him shooting Luke a black look. ''I haven't been home,'' she added, unlocking the door.

The second she opened it, Sam rushed out to check on who was with her and get a few good pats.

"I spent last night at the hospital," she finished explaining to Rayland. "Would you like to come in for a beer or something?"

"Yeah ... yeah, that sounds great."

Luke looked distinctly annoyed by her invitation, which started her heart beating a little faster. She assumed it meant he wanted to be alone with her and ... or was it just that he didn't like Rayland?

Sam apparently decided she was safe with Luke and Rayland and went trotting off to do his dog thing. The two men followed her inside.

"Why don't you go on out to the deck," she suggested to them. "I'll bring the beer out there. You'd like one, too, Luke?"

When he nodded, she started for the kitchen.

"Ahh ... Cait, sugar?"

She stopped and looked back.

"I was wanting to talk to you privately about something."

There was a long silence, then Luke said, "I think there's a ball game on TV. So why don't I just watch that while you two have your talk."

RAYLAND HAD MOVED one of the other deck chairs so close to his own that the arms were touching. Caitlin handed him the bottle of beer, then angled the other chair away from his a little before she sat down.

"So," she said, "what's up?"

He chewed on his toothpick for a minute. "Well, Cait," he finally began, "you and I go way back, so I didn't want any hard feelings between us."

"Why would there be hard feelings?"

"Well...I knew that after Luke told you about my report, you'd be thinking I held out on you. So I wanted to tell you why it was I ... I just wanted to explain why I didn't mention it."

"Oh ... all right," she said as calmly as she could. But what was the "it"?

"It wasn't that I was trying to keep anything from you," Rayland went on. "Well ... I mean, I was, but only because I didn't want you hurt any worse than you already were."

She nodded, surreptitiously glancing along the deck and into the family room—where Luke was watching the baseball game.

He'd said there was nothing in that report she didn't already know. But that obviously wasn't true.

"So," Rayland was saying, "I told Lonnie and Trout to keep their mouths shut. There was no need for anybody else to know. Especially not you."

"Oh," she said again, but she still had no idea what Rayland was talking about. Except that now he was saying there'd been a whole conspiracy to keep her in the dark about something.

"So ... what did you think when Luke told you?" Rayland asked. "Were you damn ticked off at me or ... ?"

She hesitated, not really wanting to tell him Luke had apparently been holding out on her, too. But she could hardly get away with another "oh" in answer to a direct question.

"Actually," she admitted, "Luke didn't say a word about whatever you're assuming he did."

"No?" Rayland suddenly looked as close to being unsure of himself as she'd ever seen him.

"So what is it? What is there about Mike's death that I don't know?"

"It's not really a big deal, Cait, sugar."

"Oh? Then why did you come out here on your own time to talk about it?"

"I told you. Because I didn't want you to think I'd been keeping something important from you, when all it was . . . well, like I said, I just didn't want things to be any worse for you than they already were. And I thought, if you knew . . ."

"Knew what? Rayland, would you please get to the point? What don't I know?"

He shrugged. "I didn't want to tell you this, Cait. And if it weren't for your friend in there I wouldn't have to. I was trying to protect you from the truth— Mike wasn't *working* in his office the night he died. At least not right before he shot himself."

"What are you talking about?" she asked uncertainly.

"Cait, there was no work on his desk. But there *was* a bottle of bourbon. He'd been sitting there drinking."

Caitlin's mouth suddenly felt dry. She stared at Rayland. "Mike wasn't much of a drinker," she managed to say evenly. "And he almost never drank hard stuff. You know that."

"Well . . . the truth of it is, the months before he died he was drinking pretty regularly. You just didn't know about it. And that night, according to the blood sample, he'd had a lot. And see, that's why neither the medical examiner or I had any doubt it was suicide. Mike was depressed . . . had a drink . . . then another. . . . Gradually he lost his inhibitions and started thinking how easy it would be to pull that trigger. Hell, Cait, it was just so obvious what happened."

The dryness had spread down her throat, making it impossible to swallow, and her chest felt as if there were steel bands pressing in on it.

It was just so obvious what happened—unless some of the facts were withheld from you. Until now, she'd never known why Rayland seemed so positive. Until now, she'd been deluding herself because they'd kept this from her.

"But I thought," Rayland went on, "well, I knew how bad you'd feel about the suicide. And I figured it would only make you feel worse if you knew Mike had been sitting in his office hitting the sauce at night, instead of going home to you."

Rayland's final words hit her like a fist to the solar plexus. Then a wave of nausea struck her. It was followed, in turn, by a rush of all those haunting questions she'd thought her bereavement group had helped her put to rest. Just thinking about them again made her throat hurt and brought tears to her eyes.

"Oh, God," she murmured, unable to keep the tears from escaping.

"Cait, sugar," Rayland said. He reached for her hands, but she pulled them away.

"Cait, sugar," he said again. "This is exactly why I didn't want you to know. I was just trying to spare you. When you calm down I want you to think about that, huh? The only reason I didn't tell you everything was because I knew it would hurt you."

"Go home, Rayland," she whispered. "Please, just go home." She squeezed her eyes shut, trying unsuccessfully to stop those damn tears. The pain she'd thought was gone hadn't really gone at all. It had just been hiding somewhere inside her, waiting for an opportunity to strike again.

"Not a good time, buddy," Rayland was saying. "Go back and watch some more of your game."

Caitlin opened her eyes. Both Rayland and Luke were standing in front of her, but her vision was so blurred they were fuzzy around the edges.

"What the hell's going on?" Luke demanded. "What did you say to her?"

"Nothing you wouldn't have said to her, if you ever got around to it."

"We were talking about Mike," Caitlin managed to say.

"Yeah?" Luke glared at Rayland. "Well it looks like Caitlin's had enough talking for tonight. Caitlin?" he added more quietly. "Is there anything I can do?"

She shook her head. All she wanted either of them to do was leave her alone. "Just go," she whispered. "Just go, okay, Rayland?"

CHAPTER ELEVEN

LUKE FOLLOWED ALONG to the front door after Rayland, in case the sheriff had second thoughts about leaving. He was clearly damn mad—looked as if he'd like nothing more than to stick around and throw some punches.

And Luke almost wished he would. The sheriff might have thirty or forty extra pounds on his side, but Luke figured he was in better shape. And *he'd* like nothing more than to deck Rayland. Whatever it was that he'd said to Caitlin, she'd obviously have been a lot better off if he hadn't said it.

Rayland yanked the door open, then turned back to Luke.

"What got her crying?" he demanded before the sheriff could utter a word. "What did you say to her?"

"I said something about Mike's drinking," Rayland snapped. "Trout said he told you about it. So between that and reading my report, I figured you'd have already told her. And I wanted her to understand why I never said anything to her before."

Luke nodded. He'd buy that, but now he had Rayland alone he might as well try asking a few more questions. "Trout said a couple of other things I was wondering about."

"Look, fly-boy, how 'bout you mind your own business? Mike's graveyard dead, so just leave it at that, huh?"

"No, I don't think so, Rayland. Mike was a friend of mine."

"Yeah, well Mike was a friend of a lot of guys. And it's too damn bad he killed himself, but that's what he did. And I don't need some amateur detective coming into *my* county, all the way from Pen-*seee*cola, and asking questions that just get folks upset."

"Caitlin's the only person I've seen get upset," Luke snapped. "And it sure as hell wasn't me who upset her."

"You know, buddy, you're just asking for trouble."

Rayland looked even closer to throwing a punch, but Luke was getting so hot he'd gone beyond hoping that's what the sheriff would do. He wanted to throw the first one himself. The only thing holding him back was the certainty it would land him in Rayland's hoosegow for the night.

So instead of taking a shot at the guy, he said, "Why did you call Lonnie and Trout out to the hangar after you found Mike's body?"

"Because they'd been with him all day and I wanted to ask them some questions. And it was a hell of a lot faster to get them out there than for me to go driving around to their places. And that's the last of your damn questions I'm answering."

"So you just got them out there and had them wandering all over the crime scene."

Rayland let out a string of obscenities. "Who the hell do you think you are, Dakota? A one-man inquiry board? I was looking at a damn suicide. That was as clear as the nose on your face. And I saw everything I needed to see at the scene before Lonnie and Trout ever got there. So look, why don't you do us all a favor? Why don't you just get into that Mustang of yours and drive yourself back to Florida?''

"Because I'm doing some flying for Sky Knights. Or did that slip your mind?"

"No, it didn't slip my mind. But the way I hear tell, you won't be doing it for long. I hear Lonnie hired himself a new pilot this afternoon. So as soon as he starts, they won't be needing you."

CAITLIN SAT STARING out over the pool, completely cried out and left feeling . . . nothing. Just emptiness inside.

The black sky was clear, studded with diamonds. In the distance, moonlight softly outlined the shapes of the foothills. The beauty of the desert night, though, was lost on her. The only thing she was really aware of was the dull ache in her heart.

All this time, she'd never believed that Mike had killed himself. But he had.

All this time, she'd suspected Rayland might have been concealing something he knew—to protect one of his buddies. But it had been her he'd been protecting.

She wished he hadn't. It only meant she'd wasted all that time believing the wrong things when she should have been accepting the truth. But Rayland's trying to protect her was typical of the men around Culpepper. To them, equal rights for women meant equal rights under *some* circumstances. And the same obviously held for equal access to the truth.

Rayland had decided she hadn't been up to handling the details of Mike's death. And Lonnie and Trout had gone along with it, keeping the knowledge of his drinking from her.

And Luke... she'd thought Luke was so different from Culpepper's good ol' boys. But it turned out he was just the same. What he didn't want her to know about, he conveniently *forgot* to mention. Like letting the dog get away on him. Like Rayland's phone message.

But those were minor compared to his not telling her what he'd read in that report. And she felt more betrayed by him than by all the rest of them put together. She'd come to expect so much better from him.

She heard the front door slam... then the throaty purr of a car coming to life. A moment later it roared down the drive, and the sound of its engine gradually faded into the night. Rayland had finally gone on his way.

"Caitlin?" Luke said.

She looked wearily across the deck. He'd come through the family room and was standing outside its sliding door. She tried to tell herself he wasn't the man she'd thought he was, that she hadn't actually been at risk of falling in love with him at all. But he looked so damn rugged standing there, so damn take-your-breath-away handsome, that even now...

He was really just like all the others, though. "Why did you lie to me?" she said.

He started toward her, saying, "I didn't lie, I—"

"No? Well what do you call it? You told me there was nothing in Rayland's report I didn't already know. And according to my dictionary, that definitely qualifies as—"

"Caitlin, listen to me." Luke sat down on the chair beside her. "I intended to tell you. I was just waiting for the right time."

"Oh? And when did you figure that would be? Obviously it wasn't while we were in the hospital. Or in the restaurant. Or during the drive home. So when?"

"Look, maybe I should have said something earlier, but you were so happy about the baby, I didn't want to say anything to make you unhappy."

"Luke, I—"

"I'm sorry, okay? It was a judgment call."

"You called it wrong."

"All right. The way things turned out, I guess I did. But how the hell was I supposed to know Rayland would be waiting at your front door? I intended to tell you as soon as we got home. I really did."

She didn't know whether or not to believe him, didn't know if it even mattered whether she did or not. She felt so utterly down, so utterly drained, that nothing seemed to matter.

"Caitlin?" he said softly.

Her eyes filled with tears again. She blinked fiercely, determined not to give in to them.

"Do you want me to tell you about it now?"

"No, I already know. I've been wrong all along. Mike really did commit suicide."

"No, Caitlin, I—"

"Yes! Don't lie to me anymore, Luke. Rayland finally gave me the missing piece of the puzzle. That's why it was so obvious to them what happened. And he said it was in his report. The report *you* read. Or are you going to tell me you missed the fact Mike drank enough that night to push him over the brink. To lose his inhibitions, as Rayland put it.''

"I was only trying to—"

"I *know* what you were trying to do. But don't *you* try to protect me, too. I'm not a child. I can face the facts. Even the worst one of all.''

"Caitlin—"

"No! I can face it, Luke. There must have been something I could have done that I didn't. Some way . . . some way I didn't know of that I could have kept Mike from killing himself."

Luke moved to kneel in front of her and rested his hands on her shoulders. "You don't really believe that."

She shook her head, tears streaming down her face now. "I wasn't a good enough wife, Luke. I did something wrong. Maybe I could have loved Mike more. Or been a better wife so he'd have loved me more. Loved me enough to have come home to me at night instead of sitting in his office drinking. Loved me enough that he wouldn't have killed himself."

"Oh, God, Caitlin." Luke pulled her up from her chair and wrapped his arms around her.

She stood sobbing against his chest, not wanting to lean on him but unable to stop herself.

"Caitlin, Mike couldn't have loved you any more than he did. He talked about you all the time in the Gulf. You meant the world to him." Luke stopped right there. It seemed crazy to be standing here, with the woman he loved in his arms, telling her how much another man had loved her.

He lightly rested his chin against the top of her head, his throat suddenly tight. Until now, he hadn't realized she wasn't really over Mike.

She'd said she was, back on the night she'd talked about how he'd died. She'd said that she'd never forget Mike, that part of her would always love him, but she'd accepted the fact he was gone.

That wasn't true, though. She wasn't over him. Luke's sister sometimes used a term he couldn't quite think of...

Emotional baggage, that was it. Sarah would say that Caitlin was still carting around all kinds of emotional baggage.

And if she wasn't over Mike, how could there be room in her heart for another man? For him? There was no point in thinking there might be a future for them. Not with the ghost of Mike Alexander between them.

Luke stood stroking Caitlin's hair, inhaling her meadows-in-moonlight scent, and knowing he was never going to have her. The certainty of that turned his heart to stone.

There he'd been, starting to think he'd finally found the woman he could make a life with. He'd even been thinking fate must have brought them together. But if it had, fate played dirty.

Because until Caitlin was really over Mike, she wouldn't be ready to love again. And long before that time came, Luke would be back in Florida.

LUKE SIMPLY HELD Caitlin for a long time.

"Sorry," she whispered at last, moving out of his embrace. It left his arms feeling horribly empty.

"The last couple of days," she murmured, "have been kind of rough."

"Caitlin, you don't have to apologize. They've been more than *kind of* rough. And I guess you're not really over losing Mike, after all."

She gazed at him with those gorgeous dark eyes, making him wish that his words weren't true.

"That's not what's so upsetting," she finally offered.

"Then what is?"

"It's hard to explain—even after all the sessions I had with my bereavement group. But people there told me there was a whole progression of feelings I'd have to work through. And I did it. I got to the stage of accepting that you can't hold on to the past, that you've got to let it go. The problem at the moment is..."

"Is?"

"Is...one of the feelings I was supposed to work through was guilt, and I didn't."

"Guilt. Why would you have any feelings of guilt?"

She shrugged. "Feelings aren't logical, are they? And as I said, I didn't bother trying to deal with the guilty ones. Instead, I just kept them at bay by clinging to the possibility that Mike didn't really kill himself. But now that I know for sure he did...well, suddenly I started thinking thoughts I should have put to rest long ago. *They're* what got me so upset."

"And these thoughts are what? That stuff you were saying before? About not being a good-enough wife?"

"Kind of," she murmured, nodding slowly. "The minute Rayland told me Mike had taken to drinking, it was like a little voice started asking why I hadn't clued in. It told me I should have realized he was thinking about suicide, that I should have done something to keep it from happening."

Luke hesitated, but finally said, "You realize that isn't a very rational way of thinking, don't you?"

"Yes, I realize it. But that doesn't make the thoughts go away."

"No... no I guess not." He stood gazing at her, trying to understand, trying to come up with something comforting to say. But he didn't know much about what helped unload emotional baggage. "Come on," he finally said, reaching for her hand. "It's getting chilly out here. Let's go in and I'll fix us some coffee. There's something more we've got to talk about."

They wandered inside and he started making the coffee, but after a minute Caitlin said, "Why don't I do that? You just forgot the filter."

"Oh... guess I wasn't concentrating." He moved away and let her take over, his mind churning.

That little news flash of Rayland's, about Lonnie having already hired a new pilot, had added a fresh wrinkle to things. As the sheriff had been quick to point out, it meant Luke Dakota's services would no longer be required in Culpepper.

But he wasn't anywhere near convinced that Mike had killed himself, regardless of what Rayland had Caitlin believing. So he'd have to make a choice— decide whether he should just pack up and leave, or see if she wanted him to stay and keep trying to get to the bottom of what really happened in Mike's office that night.

If there wasn't a chance for him and Caitlin, though, if she wasn't ready to face a new future, he'd only be torturing himself by staying here.

Then he remembered what she'd said—that she *had* accepted his death. And if it truly wasn't so much Mike she couldn't let go of... if what really had her upset was this crazy guilt thing... guilt because she hadn't kept him from killing himself... and if he *hadn't* actually killed himself...

Luke stood rubbing his jaw, letting himself think how incredible it felt just to hold Caitlin. Remembering how heavenly it was to kiss her. Fantasizing about what making love to her would be like.

He wanted her so badly, more than he'd ever imagined wanting a woman. And if he stayed right here and tried to help her put the past completely to rest...

Hell, if there was any chance at all of having a future with her, how could he consider keeping quiet? How could he leave and let her go on thinking she was somehow responsible for Mike's death—especially if someone else actually was?

Just then she turned toward him, gave him a fragile little smile, and he knew he couldn't.

THEY'D BARELY TAKEN their coffee into the living room when the phone rang in the kitchen. Caitlin glanced around, wondering why she didn't hear the cordless, then realized she'd left it out on the deck.

"I'll just be a second," she told Luke. "I'd let the machine take it, but it could be the hospital." She practically ran to the kitchen, praying it wasn't.

When she picked up she breathed a sigh of relief, but her relief was short-lived. It might not be the hospital, but it *was* bad news. At least it was from an entirely selfish point of view.

She didn't say much, just listened.

"So that's great, huh?" Lonnie finally said.

"Yes...yes, of course it's great. I really thought we'd have trouble finding someone."

"Hey, I told you we wouldn't. You should know by now you can trust me."

She could feel her face flush when he said that. All those suspicions she'd had about Lonnie. All those times she'd lain awake at night, wondering if he'd killed Mike. And, all along, her suspicions had been unfounded and Lonnie had been perfectly innocent.

"So you'll tell Dakota?" he was saying.

"Sure."

"And remind him there's no mission tomorrow, huh? I'm booked pretty solid with lessons. Hey, you don't think he'd get a kick out of taking a couple of them for me, do you?"

"No, I don't really think he would. He *is* on leave, remember?"

"Yeah, yeah, I guess you're right. Well, bye, Caitlin."

"Bye, Lonnie."

Slowly, she put down the receiver, then wandered across to the kitchen doorway and just stood looking through the house to where Luke was sitting on the living room couch. She didn't want to tell him, didn't want to think about what this meant.

Had she actually been wishing, only an hour or so ago, that he'd just leave her alone? And now...now he'd be doing exactly that.

She swallowed hard, ruefully thinking how well that illustrated the old saying—the one about being careful what you wished for, because you just might get it. Luke's leaving her alone was the last thing in the world she wanted.

She felt like staying right where she was, gazing at him all night, but she made herself walk back to the living room.

Luke glanced over when he heard her coming. "Was it the hospital? Is everything all right?"

"No, it wasn't the hospital. So, yes, everything's all right." It wasn't, though. Everything was far from all right.

"It was Lonnie," she said, sitting down beside Luke. "That pilot he interviewed this afternoon?"

Luke nodded.

"He's got the right experience, and Lonnie thinks he'll work out fine. And he can start in a couple of days."

"Yeah, Rayland kind of told me that before he left. He'd been talking to Lonnie earlier."

She tried to make a joke, by telling Luke he was going to have to stop forgetting to mention things to her. But her sense of humor had deserted her and the words stuck in her throat. So she simply sat watching him—detailing his chiseled face, resisting the urge to trace the cleft in his chin with her finger. But it was almost impossible to keep from losing herself in the deep gray-blue of his eyes.

"A couple of days," he said at last. "Rayland didn't mention it would be so soon. I guess maybe he didn't know. So... you won't be needing me around here after that."

She forced her eyes from his, afraid that if she didn't he'd see how very much she *did* need him. And she wasn't sure if she wanted him to or not.

Should she seize the moment? Or should she deny herself what she wanted, because she knew how soon Luke would be gone?

"Unless . . ." he said.

Looking at him again, she could see that he didn't want to go any more than she wanted him to. It started her pulse racing.

She knew this thing that had happened between them was a mistake, because it couldn't possibly have a happy ending. But mistake or not, she was suddenly sure she didn't want to deny herself what she wanted for even one more minute.

"Unless?" she finally murmured.

"Caitlin...the way Mike died. Regardless of what Rayland says, I'm just not sure we've got the truth. Not all of it, at any rate."

Slowly, she shook her head, not understanding what he was getting at. Rayland had finally put that missing piece of the puzzle into place. And hadn't that given them the entire picture?

"Actually," Luke went on, "it isn't just that I'm not sure we've got the truth."

"What is it, then?" she made herself say.

"Well, after today I'm almost convinced Mike *didn't* kill himself. At least, I'm convinced that whatever happened . . . well, I just don't think it happened the way Rayland's report lays it out."

She was beginning to feel as if someone had put her on an emotional roller coaster and wouldn't let her off. After all the time she'd refused to believe Mike had committed suicide, tonight she'd finally accepted it. And now Luke was telling her she shouldn't have?

"There's something else," he said. "Something else I was holding off telling you until we got home. I had a talk with Trout—before I went to Rayland's office. And when I asked him what *he* thought about Mike's death, he got so damn nervous that I'm certain there's got to be more to the story than you ever heard. And more than what's in Rayland's report."

"But if Mike had started drinking..."

"Caitlin, you said earlier that you hadn't clued in to that. But doesn't it seem awfully strange that you didn't know?"

"I...I haven't had time to think about it...but no, I don't really think it does. I guess it simply never occurred to me. But it *does* make sense. Those last months he'd been staying late at the hangar fairly often. Working, he told me."

"So maybe that's exactly what he was doing."

"But Rayland said..." She paused, close to tears again. What Rayland said had hurt so much that his words wouldn't leave her mind.

"What?" Luke murmured. "What did he say?"

"That Mike...the way he put it was that Mike had been hitting the sauce at night, instead of coming home to me. As if...as if it was somehow my fault he was there that night. My fault that..."

Luke reached for her and pulled her close.

"Lord," she whispered against his chest, "you asked me before why I'd be feeling guilty. Well it's partly people saying things like that. All it takes is a little help from your friends."

"Rayland," Luke murmured, shifting so he could see her face, "is not your friend. Rayland's an insensitive bastard. But are you okay?"

She nodded, keeping the tears at bay.

"Good, then let's just think about this. Because as soon as Trout mentioned Mike's drinking, I started wondering how you could possibly *not* know."

"But I didn't, I really didn't."

"I know. And that makes me wonder how much we've got here is true, and how much isn't true. If Mike was sitting around nights drinking bourbon, I can't believe you wouldn't have smelled it when he got home. Or realized he wasn't exactly sober. And how the hell was he flying missions first thing in the mornings if he was getting half tanked at night? As well as being sick at the time?"

"Then...you think Rayland was lying? That Trout was lying?"

"What I think is that it would have been just about impossible for Mike to have started drinking without your suspecting. And as I said, Trout got damn nervous when I started asking him questions. And there's another funny thing."

"What?"

"You know the girl who works at the snack bar in the terminal?"

"Conchita? Yes, but really just to say hello to. I never eat there."

"Well, she started to tell me something today. Something about Mike. Then Lonnie came along and she stopped midsentence. And I started thinking... Lonnie's the one you've always suspected. So what the hell does Conchita know about Mike that she didn't want to say in front of Lonnie?"

Caitlin leaned back against the couch and closed her eyes. She wasn't sure how much more of this emotional roller coaster ride she could take. But for months, she'd agonized over not being sure of the truth. And if Luke thought they still didn't have it, she was just going to have to hang on for a little longer.

"So I'll talk to Conchita again tomorrow," he said, "and find out what she wanted to tell me."

"No, you won't be at the airport tomorrow. There's no mission booked."

"So what? Once we get the Chief home from the hospital, you'll be so busy with him that I'll bet you won't have time to make me any lunch."

"You could do the making," she said, then realized he was teasing.

He smiled. "So," he went on, "I'll probably just decide to drop by the snack bar to eat . . . and just casually talk to Conchita. Okay?"

"Okay," she murmured.

"Good, then we know where we're going next with this."

Luke simply sat looking at her after he finished speaking. Then he reached out and touched his hand to her cheek. His eyes didn't leave hers for a second, and his gaze kindled a tiny flame of desire deep inside her.

She reminded herself that he'd be leaving soon, but his hand felt so gentle on her face that she didn't want to remember. "Luke?" she murmured.

"Uh-huh?"

"If we keep digging . . . and we still haven't gotten to the bottom of things by the time the new pilot starts?"

"Uh-huh?"

"What happens then?"

He gave her a lazy, sexy shrug. It sent that flame spreading down to her belly.

"What would *you* want to happen then?" he asked.

She gazed at him for another moment, desire melting her from the inside out.

Luke slowly trailed his fingers down her cheek ... down her throat ... down her bare arm. He let his hand come to rest on hers, then began to draw little circles on it with his thumb.

The flames began to leap and crackle. But how could a simple touch be so erotic? And how could it make her crave his touch everywhere? How could it make her liquid with desire?

She lifted her other hand to his face and rested the back of her thumb in the cleft of his chin, brushed her fingers slowly across his lips. He kissed them and she could almost hear his breath quicken.

"What I'd want to happen, even if the new pilot has started," she finally murmured, having to remind herself what his question had been, "is I'd want you to stay here longer."

"Good," he whispered, leaning closer and framing her face in his hands.

CHAPTER TWELVE

LUKE DRAPED HIS ARMS over Caitlin's shoulders, edged closer and captured her lips with his. His kiss began as slowly and gently as his fingers had trailed their way down her arm.

Then he teased her lips apart, and his tongue began playing with hers. The kiss grew devastatingly arousing.

This was no kiss shared in a hospital lounge full of people. This was a kiss shared in the solitude of her living room, with only the two of them in her little corner of the world. *Their* little corner of the world.

And as heavenly as that first kiss had been, this was even better. It was raw and sexy and hot enough to set the couch on fire—as if Luke were branding her his own and telling her exactly where it would lead them.

For an instant she thought of Mike and felt a rush of guilt. But like her other guilty feelings, she knew this one was irrational. And hadn't she finally put this particular one to rest? By realizing that Mike would have wanted her to be happy.

Rayland had upset her earlier, but the truth was that she *had* been a good wife to Mike. She'd loved him, and she'd mourned him. But he'd been gone a long time and she'd come to love Luke. And how could loving a man like Luke be wrong?

He shifted so his body was even more closely pressed to hers, and a tiny sound rose in the back of her throat—a tiny sigh of contentment. It felt so right to be with him like this. He was arousing feelings that had lain dormant for so long, arousing them with the strength of his body against hers, the sea-breeze scent of his after-shave mingled with the underlying essence of his masculinity.

She ran her fingers through his hair, kissing him deeply, feeling as if some sensual animal had been unleashed inside her. Some primitive jungle cat that had been caged for eternity and was suddenly on the loose. On the prowl. Looking for love. Finding it.

There was a fierce hunger in Luke's kiss that she wanted to feed, a need in him she felt a primordial urge to satisfy.

When he slid his hands down her body, firmly molding them to her breasts, she moaned. When his thumbs found her nipples and began stroking them, heat seared her insides and a heavy pulsing started deep within her.

She wanted this man. Regardless of anything else in the world, she wanted to make love with Luke Dakota. She began nibbling gently on his lower lip and moving her hands slowly down his chest.

Luke was suddenly having trouble breathing. Caitlin's kisses were enough to drive him to the brink of insanity, and what she was doing with her hands was enough to push him over.

Slowly...ever so slowly...those clever hands slipped south until she'd reached his belt. When she finally touched him, he groaned at the exquisite agony of it.

"My God, Caitlin," he whispered, his breath ragged against her mouth. "Do you know what you're doing to me?"

She moved away an inch, still caressing him through his jeans, and smiled a little. "I've got a pretty good idea."

He just looked at her for a moment, giving himself time to think with his brain instead of another part of his anatomy. She was so damn gorgeous that he'd wanted her almost from the start.

She *was* Mike's widow but she was also the woman he loved. And which of those two facts was more important?

There was no question at all about the answer. What was important in life was the here and now, not what had once been.

"Caitlin?" he murmured.

She simply continued to gaze at him, looking incredibly beautiful, with her lips red from kissing him and her skin flushed with desire.

"Caitlin, are you sure about this?"

She still didn't say a word, just leaned closer and kissed him again—a hard, sensual kiss that left him breathless. "I was just thinking," she whispered.

"I'm amazed," he whispered back. "Because you've got me beyond thinking."

He could feel her smiling against his mouth. And he loved the feel of her smile as much as the sight of it.

"Don't you want to know *what* I was thinking?"

"Sure," he managed to say.

"I was thinking there's a bedroom just down the hall."

"Actually...several."

"But we only need one."

"Mine's closest," he said, taking her hands and pulling her up off the couch. He gave her another lingering kiss, then picked her up in his arms and started for the bedroom.

Caitlin laughed with surprise. Luke was making her feel like a heroine in an old movie. "You don't really have to carry me," she told him.

But his lips got in the the way of further protests, so she just clung to him and kissed him back . . . and grew more and more aroused in his arms. By the time Luke put her down on the bed her heart was pounding with excitement.

The drapes were open to the night; the bedroom was dappled with moon shadows that turned his dark hair silver. Then he covered her body with his, making the the moonlight disappear. Or perhaps she'd become oblivious to everything except the way he was greedily kissing her, his tongue hungry in her mouth.

He tangled his hands in her hair and pinned her head to the pillow—as if he thought she might try to escape. She assured him with her kisses that there wasn't a chance she would.

Then he rolled onto his side, pulling her with him, and his hands began roaming over her, leaving a trail of heat in their wake. His touch warmed her skin through her clothes. It warmed the blood beneath her skin and sent such an intense surge of need through her that she moaned.

"Oh, Luke," she whispered, tugging at the bottom of his T-shirt and pushing it up, smoothing her palms across the warmth of his back.

He left her for a moment and stood with his back to her, taking off his clothes. She watched him undress in the moonlight—this man she'd come to love.

She'd seen him in the pool, already knew what a lean, muscled body he had. But when he turned toward her—his sex large and erect—it took her breath away. And made her liquid with wanting him.

Sitting down on the bed beside her, he pushed her T-shirt up over her breasts. With his mouth following his hands, he kissed her eager nipples through the lace that covered them while he finished tugging her shirt all the way off.

He quickly removed her bra, and his mouth was back on her breasts, hot and wet against her nakedness. He kissed and suckled, making her nipples hard with longing and intensifying the aching throb deep within her.

As if he could feel her need, he slid one hand down between her legs and began rubbing it back and forth. She whimpered and arched against him. His hand was moving with such slow, torturing progress that she almost wanted him to stop. But she'd die if he did.

She reached down and unsnapped her jeans, desperate to be rid of them. Luke unzipped them, then helped her wriggle out of them and her panties.

"Oh, Luke," she whispered. "I can't believe this."

He smiled at her in the moonlight. "Can't believe it good? Or can't believe it bad?"

"Can't believe it incredible."

He moved over her again, kissing her eyes, her ears, her throat, her mouth. And all the time, his hands were working magic on her breasts and his hardness was pressed to her lower body, grinding against her, teasing her with its presence and making her squirm with need.

She reached for him, encircling his hard length with her fingers. "Luke, I can't wait," she murmured, her voice breathless.

He slid his hand back down once more, but this time there was no denim in the way. This time there was nothing but his hand caressing her hot, wet desire, making her moan, finally making her shudder with ecstasy—again and again, until she was gasping for breath, until that sensual jungle cat Luke had unleashed inside her was making throaty, erotic sounds.

When he finally lifted her hips and entered her, she felt as if he was filling a terrible emptiness in her. And when he came, collapsing against her and whispering her name, she smiled into the hollow of his neck, certain she'd filled whatever emptiness there'd been in him.

THE FIRST MORNING LIGHT found Caitlin still in Luke's arms.

They'd made love off and on all night. Marvelous, passionate love. It had left her satiated and languorous and so ecstatically happy that she kept drowsing in and out of sleep with a smile on her face.

She reached up and lazily stroked his jaw, not able to stop herself from touching his face. The entire lengths of their naked bodies were intertwined, which should have been enough to satisfy her. It wasn't, though. Luke's face was irresistible in the morning. Dark with stubble, and oh so beautiful.

He mumbled something incoherent, caught her hand in his and began kissing her fingers . . . slowly, each one in turn. Then he tucked her hand to his chest and nuzzled his rough face against her throat.

His warm breath fanning her skin made her smile again. Luke was such a special man, and he'd taken such a special place in her heart. If only. . .

She tried to force the next thoughts away but they refused to leave. In her imagination, she could actually hear them arguing about their right to have their say.

"We're thoughts of the future," they taunted. "And you can't do anything to keep the future at bay. No matter what, it's coming."

She hated those thoughts. The future was going to get here soon enough, without her dwelling on it now. And she was so happy that she wanted the present to stay forever.

No, that wasn't precisely it. It was Luke she wanted to stay forever. To stay with her and never leave.

But what you wanted wasn't always what you got. She knew that every bit as well as she knew what it was like to love and lose. . . and every bit as well as she knew she was going to lose what she loved again.

What she loved. There was no use trying to deny what she was feeling any longer. Ready or not, frightened of the idea as she'd been, she'd fallen in love with Luke. But she was going to lose him. Not in the same way she'd lost Mike, but she'd lose him just the same.

She'd tried her hardest not to think about that last night. She'd decided she wanted to make love with him and damn the consequences.

Now, though, now that thoughts of those consequences were scurrying around inside her head, she wasn't at all sure she'd done the right thing.

She snuggled even closer to Luke's solid warmth, telling herself this felt so good it *had* to be right. But she'd once read somewhere that the risk of loving was losing. And the price of loss was pain.

Yet she'd gone ahead and walked right into what hadn't even been a risk situation. It had been a sure thing. A sure thing for which she was going to end up paying the price. So what had happened to all her good intentions?

Her eyes suddenly filled with tears, and she couldn't keep them from escaping—no more than she'd been able to drive those hateful thoughts out of her head.

She lay as still as she could, just letting the tears trickle down her cheeks. She didn't want Luke to know, didn't want him to think—

"Caitlin?" he murmured. "Caitlin, what's wrong?"

He brushed her cheek with his hand, and she realized some of her tears had trickled right off her face and onto him.

"Oh, God," he said, propping himself up on one elbow. "It's Mike, isn't it? You're—"

"No." She wiped her eyes and shook her head fiercely. "It has nothing to do with Mike. It only has to do with you."

"But I thought..." He tucked his fingers under her chin and gave her one of his easy smiles. "Hell, if I was *that* bad, you sure put on a terrific act last night."

She tried to smile back at him, but it was awfully difficult.

"So what's the problem?"

"I just . . . you're going to leave, Luke. I want this to last, but it can't. You're going to leave any day now."

"Uh-uh," he whispered, snuggling back down on his pillow and pulling her close again. "We decided last night that I was going to stay on. Even after the new pilot started. Don't you remember?"

"Yes. But I also remember you have to be back in Florida by the end of July. And that's . . . that's practically any day now. It's no time, Luke. No time at all."

He was quiet for a minute. "You said you want this to last," he finally murmured.

She silently nodded her head against his chest. There was nothing more to say. She'd said she wanted him to stay, but she knew he couldn't.

"Okay," he said, so slowly that it sounded as if he'd just made a major decision. "You want it to last and so do I."

For a moment she simply let his words echo inside her head. He wanted the same thing she did, which should make her ecstatically happy. But she was almost afraid to hope they could actually have what they wanted.

"You do?" She finally murmured, sitting up in the bed a little so she could see his face better. "You really do want it to last?"

"Caitlin, I love you. Haven't you figured that out?"

She bit her bottom lip, not sure if she felt more like laughing with joy because he loved her or crying because their love seemed impossible.

"So . . ." He lay gazing at her.

"So?"

"So aren't you going to tell me? You *do* love me, don't you? You don't just like having me around because I'm handy around the house and good in bed, do you?"

That tipped the scale and she laughed out loud. "Luke, you're great around the house and you're *fantastic* in bed. Of course I love you. Love you, love you, love you," she added, nibbling her way up to his mouth and giving him a four-alarm kiss.

"Mmm," he said when she finally stopped. "If I wasn't already so sore, I'd follow up on that. But... God, I can't think straight this close to you, Caitlin. But we still have some time to figure things out. And even after I leave, Florida isn't a million miles away."

"No," she whispered. "Only two thousand plus." But she was terribly afraid it might as well be a million. Because once Luke was gone... well, no matter what he said about wanting this to last, she really didn't see how it could.

LUKE LEANED AGAINST the doorframe of the Chief's room and looked over to where Caitlin was still standing by the crib. They'd gotten back from the hospital over an hour ago, the baby looked great, but she still hadn't been able to tear herself away from him.

"See?" he said after he'd silently watched them for a minute.

"Da-da!" the baby cried, peering through the bars at him.

That went straight to his heart, even though he knew the little guy called a lot of people Da-da. Now that he'd finally let himself admit he was in love with

Caitlin, he didn't want to just leave it at that. He wanted the three of them to be a family.

But he couldn't see a family working via long distance, and the navy sure as hell wasn't going to move the Pensacola Naval Air Station to Arizona. So the only solution was for Caitlin and the Chief to move to Florida.

The problem with that, though, was she'd said there was no way she could leave Culpepper. Not when everything she had was tied up in the ranch and Sky Knights. He'd have to find a way around that little obstacle.

"See what?" Caitlin asked, finally looking over.

It took a second before he recalled what he'd been going to say. "Didn't I tell you that once we got the Chief home you wouldn't even have time to make me lunch?"

"Oh, no." She shot him a smile. "You aren't one of those people who loves to say I told you so, are you?"

Her smile made him want her, so he decided he'd better get going before the urge to do something about it overwhelmed him. He had other fish to fry, and Caitlin needed some time to assure herself the Chief really was all right.

"I'm heading for the airport now," he told her. "But I'll probably just clear up the mystery of what Conchita wanted to tell me and come straight back. Shouldn't take long."

When Caitlin nodded he started down the hall. He didn't intend to be gone a minute longer than necessary. He didn't intend to spend any time away from her that he didn't absolutely have to. Because the time he had here was already going by too damn fast.

If he drove home hard, avoiding the detours that had added miles on the way here, he figured he could get back to Pensacola in three days. So he could stay with Caitlin through the twenty-eighth and still make it back for August first. But he *had* to leave first thing on the twenty-ninth. And it was already July 12.

He stepped from the house into the oven outside and strode over to the Mustang. He had only sixteen days after today to do what he had to do. So he'd just have to get down to serious business.

He climbed into the car, started the engine and switched the air conditioner on full blast. The vents began pumping out scorching air, but there was no point in rolling down the windows. It wouldn't do a damn bit of good.

He wheeled down the drive and onto the road, telling himself not to dwell on how little time he had. Instead, he concentrated on coming up with a solution to the problem, and he'd be damned if something hadn't come to him by the time he reached the main highway.

He'd been so focused on the prospect of having to go back to Florida while Caitlin stayed here that he hadn't been thinking of much else. But hell, he'd been forgetting all about Mike's insurance policy. And now that he remembered it, the big picture started coming together.

Halfway to the airport, he was still wondering how he could have forgotten about that policy. But with everything else that had been happening, all thoughts of it had been shuffled to the bottom of the deck.

And Caitlin obviously hadn't been thinking about it, either, or she'd have said something. Because the insurance money was their solution.

If they could prove Mike hadn't really killed himself, she'd still get that money. Then she'd be able to pay off her debts and there'd be nothing to stop her from selling out and moving to Florida.

The only stumbling block was that they had to come up with some proof. And that was assuming, of course, proof existed. But at this point, that seemed like a pretty good assumption.

Mike hadn't been a quitter. Not the kind of guy who'd have run out on Caitlin. And the more people said, the more Luke thought about it, the more convinced he was that her suspicions had been right all along—somebody had murdered Mike.

He drove on, trying to figure out the best way of reminding her about the policy... wishing once more that he were better with words. He knew she was bound to feel funny about using money from Mike's insurance policy to start a life with another man.

But how could that be wrong, when the other man loved her so damn much it hurt?

Flicking his signal for the turn onto Airport Road, he began wondering what would happen if they couldn't find any evidence. Was Caitlin too stubborn to let *him* worry about her debts?

He had a horrible feeling she was. Even though he'd take on the debt of the entire Third World if it meant having her.

When he reached the airport, he parked outside the terminal and went in. There were no customers at the snack bar, which meant Conchita would be able to speak freely. But when he was about halfway there, he realized the girl behind the counter wasn't Conchita. She was a skinny kid who looked about sixteen.

He swore to himself. He'd been hoping that whatever Conchita had wanted to tell him, would give him the clue he needed.

He slid onto one of the stools and nodded to the girl.

"Coffee?" she asked, reaching for the pot.

He nodded. "This Conchita's day off?"

"Uh-uh. She's on vacation."

"Ahh . . . she was here yesterday."

"Well, she's not here today. Like I said, she's gone on vacation. For a week."

A week. Luke's gut clenched. That was seven of his days. "Do you know if she actually *went* anywhere?" he asked. Hopefully, she hadn't. Then he could just find out where she lived and—

"She's gone home. To visit her family."

"Home. You mean, to Mexico?"

The girl looked at him as if he was simpleminded. "Yeah," she said, popping her gum. "Yeah, a lot of Mexicans come from Mexico, you know."

He forced a grin. "So where exactly is home?"

"You a cop or something? She's legal, you know."

"Yeah, I know she is, and I'm not a cop. I'm . . . a friend of a friend."

"Oh? Well, home is a little farm somewhere in Chihuahua."

"Is it very far from here?"

She shrugged. "A day or so's drive, I think."

"And . . . what's her last name?"

The girl's expression turned suspicious. "You're not a friend of a very *good* friend, are you."

"No, but I'm definitely not a cop. Look." He pulled out his wallet and produced his ID from the air station. "I'm in the navy. I train pilots."

The girl stared at his card for a minute, then shrugged. "Her last name's Sanchez. Conchita Sanchez."

"Ahh," he said, trying to decide where to go from here. He wasn't any whiz at geography, but he knew Chihuahua was one of the biggest states in Mexico. So heading down there to try to find somebody named Sanchez would be like heading into the state of Texas to try to find somebody named Smith. Which meant he wasn't going to learn what Conchita had wanted to tell him until she got back.

"So *exactly* when will she be at work again?" he finally asked.

"Like I said, in a week."

"Next Tuesday or Wednesday or . . . ?"

The girl cracked her gum again, then shrugged. "Just a sec and I'll check the schedule for you." She ducked down behind the counter for a minute, then popped back up. "Next Wednesday. The nineteenth. She'll be back then."

"Thanks." Luke slapped down a couple of dollars and left, his coffee untouched.

Coming out of the terminal, he glanced over toward the Sky Knights hangar. Both planes were on the apron, so Lonnie was obviously between lessons.

Luke started across the tarmac, although he didn't have the slightest idea where talking to Lonnie or Trout would get him. Probably nowhere, but he had nothing to lose.

When he walked into the hangar, he stopped dead. What was usually empty space in the far half of the structure now looked like the storage area of a major appliance manufacturer—filled with gigantic cartons and wooden crates.

"Hey, Dakota," Lonnie called from the office. "I was just going to phone you."

Luke wandered across the hangar and into the office. Lonnie was sitting behind the desk, his feet up on it. Trout was straddling a chair across from him.

"What's with all that?" Luke gestured back out into the main area.

"Just doing my old man a favor," Lonnie said. "One of the bank's big customers had a fire in his warehouse, so they trucked that stuff over here this morning. We're going to store it for a few weeks—until the guy gets things back together. But, hey, what are you doing here?"

"Nothing much. I just came out for lunch. The baby's home from the hospital, and Caitlin's busy with him, so I was kind of at loose ends."

"Well, you won't be for much longer. I had a call from the pilot I hired—Joe Onsager's his name. And he got done with the stuff he was wrapping up faster than he expected. He can start tomorrow, so you won't have to stick around Culpepper any longer. But listen, thanks a lot for helping out. We'd really have been in a jam if you hadn't come along."

"No problem. I enjoyed it."

Lonnie grinned. "Well, I reckon you'll enjoy getting on your way a lot more. Caitlin mentioned you had some buddies in San Diego you wanted to see."

"Yeah . . . well." Luke hesitated, but the news that he wasn't leaving yet would hit the grapevine in no time, so he might as well see how Lonnie and Trout reacted to it.

"Actually," he said, "I've decided to stay here for the rest of my leave. Caitlin could use a hand with some things around her place."

"Hey," Lonnie said slowly. He glanced across his desk at Trout, then focused on Luke once more. "That'll be real nice for her, then, won't it. Having someone to help her out for a while."

CHAPTER THIRTEEN

EVEN THOUGH IT WAS STILL early when the Chief finally dropped off to sleep, Caitlin began getting things organized for dinner. Fortunately, there was steak in the freezer and wine in the fridge. She wanted to make something special for Luke. Lord, she wanted to make everything special for Luke.

She smiled, just thinking about him. She seemed to smile every time she thought about him. And she seemed to be thinking about him twenty times a minute. She still couldn't quite believe he loved her... or that he was staying until the end of the month. Well, until almost the end. And after that...

She concentrated on the potato she was scrubbing and tried to reassure herself they'd work something out. Eventually, they just *had* to end up together. She loved him too much to lose him. The problem was, she was afraid that eventually might be a long time away. And sometimes, eventually turned into forever.

Before she had time to dwell on the uncertainty of the situation, the phone rang. When she picked up, Lonnie was on the line, and she only needed to hear his hello to know he was angry about something.

"What's the deal with Dakota staying on here?" he demanded.

Apparently, Conchita wasn't the only one Luke had talked to at the airport. "What do you mean . . . the deal?"

"I mean *why's* he staying?"

Caitlin resisted the urge to ask Lonnie why he thought it was any of his business. But his temper was bad enough without her deliberately antagonizing him. "He's staying because I invited him to."

"And why'd you do that?"

The urge grew irresistible. "Lonnie, did somebody put you in charge of my life and forget to tell me about it?"

"Very funny," he snapped. "I just don't like the idea of his staying on."

"Oh? Any why not?"

"Hell, Caitlin, it just doesn't look good—you and him out there alone in that house."

She almost laughed. Lonnie sounded like her grandmother. But her grandmother cared about her reputation, and she knew Lonnie didn't give a damn, so what was he up to?

"Lonnie, I'm a grown woman, and if I'm not worried about what it looks like, I don't think you should be, either. So . . . do you have any *other* problem with Luke's staying?"

There was a silence at the other end of the line, then Lonnie said, "Yeah. Yeah, as a matter of fact, I do. Trout and I were just talking about it, and we don't like the way he's been asking questions about how Mike died."

Caitlin's brain went on full alert.

"And Rayland doesn't like it, either."

"Oh?"

"No. If Dakota keeps going around trying to stir up trouble, what are people going to think?"

"I don't know, Lonnie. What *are* they going to think?"

"Dammit, Caitlin, you know what I'm saying. Dakota's as much as telling people he doesn't believe that things happened the way we said they did. And, hell, we understood when you didn't want to accept the truth at first. But for some guy to come along after all this time and start sticking his nose where it doesn't belong . . ."

"Lonnie, I don't want to talk about this anymore, okay? Luke is staying on as my guest. And he's more than welcome, because he did us a big favor by flying those missions with you. He did *both* of us a big favor. I think you should keep that in mind."

"Dammit, Caitlin, you're weren't listening to what I said."

"I *was* listening. I just don't agree. And I've got to go now. Bye." She hung up, her hands shaking just a little. Why did Lonnie want Luke to leave so badly? Was it because some of his questions had hit too close to home?

She didn't have long to speculate before Luke arrived back. She listened to a brief account of his trip to the airport, then filled him in on Lonnie's call. After that, she stood watching him pace across the kitchen, wishing she could read his mind.

"What do you think?" she finally asked.

"I think it seems damn suspicious. Why would he be so concerned about my asking questions if he wasn't hiding something?"

Caitlin sank into a chair, her knees suddenly weak. All the times she'd wondered about Lonnie, the times she'd thought that maybe he'd had something to do with Mike's death. And now Luke was saying he thought she might be right.

"We need proof," he was muttering. He paced past her again. "At the very least, we need some sort of evidence—something that would force Rayland to reopen the case."

"How do we get it?"

Luke shook his head. "I was hoping to hell Conchita would tell me something that would help. But until she's back . . . I guess our best bet is to try talking to other people at the airport. Maybe somebody who was around there that night. Somebody who can give us a lead."

"A lead. Such as . . . ?"

"Hell, I wish I knew. But all we can do is ask around and see what we come up with."

"Lonnie will know what we're doing, Luke. I can think of a hundred different excuses to drop by the hangar. Some of our records are there, and I need them now and then. But Lonnie will know why we're *really* out there."

"Well, I don't see any way around it, so it's probably not worth while even trying to hide what we're up to. I mean, if you're still sure you want to pursue it . . ."

She nodded. "I am."

Luke stopped pacing and leaned against the counter, looking over at her. "You know, you once told me you wanted to know the truth for a whole lot of reasons. But you never really told me what they were."

"Well . . . mainly because I feel I owe it to Mike. I think I *did* mention that one."

"And the others?"

"Because of the baby. Maybe there shouldn't be a stigma about suicide, but there is. And if Mike *didn't* kill himself, I don't want the Chief growing up thinking he did. It just...well, according to my group, it can cause a lot of problems for children.

"And then...well, it's partly for me, too. Even though I try not to feel guilty, if I was certain it really wasn't suicide I'd feel as if a weight had been taken off my shoulders. I'd know for sure that it wasn't somehow my fault."

Luke nodded. "You've didn't mention the insurance—the money you'd get if it wasn't suicide. You'd forgotten all about Mike's policy, hadn't you."

"I...yes, I guess I haven't thought about it for a while. But Luke, I told you way back, I never really cared about the money. And I thought you believed me."

"I did." He wandered over and sat down across the table from her. "But I got to thinking that if we get our evidence, you'll get the money."

"Yes, I guess I would."

"Enough to let you get out of debt. Enough to let you do whatever you want with this place and with your share of Sky Knights."

"I..." She suddenly realized what he was getting at and the funniest feeling settled in the pit of her stomach. She wasn't sure if it was uncertainty or guilt. "I...oh, Luke, why am I thinking that would be like using *blood money* to—"

He reached across and silenced her lips with his fingers. "Listen to me, Caitlin. Before you start thinking there's something crass about what I'm saying, think about everything you just told me. You didn't start off wanting to know the truth because of the money. But that doesn't make the money bad. You should get it if you're entitled to it.''

"I know, but—"

"No, keep listening. You once told me that after Mike got sick, he used to talk about how glad he was he'd taken out that insurance policy—that he wanted to provide for you. He wanted you to be okay if he died. I'm right, aren't I?''

She merely nodded, her throat too tight to speak.

"And he'd have wanted you to be happy, right?''

She nodded again. She'd been telling herself that only yesterday.

"Caitlin, I'll make you happy. I swear, I'll make you and the Chief as happy as two people can be. And if that money gives you the means to leave here and be with me, I think Mike's going to be up there cheering.''

"Oh, Luke,'' she whispered, tears spilling down her cheeks. "Oh, Luke, sometimes this is so hard.''

A moment later he was pulling her to her feet and wrapping his arms around her.

"I know,'' he murmured. "I know. For a while there I was having trouble, too. Mike was my friend. And you'd been his wife. But hell, if he had any say in things, don't you think he'd want you to end up with someone he knew and liked?''

Luke kissed the top of her head and brushed away her tears. "Caitlin, we decided days ago that we were going to try to discover the truth. So let's just do it. And as for the rest...well, let's just assume Mike would have wanted us to be together and try not to worry about all this stuff my sister would call emotional baggage. Okay?''

When she nodded, Luke smiled at her. And then he kissed her. A tender, loving kiss that said he'd make her the happiest woman in the world. If only she'd let him.

CAITLIN FINISHED READING the report and looked across the desk at the medical examiner. Dr. Brownly was in his late fifties, with the florid complexion and large nose of a dedicated drinker. And at the moment, he was watching her through extremely blood-shot eyes.

She glanced at Luke. He'd looked through the report first, so he'd seen both it and Rayland's, whereas she'd never read Rayland's.

"It says pretty well the same things as the sheriff's report does," Luke told her.

"Well, that's how it's supposed to be," Dr. Brownly muttered. "It was the same incident."

"So..." Luke said to him, "when Rayland called you out to the hangar that night, it must have been pretty late."

"Uh-huh. So if there's anything that seems vague in what you read, that's why. Takes me a while to wake up late at night."

Caitlin mentally substituted *sober up* for wake up. "Well, thank you for fitting us into your busy schedule," she told him—using the same phrase he'd used to put them off for the past three days. "I guess there's nothing else we wanted to ask you."

When she stood to go, Brownly looked decidedly relieved. "Any time, Caitlin," he said. "Any other questions you have, you just let me know."

Luke took her hand as they left, but even his touch wasn't enough to make her feel any better. This visit had turned out to be an exercise in futility—just like everything else they'd been doing lately.

As they started down the block to where the Mustang was parked, she glanced up. Above, black thunderclouds were rapidly rolling in over the clear morning sky. Monsoon season had arrived right on schedule. And right on schedule meant they'd reached mid-July. July 15—to be precise.

She glanced at Luke, wondering if he was as discouraged as she was. It seemed as if all they'd done for the past few days was waste precious time banging their heads against brick walls.

Each morning, her grandparents had come out to look after the Chief for a few hours, while she and Luke played detective at the airport.

And since they'd decided Lonnie would realize what they were up to, they hadn't bothered to pretend they were only dropping by so she could pick up things at Sky Knights.

Oh, they'd made a point of meeting Joe Onsager the first day he'd flown a mission. And they'd check in with Lonnie, the next day, to make sure that their new pilot was doing all right. But aside from that, they'd just talked to people about Mike—ignoring the angry looks they got from Lonnie and the uneasy ones Trout gave them.

By this point, though, they'd talked to almost everyone who ever spent much time at the airport, and they'd gotten absolutely nowhere.

Caitlin told herself not to dwell on their failure. The entire world wasn't as black as those clouds overhead. After all, the most important thing had turned out just fine. The Chief already seemed back to normal. He'd recovered even faster than Dr. Peterson had predicted.

"You were sure right about that report," Luke said, bringing her back to the moment. "Way back, you told me it would probably be a copy of Rayland's, with a few medical terms added in."

She nodded. "I'm almost surprised they didn't just write up one report between the two of them and photocopy it."

They'd reached the Mustang, and Luke squeezed her hand before letting go of it. "You're getting cynical, Caitlin."

Is *that* what she was getting? She climbed into the car, wondering if that was really it. Maybe *desperate* would be a better word.

Impossible as it seemed, with every day that passed she fell more deeply in love with Luke. Lord, with every *hour* that passed she seemed to love him more. She loved having him in the house with her, loved sharing meals and talking into the night with him.

And the Chief was crazy about him, too. His little face lit up whenever Luke walked into the room. But she just couldn't ignore the fact that the end of July was quickly closing in on them.

Luke got into the driver's seat and glanced at her. "Want to get some lunch before we head back to the ranch? Somebody told me the chili at the Culpepper Café is pretty good."

"No, we'd better try to get home before the storm hits. There's a low spot on the side road that washes out every couple of years. And we don't want to end up with my grandparents stuck at the ranch for the night."

"No. That's the last thing we want," Luke said, his expression telling her he knew precisely what she meant.

It had taken her grandparents almost no time at all to conclude that Luke was the greatest thing since sliced bread. But that didn't mean they'd take kindly to her sleeping with him right under their noses. Or right down the hall, as the case might be.

Luke started the engine and she closed her eyes, thinking how few nights they had left before he had to leave...and about how painfully empty her arms would feel, how incredibly lonely her bed would be, after July 28.

CAITLIN GLANCED across the kitchen to where the Chief was playing on the floor. Since they'd brought him home from the hospital she seemed to be forever checking that he was all right. But he hadn't had any setbacks, and he'd been home an entire week now...the entire week that Conchita Sanchez had been off visiting her family.

The baby caught his mother looking at him, waved his fists toward the window and yelled, "Cah!"

Caitlin shook her head. "No, we can't go out in the van. We have to wait for Luke to get back from the airport." And she was waiting on tenterhooks, because this was the day Conchita was due back at work. The day Luke would finally find out what she'd wanted to tell him about Mike.

Sky Knights' records for the past month were spread out over the table, and Caitlin turned her attention back to them. But she'd barely started working again when Sam growled, the Chief yelled, "Oh-oh," and she heard a car coming up the drive. When she looked out, she saw it was actually a truck—Lonnie's pickup.

That sent an anxious shiver through her. Maybe she and Luke hadn't managed to turn up any real evidence yet, but Lonnie was still number one on their suspect list. In fact, he was still the *only* one on their list.

She firmly told herself there was no reason to be nervous. Lonnie hadn't come out here to do her any harm. He'd just come because...well, she didn't know the reason, but she soon would. She waved at him through the window, so he'd know to come around the back, then headed over to slide the door open.

Sam ambled after her, ready to take off into the wild blue yonder, but she grabbed him firmly by the collar and thwarted his plan. Her partner stomped across the deck, an angry expression on his face.

"Where's Dakota?" Lonnie demanded.

"Da-da!" the Chief cried.

Lonnie ignored him.

"He's...he went to the airport for something."

"Well there's a surprise," Lonnie snapped. "Is there a day he *isn't* at the airport?"

"Zam!" the baby said.

Caitlin shooed Sam over to him, then looked back at Lonnie.

"I heard something last night," he told her. "Something you have to know about. Luke Dakota isn't who you think he is."

"Oh?" At least she could stop wondering what Lonnie was doing here. He was obviously taking another shot at getting Luke out of the picture. "And exactly what does that mean?" she asked evenly. "If he isn't who I think he is, just who *is* he?"

"Well, I know you're going to have trouble believing this, but he's a damn spy."

"He's a what?"

"He's a spy. He didn't come all the way to Arizona to see you and the baby. And he's not on leave. That was all a cover. He's really here because he's on assignment for naval intelligence. They pulled him off flight instruction to come and do some snooping for the Department of Defense."

Lord, that was one of the most ridiculous things she'd heard in her entire life. "Lonnie, why have the words *paranoid fantasy* popped into my mind?"

"I told you you'd have trouble believing it, but it's the truth. I heard it from an impeccable source."

"*What* impeccable source?"

"I can't say."

"Oh, right. The old *anonymous* impeccable source."

Lonnie glared at her. "Look, this is no joke. I got it from somebody who has a pipeline into military intelligence. And the only reason Dakota's here is because you and I filed that compensation claim."

When she took a minute to try to sort out exactly what Lonnie was saying, he snapped, "Our *claim*. You *do* remember it, don't you? Our landmark case? Our claim against the Veterans Admin and the Defense Department? Our compensation for business losses, because the syndrome made Mike so depressed he killed himself?"

"Yes, yes, of course I remember. But this is all crazy. Mike and Luke were friends. That's why—"

"That's why they asked *him* to take the assignment. You'd hardly have let a stranger come waltzing in here, would you?"

"No, but—"

"Caitlin, just let me lay it all out for you, okay? And wipe that skeptical look off your face, because I called the lawyer first thing this morning and *he* had no problem believing it. In fact, he said it didn't surprise him a bit."

Suddenly, she felt a little less certain this was all just something Lonnie had dreamed up. But that was absurd. Luke would never—

"Here's the deal," Lonnie went on. "According to my source, Mike's far from the only guy who's killed himself because he came down with the syndrome. And if we get compensation for what his death cost our business, the government's going to be inundated with similar claims. Which means that paying us is the last thing they want to do. Are you with me so far?"

"Of course I'm with you. I *do* have a brain."

"All right. So they went through Mike's military records and learned he'd been friends with Dakota. Then they found out all the more recent stuff they needed from wherever—you know how these things work—and they got Dakota out here to snoop around and see what he could come up with."

"What do you mean, come up with?"

"Anything that can get them off the hook. Caitlin, *use* that brain, huh? *This* explains why Dakota's been nosing around, asking questions that—"

"Lonnie, Luke hasn't been *nosing around* on his own. I've been right with him. Don't try to tell me you haven't been aware of that."

"Sure, but you didn't start asking any questions until he showed up, did you? So Dakota must have instigated all this."

"No, he didn't, I—"

"All right, all right, have it your way. But the point is Dakota, and you, suddenly started asking questions that are making people wonder if Mike was *murdered*. And all Dakota needs is a few people to say something to build a case against Mike's having committed suicide."

"Luke is going to build a case? Lonnie, he's a pilot, not a private eye. And he..." She realized Lonnie was glaring at her again.

"Don't play word games with me, Caitlin. Dakota's trying to get information for the military so *they* can build the case. And if they can prove that Mike's death wasn't suicide, then they'll say there's no liability. Our claim will be thrown out and Sky Knights will get nothing in compensation."

Caitlin just stared at Lonnie. What he was saying couldn't possibly be true. Luke would never have deceived her like that.

"Well?" Lonnie said. "It all adds up, doesn't it?"

"Except for one thing. Luke wouldn't be part of something that underhanded."

"No? You'd never met him before he showed up here, had you?"

"Well, no, but—"

"But already, you figure you know him well enough to know he's not a snake in the grass?"

"I...yes, I do. You're wrong, Lonnie. I don't know where your *source* got his information, but it can't be right."

"No? Then tell me this. After I hired Joe, why didn't Dakota take off for San Diego like he said he was going to? Why's he still hanging around here?"

Caitlin could feel her face flushing.

"Well? Why?"

"Because he fell in love with me, Lonnie. And because I fell in love with him."

"Oh, hell, Caitlin, I don't believe it! You're not only harboring an enemy spy, you fell for him, too? Hell, are you *sure* you've got a brain?"

"Dammit, Lonnie, don't you—"

"Oh, just grab your socks and pull, will you? Because that's the oldest trick in the book. Any guy knows if he wants to make a woman believe what he's saying, all he has to do is tell her he loves her.

"So look, partner, we've got to get rid of Dakota. Right now, before he manages to screw Sky Knights out of that money. So you turf him out of the house, and if he still doesn't leave Culpepper, he'd better be sure he keeps the hell away from the airport."

CHAPTER FOURTEEN

LUKE WAS LATER than he'd expected getting back from the airport, and by the time he arrived at the ranch the sunny sky had turned dark and ugly. It reflected his mood perfectly.

He climbed out of the Mustang and strode into the house. Sam greeted him in the front hall, and Caitlin was working at the kitchen table. The baby, he assumed, was having his afternoon nap.

"Well?" Caitlin gazed at him expectantly.

"Conchita wasn't there."

"What?"

"She's staying with her family for a couple of extra days."

"Oh, Lord. Is a couple two? Or more?"

"I'm not sure, but I hope it's not many. The girl at the snack bar didn't know what the story was—she'd just gotten a call that she had to work today. But she said the boss was supposed to be coming by, so I waited around. That's why I took so long."

"And?"

"And Conchita had phoned him and asked for a few more days off because her mother's sick. So I'm just going to have to wait a little longer to talk to her. I left a message, asking her to call here as soon as she's back."

Outside, a streak of lightning slashed across the sky, followed by a mighty crash of thunder. It was followed by a loud wail from the Chief.

Caitlin pushed back her chair and started for his room. Luke trailed after her, then stood waiting while she tried to calm the little guy down. When he kept on wailing, she picked him up and cuddled him.

"People say you're not supposed to do this," she said, patting his back. "They say it only encourages them to cry. But I can't just let him lie there when he's so frightened."

Luke shrugged. "You can't always believe what people say."

"No...no, you can't, can you." She stood looking over the Chief's head at him, and there was something in her gaze that made him uneasy.

"Caitlin? Is anything wrong? Aside from this delay with Conchita?"

"I hope not...but I guess I need you to tell me for sure. Lonnie was here a couple of hours ago."

Luke listened while Caitlin told him about Lonnie's visit, his blood pressure climbing with every word she spoke.

"And that's basically it," she concluded. "Except that Lonnie wants me to turf you out, as he so elegantly phrased it."

"So what did you tell him?" Surely she hadn't believed a word of such an insane story. Yet there was still something in her eyes that made him wonder.

The Chief had stopped crying, and instead of giving Luke his answer right away she tucked the baby back into his crib.

While she was doing that, Luke thought up a dozen different slow and painful tortures he'd like to inflict on Lonnie McDougall.

Finally, Caitlin turned back to him. "What I told Lonnie was that I'd ask you if his story was true."

"Oh, Caitlin, don't be ridiculous. Of course it's not."

She nodded. "That's what Lonnie said you'd say. But he told me it would just be another of your lies."

Luke's blood pressure inched up another few points. He wished he had Lonnie here right now—preferably, with his hands around the guy's throat. "Caitlin... you didn't think for a minute there was anything to Lonnie's story, did you?"

She slowly brushed her hair back from her face. Something about the motion was so sexy that he wanted to wrap his arms around her and kiss her. He didn't move, though. If she could even suspect he'd be part of a scheme like that...

"Luke, I didn't believe what Lonnie said. But he believed it. He was absolutely furious. He was managing to control it, but I could tell he was really angry. And it made me sure he believed what he was saying. So I don't think he could have fabricated it. I think the *impeccable* source he told me about is for real."

"Dammit, Caitlin, how impeccable can a source be when the whole thing's a bunch of lies? And who the hell *is* this damn source?"

"I don't know. I asked a couple of times, but Lonnie wouldn't say."

"But you didn't believe any of it." That was the important thing. As long as Caitlin trusted him, it didn't really matter who said what.

"No, I told you, Luke, I didn't believe it. But...it's just that after Lonnie left, I could hear a nagging little voice pointing out that I didn't want to believe it because I love you. And even though I've been trying to pick holes in the story, everything hangs together. I mean, it sounded so absurd, and yet it all fits. So...just tell me again that it's a lie. I guess I need a little reassurance."

This time, he did move. He stepped closer, took Caitlin in his arms and held her. "It's a lie," he murmured against the softness of her hair. "I wish I could think of some way of proving that to you, but I can't. All I can do is say I love you, and that I'd never do anything to hurt you. I just want to help you get to the bottom of things before I have to leave. And you know what I want after that. Hell, Caitlin, do you think I'd be counting on making this thing between us last if it was built on lies?"

She looked up at him, and the way her lower lip was trembling made her mouth irresistible.

"Trust me, Caitlin," he whispered, and then he kissed her. But his mind was so full of dark thoughts that even her kiss couldn't drive them all away.

If Caitlin was right, if Lonnie really did believe what he'd told her, then who had concocted the story in the first place? Someone else who wanted Luke Dakota out of Culpepper?

Dammit, he was going to have to leave too soon as it was. He was going to have to leave Caitlin behind—at least temporarily—after they'd stirred up all this trouble. Leave her with a partner who had one hell of a temper, a partner who was their prime suspect for a possible murder. Leave her with a damn unidentified *source*, who for some reason didn't want them digging for the truth any more than Lonnie did.

Luke deepened his kiss, trying not to think at all. Because his thoughts were scaring the hell out of him.

THE CHIEF WAS TUCKED IN for the night, Sam was off on his evening prowl, and the house was unusually quiet.

And so, Caitlin absently reflected, were she and Luke. She glanced across the dining room table at him, but he looked as if his thoughts were miles away.

She'd tried to make dinner special, because they'd both been feeling a little down. She'd served wine with the meal and had even changed into a dress beforehand. But when it had come to conversation, there was none. They must have talked themselves out during the afternoon. Even though all they'd really done was talk around in circles.

They still had only one suspect and no evidence. They didn't know when Conchita Sanchez would be back. And to top it all off, Lonnie had tossed his mysterious unidentified source into the pot.

The bottom line was that they had too many unknowns and not a single fact.

"What," she finally asked, "are we going to do if Conchita *never* comes back?"

"She'll come back."

"But what if she doesn't? Do we just accuse Lonnie and see where it gets us?"

Luke shook his head. "I don't think that would be a good strategy."

"But he must know we think he had something to do with it."

"Yeah, I'm sure he does. But if we come right out and accuse him...hell, Caitlin, who knows what he'd do. And if I have to leave before we get our answers...well, I just don't think we should say anything."

"But what, then? Do we just..." Her words trailed off when she heard a car. A second later, headlights flashed across the front windows.

"Now what?" Luke said.

"I don't know. But at least it doesn't sound like Lonnie's pickup."

She started for the door with Luke at her heels. But before they got there, it opened and Peggy-Sue walked in—her cheeks streaked with mascara and dried tears, her eyes red.

"Peg, what's wrong?" Caitlin asked.

"I've got to talk to you." She shot Luke a pointed glance.

"Ahh..." he said, "why don't I take care of the dishes?"

Caitlin led Peggy-Sue out to the deck. The storm clouds that had been threatening all afternoon had passed through without leaving a single drop of rain. Now the sky was clear and starry.

"Lonnie and I are finished," Peggy-Sue announced as they sat down. "I broke up with him tonight. For good this time."

Caitlin told herself to be careful. She'd been through this scene with Peggy-Sue a dozen times over the years—more than enough times to know that *for good* might not last until morning.

"What happened?" she finally asked.

Peggy-Sue twisted off her diamond. "This engagement was all a mistake," she said, shoving the ring into her pocket. "I...oh, Caitlin, I lied to you about getting that job in Minneapolis. I didn't mean to, but I didn't want Lonnie to know the truth. And he was standing right there when you asked, so I had no choice."

"Wait, back up. You've lost me."

"The night Lonnie and I got engaged. When we stopped by to tell you...I hadn't actually gotten that great job in Minneapolis at all."

"But you'd told me before—"

"I know. They said I had it for sure. But Lonnie didn't want me to take it. That's the reason he finally asked me to marry him. He thought it was the only way he could keep me from leaving. But then the job fell through at the last minute. They had a budget cut and I was out of luck. I didn't want Lonnie to know that, though."

"You wanted him to think you were staying because you loved him."

"Yes, exactly. But...even that night I knew I was making a mistake. I shouldn't marry a man just because I'm twenty-nine years old and want a husband and kids and have no other prospects. Or because I didn't get a job in another city. Isn't that right?"

"Oh, Peggy-Sue." Caitlin took her friend's hands in hers. "Oh, Peg, I'm sorry. I know how hard it is, even if you do feel it's the right decision."

Peggy-Sue shrugged, looking absolutely miserable, then glanced toward the kitchen. Inside, Luke was wiping off the counter.

"I don't believe it," she murmured. "A guy who looks like that and he's domesticated, too? I can see why you bothered to dress for dinner," she added, glancing at Caitlin's sundress. "You've really lucked out. Lonnie told me you were in love with him."

"I am," she admitted, almost feeling guilty about it when Peggy-Sue was so unhappy.

"So what are you going to do when he goes back to Florida?"

"I don't know. I'll have to stay in Culpepper, for the time being, at least. You know how things stand. Between the ranch and Sky Knights, there's no way I could leave right now."

"Yeah, I guess. Too bad Trout didn't have any money, huh?"

"Trout?" Caitlin said when Peg didn't elaborate.

"Yeah...didn't Lonnie ever tell you he asked about buying into the company?"

"No."

"Oh. Well, it was a while back that they talked about it. Not long after Mike died. Trout had some idea about taking a cut in his pay and buying in gradually that way. But Lonnie said it just wasn't feasible. Not unless Trout managed to live to be a hundred and twelve or so. I guess that's why Lonnie didn't mention it to you. But it is too bad Trout isn't loaded, isn't it. If he could buy you out, that would solve at least part of the problem."

Caitlin nodded, thinking *if* had to be the biggest two-letter word in the English language.

Peggy-Sue was silent for a minute, then said, "I should have broken up with Lonnie long ago. Broken up and made it stick, I mean. I always just kept telling myself I could live with his faults, when deep down I knew I shouldn't settle for that. This time it's different, though."

"You're sure?"

"Uh-huh. I think so. Because in all the time we've gone together, I never *really* realized, until tonight, just what a selfish bastard he is."

"What happened tonight?"

"I don't even want to tell you. It was just so mean-spirited of him. And it was . . . he said things about *you*, Caitlin."

CAITLIN WAITED UNEASILY for Peggy-Sue to go on, wondering exactly what Lonnie had said. Of course, after the things she'd been implying about him lately, she was hardly in a position to criticize—regardless of what he'd said. But she *was* curious.

"It might help to talk about it," she finally said, when Peggy-Sue didn't continue.

"Well . . . maybe you're right. And maybe . . . I don't know. Maybe you *should* know."

She hesitated, then plunged ahead. "Okay, what happened was he told me about coming out here today. About Luke's being a spy and—"

"Luke *isn't* a spy. That story just isn't true. Do you know where it came from? Who Lonnie heard it from, I mean?"

Peggy-Sue shook her head. "I asked, but he wouldn't tell me."

"But did you believe it?"

"I . . . I didn't really have a chance to think about whether I did or not. Lonnie sure believes it, though. And he's scared to death that Luke is going to screw up your compensation claim."

"I know."

"Well, anyway, I was trying to convince him it wouldn't be the end of the world if Sky Knights didn't get the money. And you know what he said?"

"What?"

"He said, and I quote, 'Why the hell should Caitlin benefit from Mike's death and not me?'"

Hearing the word *benefit* started a queasy feeling in Caitlin's stomach. She'd come to hate that word. Why did insurance policies refer to *death benefits?* It was such an awful way of looking at things.

"I mean," Peggy-Sue elaborated, "what I was saying to Lonnie was that if by any chance it did turn out that Rayland was wrong...well, then, obviously Sky Knights wouldn't have any chance with its claim. But then at least *you'd* end up getting your money from Mike's policy. And that was when Lonnie said *he* was the one who'd kept Sky Knights going after Mike died, not you. So he deserved to benefit as much as you—if not more. And that just struck home to me how selfish he really is."

Caitlin did her best to keep quiet. But given the mood Peggy-Sue was in right now, she probably wouldn't feel she should cover up for Lonnie. So if she knew anything about what had happened the night Mike died...

It was just too tempting to resist. She took a deep breath and asked. "Peggy-Sue? Do you think there's any chance at all that...could Lonnie have killed Mike?"

Once Caitlin got the words out she no longer seemed able to breathe. She sat motionless, her question hanging, and waited for Peggy-Sue's reaction.

"Oh, Caitlin," she finally murmured. "Oh, no, you *have* been thinking that. Before we got to the big blowup part of the evening, Lonnie told me you've been asking people questions, and that he's sure it's *him* you suspect. But I figured he was crazy."

Caitlin's heart sank. She'd thought that Peggy-Sue might have had the key. But obviously, as far as she knew, Lonnie'd had nothing to do with what happened.

"It's been so long," Peg went on, "since you've said anything about Mike's..."

She swallowed the next word, but Caitlin knew she'd been going to say suicide. Everyone still tried to avoid using that word around her, even Peggy-Sue.

"...Since you talked about Mike's death," she said, finally finishing her sentence. "I thought, after you talked to Rayland about it, you'd come to terms with how it happened."

"No...no, I came to terms with the fact that asking questions made people uncomfortable. So I stopped. But all along I've wondered."

"You mean specifically about Lonnie? Because he wanted control of Sky Knights?"

"Yes."

"Oh, no," Peggy-Sue said softly. "Oh, no, Caitlin, Lonnie didn't kill Mike. It seems funny to be defending him, after the way I've been running him down, but I know he didn't kill Mike. Why didn't you tell me long ago what you were thinking? If you had, I'd have—"

"How *could* I have told you? You were going with Lonnie. And every time the two of you had a fight you were back together again before I got up the nerve to say anything."

"But if I'd known, I'd have straightened things out right away. Because I was with Lonnie when Mike died. I was at his place the entire evening."

"What?"

"I was."

Caitlin stared at her friend, searching for some sign she was lying. There wasn't one. Peggy-Sue was telling the truth.

The realization made Caitlin numb. It meant that all her suspicions, all her theories . . . But why hadn't she known this long ago? "Why," she said, "didn't either of you ever tell me?"

"I . . . I guess it just never came up."

"Never came up? But you're my best friend! In all this time, how could you not have thought to—"

"Caitlin, calm down. Have you and I *ever* really talked about the night Mike died?"

"We must have."

"No. We haven't. You couldn't handle it at first, so everyone got in the habit of not mentioning Mike's name, let alone talking about that night. And frankly, until tonight, it never struck me as being important where *I* was when it happened."

"But how could you not have said *something?*"

"What do you think I should have said? *'Oh, by the way, while Mike was lying dead in his office I was in bed with Lonnie?'* Look, I'm sorry if that sounded cruel, but why on earth would I have said anything? I mean, you never told me what you were thinking. If you had, I'd have straightened you out in a second. But I had no idea you thought Lonnie had anything to do with it."

"But what about now? Why didn't Lonnie say something a week or so ago? When Luke and I first started asking around? If he's sure I suspected him, why didn't he tell me he had an alibi?"

"That's what I asked him. And he said an alibi was exactly what you'd have thought it was. You'd have figured he was making it up. And that he'd asked me to go along with it. But it's not an alibi, it's a fact. I went to his place straight from work that night. And I was still with him at midnight, when Rayland called from the hangar to say...to tell him about Mike.''

Caitlin turned away and stared out into the night, feeling utterly drained. She'd never *wanted* Lonnie to have killed Mike, but he'd been the only one who'd had a motive. Had Mike killed himself, after all, then? Had she spent all this time doubting the truth?

The obvious answer to both those questions was yes.

''Talk to Lonnie, Caitlin,'' Peggy-Sue said quietly. ''Go out to the airport tomorrow and talk to him. Between what you and Luke have been putting him through, and me breaking up with him, he's not in very good shape. And he's...he does have feelings, even though he tries not to let them show.''

''I know,'' Caitlin murmured.

''And I realize Mike's death was harder on you than it could possibly have been for anyone else, but it was hard for Lonnie, too. Sure they'd been fighting. But Mike wasn't only his partner, he was his cousin. And after Rayland said they figured it was the bourbon that had triggered things...oh, maybe I shouldn't be talking about all this.''

''No, it's okay. It's been a long time. I'm all right with it now.''

''Well then, after Lonnie found out about the booze, he kept wondering if he could have done anything. For months afterward, he used to say he should have realized Mike had started drinking. That if he'd just been more observant, he'd have talked to him about it.... Maybe that would have helped.''

"Wait. You're saying Lonnie didn't know? But Trout did. He told Luke he used to see Mike sitting in the office drinking. So how could Lonnie not have known?"

"I have no idea. But he didn't."

Caitlin heard the quiet sound of the kitchen door sliding open and glanced along the deck. As she looked over, Luke said, "I don't want to interrupt, but would either of you like coffee or something?"

She gazed at him for a minute, thinking how much he'd gone through to try to help her find out the truth. And all along, she could have learned it by asking Peggy-Sue a couple of simple questions.

"Why don't you come out and sit with us for a few minutes," she said. "Peggy-Sue just told me something you should know about."

CHAPTER FIFTEEN

WHILE CAITLIN WALKED Peggy-Sue to her car, Luke forced his mind off the news flash she'd given them. He might as well wait until after she was gone to think about it.

In the meantime, he let his thoughts drift to how seldom he'd seen Caitlin in a dress. And how damn good she looked in one. Maybe it didn't quite compare to the way she looked in a bathing suit. But hell, she looked good in anything. Or out of anything, for that matter.

And every time he focused on that dress he started imagining her out of it, because the two little straps that were tied at her shoulders seemed to be the only things holding it up. Spaghetti straps, he thought they were called. But whatever the proper name was, every time he looked at them he had a strong urge to untie them.

He let his imagination wander a little further down that path as she hugged Peggy-Sue goodbye—still assuring her that breaking up with Lonnie wasn't the end of the world.

"You'll see," she said. "You just haven't been noticing all the other men out there because you've been going with Lonnie for so long. But I'll bet, any day now, you're going to meet somebody great."

Caitlin's pep talk made Luke think of the way his sister was always telling him that one day the right woman would come along. Sarah hadn't warned him, though, that when the right woman did show up, there'd be a thousand and one obstacles in the way. And the way he figured it, Peggy-Sue's news had just added one more.

Assuming she *had* been with Lonnie the night Mike died, he and Caitlin had suddenly gone from one suspect to none. And he couldn't help wondering if it was because they'd been wrong—Mike really had killed himself.

If he had, there was no chance Caitlin would be getting that insurance money—which obliterated the rosy picture of her straightening out all her financial problems and being able to leave Culpepper.

When he looked back at Caitlin, she was saying, "Your Mr. Right is out there someplace, Peg. You'll see."

Peggy-Sue smiled wanly. "Well I sure hope someplace is Arizona, because I might be stuck at my job in Tucson for a long time yet. And if I'm in Arizona and Mr. Right is in Wisconsin, it'll be a serious problem."

"Right on," Luke muttered to himself. It would be just as bad as his being in Pensacola while Ms. Right was here. And that's exactly the way things would soon be.

"Bye, Luke," Peggy-Sue called, getting into her car.

"Bye, Peggy-Sue."

As she headed down the drive, he walked over to where Caitlin was standing. When he wrapped his arm around her waist she leaned into him, her body a perfect fit against his.

Her soft warmth sent a rush of desire through him. Desire and love and an aching need that made him wonder how he was going to stand being separated from her.

"We'd better go back in," she murmured. "In case the Chief wakes up or something."

"So?" he asked as they turned toward the house. "What do you think? Was she actually with Lonnie that night?"

"Yes, I'm sure she was. Which means he hasn't been trying to run you out of Culpepper because he's been afraid we'd learn he killed Mike. He's just been afraid we'd turn up something that points away from suicide—something that would mean Sky Knights wouldn't have a prayer of winning that compensation claim. *That's* what's been making him so angry."

"Well then, at least we can stop worrying that your business partner's a murderer."

"Uh-huh," Caitlin said slowly. "And maybe... maybe there's no murderer at all. Maybe I just convinced myself there was because... oh, I don't even want to get into it."

They stepped inside and Luke closed the door. When he turned to Caitlin once more she tried to smile. But it was a very sad little smile.

"What does that old Kenny Rogers song say?" she murmured. "You've got to know when to hold 'em, know when to fold 'em? I wonder if that's where we're at here."

"You want to give up?" Luke asked gently.

She hesitated, then shook her head. "I don't know, Luke. Right now, I just want you to hold me."

He took her in his arms and breathed in her meadows-in-moonlight scent. In not much more than another week or so, that scent he loved would be a fading memory. And the woman he loved would be far away.

Tangling his fingers in her hair, he tilted her face to his and kissed her. She tasted faintly of the wine they'd had with dinner.

"Oh, Luke," she whispered against his mouth, smoothing her hands down his back. "Oh, Luke, what am I going to do when you're gone?"

He simply kissed her again, because he didn't want to think about that. All he wanted to do was hold her and drink in the warmth of her kiss. He backed her against the wall so her body was pressed more tightly to his, and when she moved against him he almost groaned with desire.

Heat was spreading from her kiss, down his throat, all the way to the throbbing in his groin. Then Caitlin tugged his shirt out of his jeans and slid her hands across his skin, turning the heat to molten lava in his veins.

He caressed her breasts, stroking her aroused nipples through the thin cotton of her dress. "I love you Caitlin," he whispered. "I love you so much it scares me."

"I know. That's how much I love you, too." She moved her hands to his zipper and he *did* groan.

Suddenly the bedroom seemed too far away to be worth thinking about. He kissed her throat while his fingers found those sexy little straps on her shoulders. And sure enough, they were the only things holding up her dress.

She was wearing only a wisp of something silky beneath it. He pushed it down and kissed her naked breasts.

"Oh, Luke," she whispered, unzipping his jeans and reaching for him.

Her hands drove him crazy. Her kisses, hot and moist against his neck, only added to the insanity. He hiked her skirt up and shoved her panties down, desperate to be inside her.

When he touched her she felt as hot and moist as her kisses. Her arousal heightened his—making him breathless with desire. Then she began to make little moaning sounds, moving against his hand, and she climaxed almost instantly.

He lifted her against the wall and she wrapped her legs around him. When he entered her, it felt like heaven on earth. When he came it felt like thunder and lightning... and then the calm after the storm.

For a few minutes, he simply held her where she was. Then he eased her down and stood with his arms around her, her body against his, wishing he never had to move.

"Oh, Luke," she whispered again, "I don't want to lose you."

"You won't," he promised. But even though he was a man of his word, he couldn't help worrying about how he was going to keep his promise this time.

THEY WERE JUST FINISHING breakfast the next morning when Luke said, "Caitlin? There's something I want to talk about before we head for the airport."

She nodded, gazing across the table at him.

"I know this isn't the most romantic time and place, but I have to say it now. I love you more than I ever thought I could love anyone. So regardless of how anything else turns out, will you marry me? Will you marry me and come to Florida...no matter what?"

Both her heart and her thoughts began to race. They hadn't really talked about what Peggy-Sue had told them last night, but she knew what Luke was asking. It was no longer looking as if Mike might have been murdered. So the chances of her getting that insurance money had dropped to about zero.

She tried to think logically—which was awfully hard when her emotions kept interfering. She loved Luke so much that she'd go with him in a minute if she could see her way clear to. But the way things were...

"Well?" he finally said. "I *am* going to get a yes sooner or later, aren't I?"

She took a sip of coffee for courage. "Luke, I want to go with you so much, but I can't. It would be impossible right now—with the ranch overmortgaged and Sky Knights just scraping by."

"So sell out. Sell the ranch and sell your interest in Sky Knights."

"I can't. I thought I told you, there's no one with any money who'd want to buy my share of the company. And until Lonnie and I can make it profitable, there isn't *going* to be anyone. And I can't sell the ranch because Lonnie's father has a lien on it. It was collateral for the business loan."

"Well, dammit," Luke muttered, rubbing his jaw. "There's got to be a way around this. What about becoming Lonnie's *silent* partner? Let him hire somebody to do what you do now, and rent this place out and—"

"Oh, Luke, I wish it were that easy. But Lonnie would have to pay somebody else a lot more than I take out of the company to live on. And then Sky Knights would be in the red *every* month, instead of every other month. And if that happened, Quentin McDougall would pull the plug on us and I'd lose everything."

Luke reached across the table and brushed her hair back from her face. The gentleness of his touch almost brought tears to her eyes. How could she have to say no to this man when she was so in love with him?

"You wouldn't be losing everything," he murmured, his hand resting against her cheek. "You'd still have the Chief, and you'd have me. And aren't people the important things in life? Aren't the baby and I more important than this place and a company that isn't even doing very well?"

"Of course you are. If I had the Taj Mahal and General Motors, you'd be more important to me. But . . ."

Her "but" made Luke lower his hand and wrap it around his mug. "Caitlin, don't say but. If you really love me, then just walk away from everything here. Let Lonnie have the company and let his father have the ranch. At least we'd have each other."

She gazed into Luke's eyes, so very tempted to say yes. But she couldn't.

If it was only her future at stake, she'd probably run off with him in a second. But she had to think about the baby, too. And she simply couldn't risk the

Chief's future until she was absolutely certain she was doing the right thing.

If she stayed here and kept working with Lonnie, Sky Knights would eventually do well. She was certain of that. *Then* she could sell out, and pay off the mortgage, and she and the Chief would have a little security behind them.

But if she walked away from the only chance she had for security in the future...

As crazy as she was about Luke, she hadn't entirely lost her common sense. The saying about love being blind was sometimes only too true. So she had to keep in mind how short a time she'd known him. And remember that things don't always work out the way you expect when you fall in love.

Which all added up to the fact that she had to stay right where she was for the time being. Even though...

She tried to ignore the other old saying that was playing around the edges of her mind. The one about absence making the heart grow fonder for somebody else. She didn't want Luke to be in Florida and her to be here. But for the moment it was the only possible arrangement.

"Caitlin?" he said.

Saying no, even with just the shake of her head, was one of the hardest things she'd ever done. "I really do love you, Luke. I really do. The problem with your idea is that I can't just walk away clean. It's not *only* that I'd lose everything. There are also those guarantees I signed for at the bank. If I walked away I'd still be up to my ears in debt."

"Then we'd pay it somehow. I'm not rich, but I make a good living."

Oh, Lord, he was making it sound so easy. And just looking at him was making her want to agree. But she could practically hear her grandmother saying, "Consider the consequences, Caitlin."

And what would the consequences be if she let Luke assume her debts? Would he come to resent her?

That was certainly a possibility, and it might not take long to become a reality. She wasn't going to say that to him because it would hurt him. But she had to take some time, give this some more thought.

"Luke...this is hard to put into words, but I feel as if...my debt is my responsibility, not yours. And the baby—"

"Don't worry about the baby. As far as I'm concerned, the Chief's a plus, not a minus. He's not just anybody's baby, he's yours. And Mike's. That makes him special. And the two of you gave him my name, so hell, that means he's partly mine already, doesn't it?"

Luke's words made her throat so tight she could barely speak. And it almost convinced her to try to ignore her uncertainties. Almost, but not quite.

"I just can't go with you the way things are," she forced herself to say. "It's...your taking everything on is just too much to ask of you."

"Dammit Caitlin! You're not asking it of me. I'm offering. There's a big difference."

Luke stopped before he said half of what he wanted to say and told himself to calm down. But dammit, he could see their future slipping away right before his eyes.

He'd finally found the woman he didn't want to hold back from, and now *she* was holding back from *him*. What the hell was wrong with the world?

"Luke...look, I just need some time to sort things through, and then maybe we can—"

"Right. But let's keep in mind that while you're sorting things through, I'll be in Florida. And by the time you're done sorting, some other guy will probably have come along and swept you off your feet and—"

"Oh, Luke, that isn't going to happen. I love you so much, I can't even imagine it happening."

He bit his tongue. But he could sure imagine it happening. Caitlin might not be the most wonderful woman in the entire United States of America, but she was sure the most wonderful one *he'd* ever met. And he wasn't the only man who'd think that.

Hell, he'd heard the way Rayland Skoda talked to her. And maybe Rayland wasn't any threat because she didn't like him much, but other guys would think she was terrific, too.

Luke sat absently rubbing his jaw, trying to figure out what he was going to do. Lose her because she was being so stubborn? No damn way! So what the hell *was* he going to do?

BY THE TIME they were halfway to the airport, Caitlin was wishing they'd taken her van instead of the Mustang. With Luke doing the driving, *she* had nothing to do but worry about what she was going to say to Lonnie.

They had to talk. Peggy-Sue had been right about that. But knowing you had to do something difficult didn't make it any easier.

When they turned onto Airport Road a helicopter was taking off. From the baby seat they'd strapped in back, the Chief cried, "Bhhrrrrr."

Luke grinned. "I tell you, Caitlin, he's going to be a pilot for sure."

She glanced at her son, thinking how much happier he seemed now that he was back to normal and getting out of the house again.

"I see we've got a noon meeting of the good ol' boys," Luke said as they neared the hangar.

Caitlin looked through the windshield again and swore to herself. She'd timed this visit so they'd arrive after the morning combat mission customers had left. She'd heard their new pilot had been driving into town for lunch—that he had something going with Merline, one of the waitresses at the Culpepper Café—so he was never around at noon. But instead of having caught Lonnie alone, he was standing out on the apron with Trout and Rayland.

The three men watched as Luke parked beside the hangar. Not a flicker of welcome crossed any of their faces.

When she got out of the car and waved, all they gave her in return were three barely perceptible nods. She took the baby from his seat and handed him over to Luke.

"You sure you don't want me to go with you?" he asked. "Lonnie's got to be more angry at me than he is at you."

She shook her head. Lonnie was *her* partner. And she was the one who'd suspected him. Luke had only gone on what she'd told him. "Lonnie?" she called. "Could I talk to you inside for a minute?"

He gave Rayland and Trout a look she couldn't decipher, then strolled toward the hangar.

Obviously, he wasn't going to make this easy. But she didn't deserve easy. You could hardly go around accusing someone of murder, even if you didn't come right and say the word, then expect him to be eager to forgive you.

She followed Lonnie into the office and closed the door. Lonnie slumped into the chair behind his desk and she sat down across from him, still not sure of the best way to start.

As a delaying tactic, she gestured through the glass at the thousand and twelve crates they were still storing and asked when they'd be getting rid of them.

"That's what you wanted to talk about?" Lonnie muttered.

"No...no, of course not. I wanted to say I'm sorry about you and Peggy-Sue. She came by the house last night and...well, I'm sorry."

He shrugged. "It's no big deal. You know how it is, she'll change her mind in a day or two."

Caitlin really didn't think that was going to happen this time, but she kept her opinion to herself. "Peg told me," she went on, "that she was with you the night Mike died."

"Yeah? You believe her or not?"

"Yes, I do."

For the first time, a flicker of emotion crossed Lonnie's face. Relief. And seeing it made her wish again that she'd known the truth long ago. "Lonnie, I'm sorry I suspected you. I know there's no way I can make it up to you. And no way I can take back all those questions I asked people. But I just didn't know. I thought maybe somebody other than Mike could have been here that night. And you were the only one who had anything to gain and—"

"Caitlin...can it, okay? I didn't have anything to gain that would have been worth killing Mike."

"I know. Lonnie, there's just no way I can apologize enough. I'll make a point of talking to every single one of those people again, and do what I can to straighten things out. But I know there's no excuse."

"No, there isn't. So let's just stop talking about it, huh?"

She nodded unhappily. "I guess it's time to admit everyone else has been right all along. Mike killed himself, and I just couldn't make myself believe it. So, instead, I started suspecting the only person I thought might possibly... Lonnie, I'm just so sorry."

"I am, too, Caitlin. Because things are never going to be the same between us. But..." He stopped and shrugged again, obviously changing his mind about whatever he'd been about to say.

"But?" she pressed.

"Oh, hell, I guess it's not going to hurt to admit this to you. If *I'd* had someone to suspect, the way you had me, I might have done just what you did."

"What? I don't understand what you mean."

"I mean, I didn't want to believe Mike killed himself, either. It just wasn't like him to have left you in the lurch the way he did. And I know I'm not the most perceptive guy, but I kept wondering how he could have been *that* depressed without my realizing it. How could he have been drinking so much without my knowing it? But... well, like I said, I had no one to suspect, so I guess it was easier for me to accept."

Caitlin's heart had begun racing. Aside from her, Lonnie had been the closest person in the world to Mike. "Lonnie, you're saying you had doubts, too? I mean, you aren't saying it was just that you didn't want to believe it, are you? You're saying you found it *hard* to believe.''

"Yeah ... yeah, I found it real hard to believe."

"Then why didn't you tell me?"

"What was the point? You were in bad-enough shape already. And Rayland was sure he was right. So the longer I thought about it ... well, hell, unless somebody had a motive that neither of us knew anything about, it just wouldn't add up to murder, would it?"

Unless somebody had a motive that neither of us knew anything about. The words began echoing in Caitlin's head. But nobody she and Luke had talked to so far had admitted to knowing anything. And there weren't many people they *hadn't* talked to ... except for Conchita Sanchez, of course.

Caitlin closed her eyes, not wanting to get her hopes up. But what if, when Conchita got back, it turned out she knew something that nobody else did?

CHAPTER SIXTEEN

LUKE PARKED IN FRONT of the terminal, praying that whatever Conchita Sanchez had to tell him about Mike would be significant. Because learning that Lonnie'd once been just as suspicious as Caitlin had changed things dramatically. And it had made them decide they weren't giving up until there wasn't a single stone left unturned.

But they'd pretty well reached that point. Conchita was their last possible source of information, the only hope they had left of uncovering the truth.

He absently glanced at his watch as he got out of the Mustang, but his gaze caught on the date, rather than the time. Conchita's *couple* of extra days off work had stretched into *several*. It was already Monday, July 24. He'd reached four days and counting.

Inside, he headed for the snack bar, relieved to see that Conchita really *was* behind the counter—and that she had no customers at the moment. When she spotted him she gave him an anxious-looking smile.

"How's your mother?" he asked, sitting down on one of the stools.

"Oh, she is much better, thank you. But it was good I was there. She had a fever for days, and my youngest brother, he is only a baby. But your message? You asked that I call, so I did."

Luke glanced around. The terminal was virtually empty and there was no one anywhere near them. "The last time I saw you," he said, looking back at her, "you started to tell me something about Mike. But we got interrupted before you could finish."

"*Sí*. But I have been thinking...I was maybe silly to say anything."

Luke's gut clenched. What the hell was he going to do if she'd had second thoughts about telling him? Strong-arm an eighteen-year-old girl?

He shrugged, trying to look casual. "Well, you mentioned you wondered about something when he died. And there's a lot I don't understand about his death, so I'd really like to hear the rest of what you started to say."

For a second he thought she was going to refuse. Then she nodded and he relaxed a little.

"I told you I had a problem, *sí?*"

"Yes. You said Mike was trying to help you with it."

"*Sí*. But it is not so easy to tell you about it. Mike, I knew."

"I understand. It's hard to talk to strangers. But I was Mike's friend. And you never know, it might not be silly to tell me at all. What you were going to say might be important."

She hesitated, but said at last, "Well...my problem was this. I have a sister, Maria. She is seventeen. But two years ago, when she was only fifteen, she comes to stay with me. And she meets this man...this part is hard for me to say."

Luke nodded, then waited while Conchita fidgeted with some napkins. Finally, she looked at him again.

"This man she meets somewhere, he says to her he can get her a job in Tucson. And I say, who is this man? What is this job? But she is so excited, and he takes her there. And I find out later that..." Conchita paused and stared down at the counter. When she looked up again, her face was flushed.

"I do not see her now," she went on quietly. "But sometimes she phones. And this job, it is being a whore. This man, he takes my sister, who is just fifteen, and another man in Tucson pays him. Then this man in Tucson, he makes Maria a whore."

"Oh, God," Luke murmured. "Who the hell took her to Tucson? Who was it?"

Conchita shook her head. "I do not know. Maria would not tell me. But she is not the only one. Maria says he brings other girls like her. Girls who come from Mexico and have no job. And he tells them all... he says if they tell anyone his name he will kill them."

Luke swore under his breath. "And this is the problem you told Mike about?"

"*Sí*. I tell him because the only thing Maria said was that I know this man. That he is here, at the airport, a lot. So I thought maybe Mike... because he knew everyone at the airport."

"And what about when he died? What was it you said you wondered about?"

"I wondered why he would kill himself, a man like Mike, with his nice wife. I wondered if... this is the silly part, my wonderings. But I thought, what if Mike, he found out who the man was? And what if the man... he said he would kill Maria and the other girls. So what if he killed Mike?"

Luke's adrenaline was pumping like crazy. Finally, here was a real motive for murder. If Mike *had* found out who the guy was...there had to be a long jail sentence for helping turn fifteen-year-old girls into hookers. But who the hell could he be? Someone who was around the airport a lot. That wasn't much to go on.

"You don't have *any* idea who this man is?" he asked.

"No...no, but there is something else. Something else I wondered about."

"What?"

"The sheriff said that Mike, he was alone all that night. But I know this is not right. So I wonder if other things the sheriff said, other things about that night, if they are not right, too."

"Good God. What else do you know?"

Conchita shrugged. "That night, I forgot my purse at work. So I came back later to get it. And the Trout was here with Mike."

"Trout?"

"*Sí.* When I go home at six, after work, his truck, it is parked outside the hangar. Next to Mike's van. And when I come back, it is still there."

"And when was that? What time?"

"Maybe eight o'clock. Eight-thirty, maybe."

"Conchita, did you tell Rayland about this?"

She shook her head.

"Why not?"

"Because I like the Trout. And I know he could not kill Mike. And I do not like the sheriff. So why should I say a thing to him that might make trouble for the Trout?"

Running his fingers through his hair, Luke tried to put everything together. Maybe Conchita didn't think Trout could have killed Mike, but if she was right, if he was here that night...

If he *had* been here, he'd lied about it. Luke distinctly remembered Trout saying he'd gone home after work that night. He'd said Mike had been sitting with a bottle of bourbon on his desk, and that was the last time Trout had seen him alive.

And he'd obviously lied to Rayland, as well, because as far as the sheriff was concerned, Mike had definitely been alone. So unless Conchita was wrong...

He looked at her again. "You aren't positive Trout was here, are you? I mean, you saw his truck, but maybe he could have just left it here. Maybe it wouldn't start or something. Or maybe somebody had borrowed it from him or—"

"No, I saw the Trout. Not just his truck. When I came back, I saw him. He was at the door of the hangar."

"But he didn't see you?"

"No. He did not look my way. He just looked down the road. Then he went inside the hangar again."

CAITLIN PACED ACROSS the kitchen once more, glad she'd put the Chief down for his nap before Luke had gotten back. Because the way her thoughts were racing off in all directions now, she'd be at risk of putting her son into the washing machine instead of his crib.

She turned back and looked over to where Luke was leaning against the counter. "Conchita was absolutely *positive* it was Trout she saw?"

"Caitlin, you've asked me that at least a dozen times. My answer isn't going to change. She said she's sure Trout couldn't have killed Mike, but she's absolutely positive it was him she saw."

"Well, she's right about his not killing Mike. Whatever he was doing there, he couldn't have had anything to do with murder. I'll admit he's not the smartest guy in the world, and he sometimes comes off as a little rough around the edges, but he doesn't have an evil bone in his body."

"Look, all I know is Conchita saw him there around eight or eight-thirty. And from the word go, he's claimed he went home after work and didn't head back to the airport until Rayland called him after midnight."

"But this man who's been taking those girls to Tucson, who's been..." Caitlin shuddered, just thinking that someone in Culpepper, someone she must know, was luring young girls into prostitution. "It can't possibly be Trout," she went on. "He's got girls of his own. He and Sally-Mae have three daughters, and he dotes on them."

"Caitlin, I'm not saying Trout is *that* guy—although I'm not saying he isn't, either. Hell, there's damn little here that we know for sure."

She shook her head, her thoughts still a jumble. It *couldn't* be Trout, and yet... "If Conchita said it was somebody who's at the airport a lot, that *could* be Trout, couldn't it. Even though I can't believe it. Conchita must have meant someone who works there, right?"

"Well, that's what I assumed at first, too. But she was only repeating what her sister told her, so who knows? Maybe it's someone who keeps a private plane there. But whoever he is, let's not get sidetracked. Because he wasn't necessarily involved at all. Conchita just said she wondered if Mike had found out who he was. So I think we've got to concentrate on the one thing we do know—that Trout was at the hangar that night, even though he's said all along he wasn't."

"All right. Then let's concentrate on that." Caitlin waited, hoping Luke had an idea where to start.

"Is there any possible reason," he finally asked, "that Trout might have wanted Mike dead?"

She shook her head, then suddenly thought of something Peggy-Sue had mentioned the other night. "No, wait. I doubt this is anything. But after Mike died, Trout asked Lonnie about buying into Sky Knights. So...no, I'm just reaching."

"No, tell me the details."

"I don't know them. All I know is that apparently he was interested. But he has no money. He just had an idea about forgoing some of his wages and buying in a little at a time—which Lonnie said wasn't feasible."

"You don't figure he might have thought that maybe, if Mike was out of the way...?"

"Oh, Luke, that sounds like an awfully weak motive for murder."

Luke shrugged. "Well, you said he wasn't the smartest guy in the world."

"I know, but he's a long way from being an idiot." She stood silently gazing across the kitchen.

"What?" Luke said at last. "You look as if you're thinking about something."

"I am, but . . . oh, it really does seem like we're grasping at straws here. I always had the feeling though, that Trout kind of resented the setup at Sky Knights. I mean, the fact that Mike and Lonnie started the company and asked him to work for them without letting him in on a share of it."

"But you said he has no money."

"I know. I didn't say it made sense. I just said it was a feeling I always had."

"So . . . where are we here? Have we gone from it couldn't possibly be Trout to it just possibly might be?"

"I guess," she admitted reluctantly. "So what do we do now?"

"Well, either we pay Trout a visit, or we talk to Rayland and let him take it from here."

Caitlin gnawed on her bottom lip for a minute. "I don't suppose you've got a third alternative up your sleeve, have you?"

"'Fraid not. You don't like either of those two?"

"No. I've already been wrong about Lonnie, and things will never be right between us because of it. And I don't really believe Trout could have had anything to do with it, so if I go accusing him . . ."

"You think we'd be better off just telling Rayland?"

"No, what I think is that we're between a rock and a hard place. What do you figure will happen if we tell Rayland?"

"Frankly, not much."

"Exactly. There's no way he'd believe an eighteen-year-old Mexican girl over his buddy."

"Which leaves us with talking to Trout."

"I guess."

Luke nodded. "Okay, then let's get going. The Chief probably won't like your waking him up, but if you do we've got time to drop him off at your grandparents' place and still get to the airport before Trout leaves. I don't want to be left holding the baby this time around."

"You mean you think we should do it right now?"

"Caitlin...we don't have all the time in the world."

She nodded, although she didn't need the reminder that Luke could only stay in Culpepper for a few more days. A *very* few more days. And remembering that made her throat hurt.

"Caitlin?"

"You're right. This is a perfect time to go. There are flight lessons scheduled all afternoon, so neither Lonnie nor Joe should be around. We'll have Trout to ourselves."

"Good. And you once mentioned there's a handgun in the house. Where is it?"

"In my bedside table, but—"

"Just in case, Caitlin. We'll take it along just in case."

FOR THE FIRST DAY that week no thunderheads had rolled in, and the afternoon sun was glaring down on the Mustang as it sped along Airport Road.

Luke glanced fleetingly at Caitlin, wishing to hell he could have left her at her grandparents with the baby. But he knew there was no way she'd have agreed to that.

Besides which, talking to Trout without her wouldn't make sense. There had to be a lot of things she'd think to ask that he wouldn't. She'd known the guy all her life—she'd be able to read his reactions far better.

If it weren't for that, though, he'd have tied her down rather than let her come with him. He was only too aware of the pistol in his glove compartment—a deadly looking little Luger. He hadn't forgotten about the gun rack in the back of Trout's pickup, either. And unlike Caitlin and Conchita he didn't whole-heartedly believe that Trout *wasn't* a murderer.

Luke had never accused anyone of murder before, but he doubted most killers just admitted they were guilty and waited peacefully while someone called the sheriff. Or probably, under these circumstances, calling the state police would be a better plan than calling one of Trout's best buddies.

"Both planes are gone," Caitlin murmured as they neared the hangar. "I was worried someone might have canceled out on a lesson, but we're okay. We'll be able to use the office without having to explain things to Lonnie."

"Good." Luke mentally pictured the office—with its front wall that was half glass. He couldn't help imagining how a gunshot would shatter that glass into a million shards. And anyone standing in the line of fire... Hell, that was the last thing he wanted to think about.

"And there's Trout's pickup," Caitlin said. "So he hasn't gone home early."

Luke nodded. There it was, all right. Parked out-side the hangar along with Lonnie's pickup and Joe Onsager's Chevy. Trout's pickup with its damn gun rack. "So far, so good," he made himself say.

Trout wasn't anywhere in sight. Which probably meant he was either in the hangar or over in the terminal, having one of his diet snacks of a burger and beer.

"So we'll just come straight out and hit him with it, right?" Caitlin said.

"If you figure that's the best way."

"I think it is. He's not very quick on his feet, so the less time he has to think, the better."

"Okay, then that's the way we'll play it."

Luke parked beside the hangar and reached over into the glove compartment for the Luger.

"You don't really think you'll need that, do you?" Caitlin murmured.

"Let's hope not." He tucked it against the small of his back and pulled his T-shirt down over it. Its shape was probably still visible but that was the best he could do.

When they climbed out of the car and headed inside, they found Trout working on some engine parts—the mountains of giant crates still stacked beyond his workbench.

"Hey, Caitlin. Luke," he greeted them, waving a large screwdriver in their direction.

"Could we talk to you for a minute?" Caitlin said.

He shrugged. "Sure. Talk away."

"In the office? So we won't be interrupted if anyone comes in?"

"Ahh . . . sure," Trout said, letting Luke breathe a little more easily by putting down the screwdriver.

The three of them filed into the office and Caitlin closed the door. Luke leaned against the wall so Trout wouldn't notice the gun.

"So?" he said, glancing uncertainly from Caitlin to Luke, then back at Caitlin. "What's up?"

Caitlin looked at Luke, silently reminding him the opening lines were his.

He took a deep breath and began. "A while back, you and I were talking about the night Mike died."

"Ahh . . . yeah."

"And you told me the last time you saw him alive was when you went home after work that night."

Trout cleared his throat, looking even more uncertain. "Yeah," he said at last.

"Well, the thing is, we've got a witness who saw you here later on."

"Sure. I told you that, too. Rayland called me an' Lonnie to come out here after he found Mike's body."

"Uh-uh. Rayland's report says he found Mike's body just before midnight. This witness saw you here about eight or eight-thirty . . . closer to the estimated time of death."

Trout's face went pale under his tan. "Your witness is lyin'."

"I don't think so," Luke said quietly.

"Well I say they are," Trout snapped. "So if that's what you wanted to talk about . . . people are sick of y'all pokin' round with your questions, you know. And you might own half of this here business," he muttered to Caitlin, "but that don't give you the right to go sayin' things like this. I'd never hurt Mike, and you oughtta know it. What the hell's gone wrong with you, Cait? You forget who your friends are?"

"What were you doing here that night?" Luke pressed. "Your truck was parked right beside Mike's van."

"Oh…that. Oh, well I can explain that. See, Sally-Mae came by and picked me up in her car that night 'cuz we was…we was goin' somewhere. So we left my truck here and—"

"Uh-uh," Luke said. "Our witness didn't just see your truck. You were standing in the hangar doorway. Looking down the road." Trout's face went even whiter.

"You were in here with Mike. So what the hell was going on? What really happened?"

"I don't have to put up with this. I'm gonna call Rayland and you can tell *him* about your damn witness. See if he believes you."

"Uh-uh. When we call someone, it'll be the state police, not Rayland."

"Trout?" Caitlin said quietly. "We really *do* have a witness. And I know you'd never have intentionally hurt Mike. But something happened you're not telling us. And if you drag Sally-Mae in, if you make her try to give you an alibi, you'll only be getting her in trouble, too. Because we *are* going to call the state police. And they're going to find out what happened here that night. So what was it? Was there an accident with Mike's gun? And did you and Rayland try to cover up the truth?"

"Oh, God," Trout said. "Oh, God, Cait, why couldn't you have left well enough alone?"

"What's the real story?" she murmured.

"Caitlin, I swear I didn't know what was gonna happen. I shoulda been suspicious, but I wasn't. He said he just needed to talk to Mike alone, so could I hang around and make sure Mike didn't leave before he got here. But he was settin' me up. And after it was over he said I had my choice. Either I could swear by

the story he made up or he'd put the blame on me—
say I was the one who done it, that he wasn't even
here. And he said I'd go to prison for murder. So I
had to go along with him. But I didn't do nothin'
Cait. You gotta believe that.''

"Who was saying all this?" Luke asked. "Who's
the he?''

Trout simply shook his head. "I shoulda wondered, 'cuz there was a million times he coulda talked
to Mike alone. But I didn't think about it.''

Luke was about to ask *who* again, when Caitlin
shot him a look that told him to be patient. Trout
would get to the *who* in his own time.

"He told me," Trout went on, "that I probably
wouldn't have to do nothin'. 'Cuz a lot of nights Mike
was here workin' till eight or nine. But he said if Mike
went to leave I should have a bottle of bourbon here
and have a couple of drinks with him. Keep him here.
And I just said sure.''

"You mean that was *your* bourbon?" Luke said.

Trout nodded. "The stuff about Mike drinkin'...it
was just part of the story. I mean, he did have a couple of drinks with me that night, but he hadn't taken
to drinkin' regular, not like I said.''

"That's why Lonnie didn't know about it," Caitlin murmured. "And why I didn't. Because it wasn't
true.''

"No... no, it wasn't, Cait.''

"And Mike didn't kill himself, did he," she barely
whispered. "That wasn't true, either, was it?''

CHAPTER SEVENTEEN

AND MIKE DIDN'T KILL himself . . .

Caitlin's words hung fire while she and Luke stood staring at Trout. At last, he said, "No, Mike didn't kill himself."

She exhaled slowly, only then realizing she'd been holding her breath. After all this time, she was finally learning the truth. She felt as if she'd been trapped under water for an eternity, and was now bursting through the surface into the air above.

"Tell me," she said softly. "Tell me what really happened, Trout. I've agonized about it for so long."

He gave her a weary shrug. "Like I said, Rayland asked me to make sure Mike stuck around here until—"

"Rayland?" she whispered, feeling as if she'd been struck. "*That's* who you've been talking about? It was *Rayland* who killed Mike?"

"Yeah, it was Rayland."

Luke swore, then muttered, "At least we picked the right one to talk to."

Caitlin wrapped her arms around her chest, trying to keep from trembling. "But why?" she managed to ask. "Why on earth would Rayland . . . ?"

"Mike had something on him," Trout said. "Something about him and a girl named Maria."

"Oh, God." Luke looked at Caitlin. "Maria is Conchita's sister. So *Rayland's* the guy who's been ... and Mike *did* find out."

"You two know what was goin' on with Mike and Rayland?" Trout was asking.

"I think so," Luke told him.

"Yeah? Well I never to this day figured it out."

Luke glanced at Caitlin again. "No wonder Rayland was hoping I'd leave as soon as Lonnie hired his new pilot. He must have been damn worried about all the questions we were asking."

"Yeah, he was worried, all right," Trout said. "That's why he came up with that story he fed Lonnie."

"What story?" Luke asked.

"The one about you bein' a spy for the military. That you was tryin' to find out somethin' to keep that claim from goin' anywhere. Rayland figured if Lonnie believed that, he'd convince Caitlin to throw you out."

"So Rayland was the impeccable source," Luke muttered.

Caitlin's head had begun to throb, and her stomach was churning faster by the second. Rayland had killed Mike. And it was Rayland who'd been taking those poor girls to Tucson.

"But what happened that night?" Luke asked Trout. "After Rayland got here?"

"Well, Mike was surprised to see him. They didn't talk much, but Mike asked somethin' about whether Rayland had fixed it to get this Maria back from Tucson. But they were tryin' to talk so's I wouldn't catch on to exactly what they were saying, and I didn't. But then ..."

"Then?" Luke prompted when Trout paused.

Caitlin gave him a grateful glance for pressing. After coming this far, she had to hear the whole story, no matter how painful the truth would be.

"Then," Trout went on, "Rayland says, 'You know, Mike, I've gotta feelin' I can't really trust you on this.' And Mike says, 'What's that supposed to mean?' And Rayland says, 'It means I don't think you're gonna keep your mouth shut. It means that even if I do trot Maria on back here, I gotta a feelin' the day after she's back, I'll have a couple of guys bangin' on my door with an arrest warrant.' "

"And?" Luke said when Trout paused again.

"And then Mike says, 'I told you I'd have to think on what I'm gonna do, Rayland.' And then . . . oh, hell, Caitlin, I'm real sorry. But the next thing I knew Rayland had a gun in his hand and it was all over. One shot and Mike was lyin' dead on the floor. There was nothin' I coulda done to stop it."

Tears had begun streaming down her face and she wiped at them fiercely. Then Luke moved closer and wrapped his arm around her shoulders.

She buried her face against his chest. She hadn't expected the truth would be as hard to listen to as the lies had always been.

"Are you going to be all right?" Luke murmured. "You want us to stop talking about it?"

She shook her head. She didn't want to hear another word, yet she wanted to hear the whole truth—once and for all. *Then* she'd finally be able to make her peace with it.

"I don't think he coulda felt anything, Cait," Trout said quietly. "I don't think he even saw the gun."

"Good. Thank you for telling me that," she whispered, fighting for composure. Her tears wouldn't stop flowing, though.

Luke pulled her even closer to him, as if to give her some of his strength. "But according to Rayland's report," he said to Trout, "Mike was killed with his own gun. Was that true?"

"Yeah. Mike never locked his desk, and the gun was always in there. Rayland had lifted it. And after...after it was over, he wiped it clean. Then he put Mike's prints on it and left it on the floor beside him. And then...and then that's when he said I had my choice. Either he told people he'd just come in to see why there was a light on, and he'd found Mike's body, or he'd tell them he'd come in and found me here *with* the body. But I didn't murder him. You believe me, Cait, don't you?"

She nodded. Hard as it was to believe Rayland had murdered Mike, it would be almost impossible to believe it of Trout.

"I didn't want to lie about it," he went on. "Especially not to you. And at first I told Rayland he was crazy to think I would. I said I'd tell everyone what *really* happened. But he just stood there chewin' on his toothpick, with that cocky look he has, and he says, 'Whose version do you think folks are gonna believe, Trout? Yours or their sheriff's?' So...I know I shoulda just told the truth and taken my chances. But I was scared I'd be the one to end up in prison. And no matter what story I told, there was no bringin' Mike back."

"So you agreed to go along with Rayland's version," Luke said.

"Yeah . . . yeah, I did. Then he fixed up everythin' in the office. He washed the glass I was usin' and put it away and stuff like that. Made it look like nobody but Mike'd been here. After that we just waited for a while. Spooky as hell it was, what with Mike bein' there and all. But Rayland didn't want to call the medical examiner until real late. He said we should leave him time to get good and drunk. He finally phoned him around midnight. And he phoned Lonnie to come out. And he told people he phoned me, too."

"But Sally-Mae must have known he didn't," Caitlin said, amazed she was thinking straight enough to realize that.

Trout shrugged. "I sometimes stop off for a few beers before I go home, and if I'm late she don't wait up for me. The kids get her up too early for that. So I told her she was asleep when I got home. And that she just didn't hear the phone."

Caitlin half saw, half heard, something outside the office and glanced toward the door—just in time to watch it open.

Then Rayland Skoda was standing in the doorway, a toothpick in his mouth and wearing the cocky expression Trout had just mentioned.

"Y'all having a *private* meeting here?" he said. "Or can anyone join in?"

FOR A MINUTE that seemed to last an hour, Luke simply stared at the sheriff, wondering how long he'd been outside the office and how much he'd heard. Nothing showed on his face. He just glanced casually around, taking in the situation—Luke with his arm still around Caitlin, Trout standing five or six feet from them.

As always, Rayland was wearing a gun. And seeing it made Luke very aware of the Luger pressed against the small of his back.

Letting his arm drop, he eased away from Caitlin. There was no guarantee this wouldn't end up in a shooting match, and the likely line of fire was between him and the sheriff.

"So, what are y'all talking about?" Rayland asked at last.

"I told 'em," Trout said. "I told 'em the truth."

A puzzled look flickered across the sheriff's face. "You told them what truth?"

"I told them the truth about the night Mike died."

Rayland worked the toothpick from one side of his mouth to the other. "I'm missing something here," he finally said. "They've already been told the truth about that—by now, I'd guess they've been told it six hundred times, considering the number of folks they've talked to. Hell, Luke here even read my report. And I hear tell they had a look at the medical examiner's too."

"Rayland, I told 'em the *truth*. I didn't have no choice because they turned up a witness. Someone saw me here."

"Where?"

Beads of perspiration, Luke noticed, had formed on Trout's upper lip.

"Here!" he snapped at Rayland. "Someone saw me at the hangar the night Mike died."

"What the hell you talking about?" the sheriff demanded. "You're saying you were here that night? Well, why the hell didn't you tell me that way back?"

Luke glanced from one to the other, trying to decide what was going on. Rayland really looked as if he didn't know what Trout was talking about, which made him a damn good actor. But why was he bothering when they all knew the real story?

Or did they? The realization struck like a bolt out of the blue—maybe what Trout had just told them was a lie. Maybe *he'd* been the one who killed Mike.

When Luke focused on the mechanic again, the beads of perspiration on his upper lip had multiplied and were spreading over his entire face.

"Rayland?" he said, his voice cracking. "Rayland, what are you tryin' to do here?"

Pushing his hat back a little, Rayland fixed Trout with a cop stare. "Ol' buddy, how about if you tell me what *you're* trying to do here?"

Trout made a spluttering noise and Rayland glanced at Luke. "What the hell's the deal? What's the bit about someone seeing Trout here that night?"

Luke looked at Caitlin. She was clearly frightened. And obviously as uncertain as he was about who was lying. But from the way her lips were pressed tightly together, he could tell she'd realized the less they said, the better. They couldn't reveal the identity of their witness until they were sure which of these two guys was playing fast and loose with the truth.

"Well?" Rayland demanded.

Luke shrugged. "Someone told us they saw Trout here that night. About eight or eight-thirty."

"Someone," Rayland repeated. "You want to be a little more specific?"

"No... no, I don't think I do. Not just yet."

"No? Well, how'd you feel about being charged with obstructing justice?"

"Rayland?" Caitlin said. "Rayland, we're not trying to obstruct justice. I guess we'd just feel better if we knew what was going on. Because...because Trout told us *you* killed Mike."

"What?" The sheriff's face turned red and he glared at Trout. "Maybe," he said through clenched teeth, "you'd better tell *me* what you told them."

"Look, Rayland, I'm sorry, but I had no choice. I—"

"Just tell me what you told them!"

"But you already know! You—"

"Tell me! Word for word what you told them!"

Trout rubbed his hands against his coveralls, looking scared half to death. "Well..." he finally began.

While he went over his story again, Luke tried to watch both men at once. Was Trout lying? Or did the sheriff just figure he could get himself off the hook?

Rayland was obviously mad as hell. And Trout was obviously terrified. But beyond that, *nothing* was obvious.

When Trout finished his second run-through, Rayland slowly shook his head. "I'm not sure," he muttered at last, giving Trout another cop stare, "what I'm finding tougher to ~~believe~~. That you actually figured you could frame me, or that you fixed the murder scene good enough to fool me in the first place. Hell, I really did believe I'd walked in on a suicide. You got everything just right, ol' buddy. You didn't make a single slip. Except for getting seen, of course."

"What...what are you sayin?" Trout whispered.

"Hey, give it up, huh? You almost got away with it, but these two did you in. Hell, if they hadn't turned up their witness, nobody'd ever have known you were here that night.''

"Rayland," Trout said, an edge of panic in his voice now. "Rayland, what the hell are you doin'?''

"Shut up," the sheriff snapped. "I get to ask the questions here. Now what *really* happened that night? Did you just shoot Mike in cold blood?''

"Oh, my God," Trout whispered. "You *know* I didn't Rayland. You *know* you killed Mike.''

"I think we'd better take this on into town," Rayland said.

"No! I'm not going anywhere with you. Not alone. I might end up as dead as Mike.''

"Just shut up and move it or I'll cuff you.''

"Wait," Caitlin murmured.

Luke tensed, praying she wasn't going to say something they'd come to regret.

"What?'' the sheriff snapped.

"I just...I just want to make sure you get the whole truth, Rayland. And there's something Trout told us before you got here that he didn't mention when he went over the story again.''

"Oh? What's that?''

"Well . . . the part where he said *you* showed up?''

"Yeah?''

"He said it's on tape.''

Luke stopped breathing. What the hell was Caitlin trying to do?

"What?'' Rayland said again.

"You know how we videotape all our combat missions? Well, we'd been having trouble with one of the cameras, and Trout said he and Mike had been fiddling with it before you got here. And...well, he didn't say there's a picture of you, but he said they had the camera running—not aimed at anything in particular, though. It was the audio levels they were concerned about. And they were testing them when you got here, so your voice is on the tape...yours and Mike's...and the gunshot. I mean, that's what Trout said."

"That's a lie," Rayland snapped. "Just another lie. There's no tape. And even if there was, I wasn't here."

"Caitlin's tellin' the truth," Trout said. "There *is* a tape."

"Oh? Then why's this the first I'm hearing about it?"

"'Cuz I forgot all about it that night. See, the camera wasn't in the office. It was out in the main hangar. Like Caitlin said, we was checkin' the audio levels—from different distances. And when I remembered about it...well, I just thought maybe I'd keep it to myself."

HER HEART POUNDING, Caitlin stood waiting for Rayland to decide what to do—and thanking her lucky stars Trout had picked up on her bluff.

She knew it hadn't been the best ploy in the world, but she'd had to come up with something. Because when Trout said he wasn't going anywhere alone with Rayland, in case he ended up as dead as Mike, she'd suddenly been certain which of them was lying. And just as certain that Trout really would have ended up dead.

She glanced at Luke. His face was so pale and tense that just seeing it sent a little shiver of fear through her. Rayland was a murderer. And they knew he was.

Which meant...oh, Lord, she didn't want to think about what it meant.

"Well," Rayland finally muttered, "I'd say if there really is a tape, we should all have a listen. Just to prove Trout made up his whole crazy story. So where is it, Trout?"

"It ain't here."

"No? Well there's a surprise."

"That's not what he told us before, Rayland," Luke said. "He told us it's right in that cabinet over there. So why *don't* we all have a listen?"

Caitlin stared at him, her blood running cold. He knew she'd made that up, knew there *was* no tape. And as soon as Rayland looked he'd realize there wasn't. So what on earth was Luke up to?

"You know," Rayland was saying, "on second thought, maybe it isn't such a great idea. That tape's legal evidence, Luke, which means you and Caitlin really shouldn't hear it right now. So I'm just going to read Trout his rights, and then I'm going to take him and the tape into town with me."

The second Rayland headed for the cabinet, Trout bolted through the door and started running across the hangar.

Rayland whirled back around, drawing his gun as he moved. "You two hit the floor," he snapped. "I'm going to get that son of a bitch."

"You heard him," Luke told Caitlin as Rayland raced out of the office. "Get down behind the desk."

She didn't move an inch, but her heart was beating a mile a minute. "Luke, Rayland's going to kill him. And then it'll be his word against a dead man's."

"I know."

She'd forgotten Luke even had the Luger, but all at once it was in his hand.

"Get down behind the desk," he said again. "In case that glass gets shot out." Then he took off after Rayland.

She hesitated for a second, then ran from the office and across to the lockers—where Lonnie kept a rifle.

By the time she had it out, all three men had disappeared among the storage crates. She raced over and tucked herself against the shelter of one, then waited in the eerie quiet, not hearing a sound except the hammering of her heart.

Suddenly someone swore, a gun blasted, and the office window exploded in a shower of glass, the sound of the shot echoing like thunder throughout the hangar. But as quickly as the sound had erupted, all was still again.

Then Rayland called, "I'm losing patience, Trout. So how's this sound? You get your ass out into the open, and I'll forget to charge you with resisting arrest."

There was nothing but silence again ... and then a soft scuffing sound. When Caitlin looked between the crates in the direction it had come from, she could see Rayland, his gun at the ready. He was no more than ten feet from her, standing almost motionless, only moving his head enough to peer between the piles of cartons surrounding him.

So what was she going to do? Nothing? While Luke and Trout and Rayland continued their deadly game of hide and seek? When one of them might end up shot? When *Luke* might end up dead? Or was she going to try and stop things before that could happen?

Her hands shaking, she took a step away from her shelter, raised the rifle and leveled it between two crates at Rayland.

"Rayland?" she called, her voice trembling a little.

He looked at her and swore. "What the hell are you doing with that thing? Get out of here!"

"No. Rayland, Trout doesn't have a gun. And I think he'd come out if he wasn't afraid of getting shot the second he showed his face. So why don't you put your gun away?"

"Yeah, right," Rayland snapped. "That's only going to happen in your dreams, Cait, sugar."

"Maybe not," Luke said.

Caitlin felt so weak with relief that her knees almost buckled. Suddenly Luke was standing behind Rayland, the Luger pressed against the sheriff's head.

"You better give me that thing, Luke my man," Rayland said. "'Cuz what you're doing right now is threatening the life of an officer of the law. And if I don't have that gun of yours in *my* hand in three seconds, you're going to be looking at a long stay in prison."

"I think I'll just take my chances on that, Rayland. So let's get on out into the open."

CAITLIN WATCHED LUKE tuck the Chief's teddy in beside him, unable to stop smiling. Luke and the baby were the two most important people in her world, and they were both safe and sound.

Everything was fine now, even though she'd been terrified that Rayland would kill Trout, then turn his gun on Luke and her because they knew the truth.

But he hadn't had the chance. She and Luke had saved the day—like a hero and heroine from an old western shoot-'em-up. And now Rayland was safely in state police custody.

"This routine could get to be a habit," Luke said, turning away from the crib.

"A good habit?"

"Yeah, a really good habit. I like tucking that little guy in at night...but I like tucking his mother in even more."

Luke drew her into his arms and kissed her. It was the kind of kiss dreams are made of—tender and loving, with just a big-enough measure of hot and sexy to make her start melting inside.

"You were smiling," he said, at last, his arms still encircling her waist.

She nodded. "I was thinking how much I love you."

"Enough to marry me and move to Florida? You can do it now, you know. Now that Trout's told his story, you'll get enough money to pay old Quentin 'Big Financier' McDougall what you owe him."

"I know. There are still a lot of details I'll have to work out, but it's almost like..."

"Like what?"

"It's hard to put into words, but I guess what happened today was what my bereavement group would call closure. Everything seems to have fallen into place. We finally learned the truth, and it's made me feel as if I've done everything I could for Mike, as if..."

"As if you can put his ghost to rest?" Luke said quietly.

"Exactly," she murmured.

"Tell me something."

"What?"

"When did you know for sure it was Rayland who was lying?"

"When Trout said he was afraid that if he went with Rayland he'd end up dead. I just...it was woman's intuition, I guess, but I just knew. How about you?"

"It was when I told Rayland that nonexistent tape was right there in the cabinet, and he backed off. I figured that *had* to mean he believed it existed and that we'd hear his voice on it."

Caitlin nodded. She'd wondered what Luke had been up to, telling Rayland the tape was right under his nose, and now she knew. But there were still a few lingering questions in her mind.

"Rayland *is* going to be convicted, isn't he?" she said after a minute. "I mean, it's still only his word against Trout's."

"Uh-uh. There's more than that now. Don't forget about all those young girls he's helped lure into prostitution. And since Mike learned Rayland was the one, Culpepper's esteemed sheriff had a definite motive for murder. So there's no way he's going to get off. The best his lawyer might be able to do is plea-bargain him out of a death sentence.

"So," Luke murmured, nuzzling her neck, "I guess hoping you'd drive back to Florida with me when I go would be hoping for too much, wouldn't it?"

She laughed against his chest. "Trust me, you don't want to drive that far with a baby and a dog like Sam in the car. Besides, my grandmother would never forgive me if we didn't get married here. So I guess you're stuck having to come back. Unless," she teased, "you think all those miles are too far to travel again."

"Too far?" He gave her another melting kiss. "Caitlin," he murmured against her lips, "the ends of the earth wouldn't be too far to travel. Not if you were waiting there for me."

EPILOGUE

ALL DAY LONG, Caitlin had been feeling as if her veins were filled with champagne rather than blood. And when the minister said, "Lieutenant Dakota, you may kiss the bride," the tiny bubbles rippled through her in a rush of delight.

She'd never been happier in her entire life. It was as if Christmas and New Year's Eve and the Fourth of July had all been rolled up into one. Then Luke took her in his arms and she felt happier still.

"I love you, Caitlin," he murmured against her lips.

And she loved him. Oh, Lord, did she love him.

His arm around her, they turned toward their guests.

The Chief, sitting on his great-grandmother's lap, grinned and waved his little fist. "Da-da!" he cried, eliciting laughter.

"You think he meant you or me?" Luke whispered.

"I think he meant you," she murmured, making her husband smile.

Everyone seemed to be smiling. Especially her maid of honor, Peggy-Sue, and Luke's best man, Lieutenant Zach Granger. Peg and Zach had hit it off like wildfire. In fact, they'd been practically inseparable in the three days since Zach and Luke had arrived from Pensacola for the wedding. And Caitlin had a feeling she wasn't going to be leaving her best friend behind in Culpepper, after all. Not for long, at least.

The organist struck a chord, then the opening notes of Mendelssohn's "Wedding March." Luke took Caitlin's hand and they started down the aisle toward the back of the church—man and wife, now.

When they stepped outside, the September day enveloped them in its gentle warmth. Overhead, a jet suddenly roared down through a cloud. As it passed over the church, it dipped a wing. Then it was gone as suddenly as it had appeared.

"It vanished like a phantom," Caitlin murmured.

Luke nodded. "Phantom. Mike's call sign. Remember what I said?" he asked when she looked at him. "That he'd be up there cheering for us? Well I think he is."

"I think so, too," she murmured. Her eyes filled with tears, half due to melancholy, half to happiness. She blinked them away as Peg and Zach and the others followed them outside and a buzz of conversation filled the air.

While the photographer began setting up for his outdoor shots, Luke's sister, Sarah, came over and hugged Caitlin. Her husband shook Luke's hand. Then Trout and Sally-Mae headed over.

"Congratulations," Sally-Mae said. "And," she added quietly to Caitlin, "I want to thank you again."

"There's no need to. It was the ideal solution for all of us. I'm just glad everything worked out so well."

And it really had. Even though Trout could have ended up facing serious charges—for unwittingly helping Rayland, as well as for lying about what had

happened the night Mike died—his lawyer had plea-
bargained him a suspended sentence. And even
though he didn't have the money, up-front, to buy
Caitlin's share of Sky Knights, now that she'd gotten
the insurance money she could afford to let him pay
her on that installment plan he'd once suggested to
Lonnie.

Lonnie. She glanced over to the fringe of their
group of guests—to where he was standing with his
new girlfriend—and thought how strangely things
sometimes worked out.

Even though the fact Mike hadn't committed suicide meant Sky Knights' claim for compensation was
dead in the water, she was sure the company would be
all right. Trout would work his heart out, and he'd
make a better partner than she ever had.

And Lonnie's personal life would probably end up
fine, as well. Peggy-Sue's breaking up with him had
finally made him admit he should try to do something about what Luke called his attitude. So he'd
been seeing a psychologist. And that gorgeous woman
he'd started dating was the psychologist's secretary.

Caitlin watched them for a moment, then glanced
around at the other guests. When her gaze came to
rest on her grandparents, she felt a pang of sadness.
Leaving them behind would be the hardest part of
moving to Florida.

As if they could read her thoughts, they started toward her and Luke—the Chief toddling along beside
them, his hand firmly clutching his great-grand-
father's.

"We'll miss you, darling," her grandmother said.
"But I know you're going to be happy."

"She's going to be as happy as I can make her," Luke assured them, sweeping the baby up in his arms and starting him giggling with delight. "But we should be able to get back for visits fairly often. I've been thinking we could get a plane of our own," he added, glancing at Caitlin. "In fact, just before Zach and I flew out here, I was looking at a nice little Beechcraft Baron six-seater."

"A six-seater?" Caitlin's grandfather said.

Luke shrugged. "Well, Caitlin and I don't want the Chief to grow up an only child."

Caitlin smiled at her husband and son, thinking she was the luckiest woman alive. And that there was nothing in the world she'd rather do than have more children—with a man like Luke.

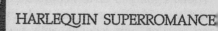

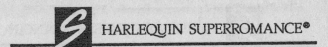

HARLEQUIN SUPERROMANCE®

The Dunleavy Legacy
by Janis Flores

For more than a century, the Dunleavy name stood behind the winners of horseracing's most prestigious prizes. The family's wealth and fame was recognized in the most powerful circles.

But times are different now, and the new generation of Dunleavys is about to claim its legacy. Meet the three grandchildren of Octavia Dunleavy, matriarch of the family, as they deal with old feuds and jealousies, with family pride and betrayal, in their struggle to restore the Dunleavy dynasty to its former glory.

Follow the fortunes of Carla, Nan and Seth
in three dramatic, involving love stories.

#654 DONE DRIFTIN' (August 1995)
#658 DONE CRYIN' (September 1995)
#662 NEVER DONE DREAMIN' (October 1995)

This eagerly awaited trilogy by critically acclaimed writer Janis Flores—a veteran author of both mainstream and romance novels—is available wherever Harlequin books are sold.

DLL-1

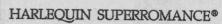

 HARLEQUIN SUPERROMANCE®

Four men of courage
Four special men
Four men who'd risk anything
For the women they love

Next month, meet the fourth of our Strong Men!

Major Nick Apostalis is used to danger. A member of the Canadian peacekeeping force, he'd been assigned to some of the world's most hellish places. But none of his tours of duty prepared him for the hell he's going through now that Kara Hartman has disappeared from his life.

Kara knows he'll try to find her but she also knows he won't be prepared for the secret she's carrying...

Watch for PEACEKEEPER, Harlequin Superromance #655 by Marisa Carroll. Available August 1995 wherever Harlequin books are sold.

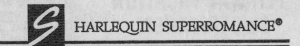

HARLEQUIN SUPERROMANCE®

Join bestselling author
Lynn Erickson
in
Apache Springs!

Gabriela and Brian Zimmerman run the Apache Springs
Hotel, relying on the spectacular scenery and local legend
to bring in the tourists. Then two of their guests die
under very suspicious circumstances, and Deputy U.S.
Marshal Jed Mallory comes to town. Gabriela doesn't
know which bothers her most, the investigation of the
hotel or the man who is conducting it—an old flame
she's never quite forgotten....

First love…last love.

Look for *Apache Springs*, Harlequin Superromance #656,
this August wherever Harlequin books are sold.

FLYAWAY VACATION SWEEPSTAKES!

This month's destination:

Glamorous LAS VEGAS!

Are you the lucky person who will win a free trip to Las Vegas? Think how much fun it would be to visit world-famous casinos... to see star-studded shows...to enjoy round-the-clock action in the city that never sleeps!

The facing page contains two Official Entry Coupons, as does each of the other books you received this shipment. Complete and return all the entry coupons—**the more times you enter, the better your chances of winning!**

Then keep your fingers crossed, because you'll find out by August 15, 1995 if you're the winner! If you are, here's what you'll get:

- Round-trip airfare for two to exciting Las Vegas!
- 4 days/3 nights at a fabulous first-class hotel!
- $500.00 pocket money for meals and entertainment!

Remember: The more times you enter, the better your chances of winning!*

*NO PURCHASE OR OBLIGATION TO CONTINUE BEING A SUBSCRIBER NECESSARY TO ENTER. SEE REVERSE SIDE OF ANY ENTRY COUPON FOR ALTERNATIVE MEANS OF ENTRY.

VLV KAL

FLYAWAY VACATION
SWEEPSTAKES
OFFICIAL ENTRY COUPON

This entry must be received by: JULY 30, 1995
This month's winner will be notified by: AUGUST 15, 1995
Trip must be taken between: SEPTEMBER 30, 1995-SEPTEMBER 30, 1996

YES, I want to win a vacation for two in Las Vegas. I understand the prize includes round-trip airfare, first-class hotel and $500.00 spending money. Please let me know if I'm the winner!

Name_____

Address _____ Apt. _____

City   State/Prov.   Zip/Postal Code

Account #_____

Return entry with invoice in reply envelope.

© 1995 HARLEQUIN ENTERPRISES LTD.   CLV KAL

FLYAWAY VACATION
SWEEPSTAKES
OFFICIAL ENTRY COUPON

This entry must be received by: JULY 30, 1995
This month's winner will be notified by: AUGUST 15, 1995
Trip must be taken between: SEPTEMBER 30, 1995-SEPTEMBER 30, 1996

YES, I want to win a vacation for two in Las Vegas. I understand the prize includes round-trip airfare, first-class hotel and $500.00 spending money. Please let me know if I'm the winner!

Name_____

Address _____ Apt. _____

City   State/Prov.   Zip/Postal Code

Account #_____

Return entry with invoice in reply envelope.

© 1995 HARLEQUIN ENTERPRISES LTD.   CLV KAL